MIDAS TOUCH

A Christmas Romance

ALEX HALL

Published by Madison Place Press
madisonplacepress@gmail.com

Midas Touch
Copyright © 2020 by Alex Hall
Cover Art by Rebekah Slather Copyright © 2020

First Edition

November, 2020

Print ISBN: 978-0-578-78282-9

Ebook ISBN: 978-0-578-78281-2

Warning: This book contains sexually explicit content, which may only be suitable for mature readers. This book also contains mention of child abuse, alcoholism, and PTSD.

❀ Created with Vellum

They say that 'home is where the heart is.' I think it is where the house is, and the adjacent buildings.

Emily Dickinson

Chapter One

Balancing on the precarious breeze, Frankie Porter lifted her arms and flattened her palms, stretching her fingers until they ached. Her arms were sleek from the humid Virginia air, her muscles buoyant. The wind lifted briefly, warm gusts flattening her hair to her scalp. Above her head and below her feet, leaves rustled. Frankie could smell the perfume of the river and hear the muffled gurgle of the water.

She tensed, straining upward, face lifted to the freedom of the sky. Her shoulders quivered, and her bare toes scraped crumbling mortar, clinging.

"Francis!"

Her lips parted and she tasted the air. Another gust wrapped around her body. She rocked, her heart singing. When she opened her eyes, she would be far above the clouds.

"Frankie Ross! You get down from there!"

Frankie swallowed a sigh. She kept her eyes clamped shut, firmly ignoring the splashing and shouts down below. Something fluttered past her cheek, and she thought she felt tiny wings. A bird, or a butter-fly. She smiled.

Another flutter of air and then a sting and a wet slap. Frankie's eyes flew open. Not a butterfly or a bird—a clod of moss, perfectly aimed. Scowling, she wiped the grit from her cheek.

"Come down, or I'll throw another!"

Still rubbing her throbbing cheek, Frankie peered between her toes. A good twenty feet below College Creek swirled, green and brown and almost as deep as its mother, the James River. Trees from the opposite bank hung over the rush. Leaves and vines brushed at the water's surface. The woods surrounding the creek were old and deeply shadowed.

A skiff floated in a small square of sunlight. From high in the air, the little boat looked bright and clean, but Frankie knew better. The paint on the hull was cracked and peeling. A hole in the stern was patched with a bit of scavenged plywood. The skiff might be usable, but it sure wasn't pretty.

The owner of the little boat stood upright and unsteady between the oars. She looked as though she might tumble into the creek at any moment. Frankie hoped she would.

"Are you coming down?"

Frankie let her arms drop. She settled back onto her heels. A chunk of old brick fell from beneath her feet, tumbled into the water. It broke the current with a splash.

"Go home, Gwen."

Even from her perch between sky and water, Frankie could see the other girl's sullen scowl. "No way. Come on down. I've brought you a birthday present."

A birthday present. Today was June 10, and Frankie had finally turned sixteen. Still one year behind Gwen Cook, who thought she knew everything—and maybe she did, but Frankie would never admit it. She preferred cataloging Gwen's faults, and there were many. For instance, when Gwen wasn't being brave and funny and quick with words, she was moody, crass, stubborn, and as bossy as a mama hen.

She was also afraid of heights, which meant that Frankie was safe on the edge of the decaying boathouse because Gwen wouldn't dare climb up and bring her down.

A birthday present. Frankie set her fists on her hips and craned her neck, trying to see what Gwen might have in her boat. She could tell her friend was in a temper. She supposed Gwen's father was on a bender again, which meant Gwen would spend all afternoon and evening on the creek, hiding.

"What kind of birthday present?" She hadn't expected any gifts to mark the day. Her mom had baked a plain poppy-seed cake, when what Frankie had really wanted was the frilly pink buttercream from the local bakery.

"There's no such thing as a perfect day," her mom had scolded when Frankie burst into tears over the homemade cake. "Not even on your birthday. So stop your sniffling, and be grateful for what you have."

Frankie understood now that there had been no money for something as frivolous as pink buttercream and that perfect days were as rare as unicorns.

"Come down and see!"

She could tell from Gwen's satisfied tone that she thought she'd won. Gwen knew that curiosity was Frankie's Achilles' heel.

Frankie rocked in place, considering. Her long hair spiraled on the wind and plastered her brow. Humidity stuck her cutoff jeans to her legs. Her tattered T-shirt clung in itchy spots to her skin. If she couldn't fly, she thought, she might as well swim.

She heard a swoosh and a plop as Gwen anchored the skiff. Bent at the knees for balance, Gwen waited, peering up. In the scattered sunlight she looked sun browned and gangly, all knees and elbows and a nose that was too big in her face. Gwen's hair was as black as a crow's wing, smooth and shiny where it fell almost to her shoulders. Her eyes were as muddy green as the creek, her temper as unpredictable as the currents below.

Frankie didn't mind Gwen's temper because it was mostly just for show. Besides, Gwen was Frankie's best friend, had been for years and would be forever—even though lately their friendship had been changing into something different.

Suspicious, Frankie frowned. "You're not thinking of kisses, are you?"

In the last month Gwen had taken a definite liking to Frankie's mouth. Frankie didn't mind the fumbling kisses. They were sweet and shy in a way Gwen normally was not. Frankie had only been kissed twice before in her life: once by Ralph MacGuillivray, whose father fished on a boat on the Chesapeake, and once by Mr. White, the man who picked up their garbage every other Thursday. She supposed she needed as much practice at the game as anyone, and Gwen's kisses usually made Frankie's toes curl up in pleasure.

But today she didn't feel like kissing.

"I might be," Gwen confessed. The wind took her voice, thinned it. "But not as your present. It's the real thing. In a box, wrapped with a ribbon." To prove it, she held up her hand. A small square box—all tied up with a pretty yellow ribbon—rested on her palm.

Frankie was suitably impressed. Gwen's family was as poor as her own, so a present, even a small one, was an unasked-for surprise of the best kind. And Frankie hadn't had a real birthday present since she'd turned twelve and Ma had scraped together enough money to order a peach-colored swimsuit from the Lands' End catalog.

"Francis!" Gwen shouted. "Stop dawdling and come down!"

The sun ducked behind a high cloud, and the breeze turned cool. Goose bumps rose on Frankie's arms. She shivered.

Curiosity killed the cat, Frankie knew. But no matter where she stuck her nose, Frankie Ross always managed to land on her feet.

"Well?" Gwen coaxed.

"Coming!" Frankie said, deciding. She turned, intending to climb down the side of the boathouse as she always did—barefoot and monkey-like, fingers and toes wormed into splitting bricks. Then she paused, struck by something as hard to catch as the breeze. She glanced back over her shoulder.

College Creek looked very far away down below, swirling around the curve of the bank. She could hear the faint slosh of the water against Gwen's boat, see the shift of light and shadow across her face.

Frankie turned back and stood again on the edge of the sagging roof. Mortar cracked and fell, raining down in a rattle and splash.

"What are you doing?" Gwen yelled.

She stretched up on her toes and lifted her arms over her head. The breeze stung her eyes.

"Frankie?" She sounded afraid. Gwen Cook, seventeen years old and frightened of heights. Frankie laughed.

Today was June 10, and Frankie Ross had gained another year. The sun was warm, school was out, and her best friend had brought her a birthday present in a box with a ribbon. Maybe the day would be perfect after all.

Frankie arched her back and spread her fingers. A perfect day to fly.

"Frankie!"

She jumped.

Chapter Two

THE BOATHOUSE HAD BARELY CHANGED in twelve years. The creek ran quite a bit deeper and wider. Brown water had swallowed up much of the far bank and licked in pools about the base of the boathouse itself. Frankie had to shove back kudzu and sumac as she walked. The soles of her boots sank inches into mud. Tiny pink-and-white wildflowers grew up between the trees, and here and there she spotted a drooping hedge bright with red berries.

She made her way cautiously through the undergrowth until she could touch the old building. Standing against the foundation, she cocked her head and squinted up along brick walls. The boathouse seemed as sturdy as she remembered. Two stories high and crumbling on the outside, it was ruler straight and strong except for the roof, which still sagged but hadn't given in to the elements and fallen.

"Used to be, they knew how to build to last." Frankie patted the warm brick.

The structure didn't tower the way it had in her childhood, but she supposed it wouldn't. She had grown—her bones had lengthened into adulthood. She'd managed to top five feet, barely. At sixteen, she'd feared she would be stuck forever just above four.

Frankie hesitated, glancing up into the sky. The trees had grown tall, and she could see less of the sun than she remembered. The place was definitely cooler, definitely shadier; but on a warm summer afternoon, shade wasn't such a bad thing.

She leaned against the boathouse and untied her boots. Stripping off her shoes and socks, she stood barefoot in the mud, regarding the brick walls. Twelve years gone and she was no longer a child. Could she do it?

Of course she could. Was it wise?

Probably not.

But her fingers and toes found the old cracks easily, and before she knew it, she was halfway up the wall. The brick brushed her khaki shorts, leaving brown stains. A branch streaked her white shirt with sap. Frankie didn't notice. At the top she hoisted herself over the edge of the roof and onto the shingles. She sat very still, holding her breath, waiting to see if the roof would protest. The shingles held, even when she rose to her feet and tiptoed across the top of the boathouse to her old perch.

She looked up and around first, admiring the oak and the dogwood and the ash with their green-as-grass leaves. She sucked in the fragrance of the creek as she brushed her bangs from her eyes. Then she took a deeper breath and looked down.

James Creek glittered below, cut into geometric shapes by dim sunlight. Shadows gathered at the edges of the water and then spread away along the bank. From where she stood, the water looked deep and inviting.

The breeze whispered and the trees moved in the wind. Something shone metallic on the far shore. Frankie shaded her eyes, squinting. Then she knew: Gwen's skiff, abandoned in the long grasses—overturned, belly to the sky. She guessed the little boat was no longer watertight. The plywood plug had certainly rotted away over the years. Probably the old oars, too.

She wondered, fleetingly, if she should rescue the old boat. Find the time to repair it, replug the hole, and repaint the skin. Maybe dig up a pair of used oars at the discount sports shop. She and Chris could sail the thing along the creek on lazy afternoons. She knew Chris would enjoy the adventure, and it had been a very long time since Frankie had dipped her toe in any creek water.

Frankie sighed and dismissed the idea. It wouldn't be stealing—not really. The skiff had obviously been forgotten for over a decade. But it wouldn't exactly be right, either.

Maybe if she skimped a bit, let the household repairs go another month, maybe then she could save enough to buy Chris a little boat.

Maybe.

Hands on her hips, Frankie turned and looked up the slope behind the boathouse. Through the trees she could just make out the Cook mansion. A two-story brick American colonial, the building had been in severe disrepair when cancer finally sent Edward to rest. Frankie had spent a good two years and much of the old man's legacy in restoring the place.

She'd repaved the long driveway and refitted the peaked roof. She'd put down new hardwood floor and rehabbed the antique bathroom fittings and replaced the dangerous wiring. Gutted the plumbing and updated the kitchen. There had been just enough money left over to landscape the wide yard and rebuild the old gazebo, where a teenaged Gwen had hidden her stash of beer and cigarettes.

Frankie had turned the house into a beauty, a gem. It had taken hard work and every spare moment, but she managed. And when at last she'd put the house on the market, it sold in less than a month, in spite of the admittedly inflated asking price.

She still couldn't quite believe her luck.

Thanks to Edward, she now had a start on Chris's college fund, and if they continued to count every penny, her Ivy League dreams were that much closer to reality.

Thanks to Edward *and* to the house's new owner, who would be arriving within the hour. Frankie glanced at her watch. She should be excited, even ecstatic. She'd taken Edward's gift and tripled it—but in the process, she'd also learned to love the house. She had put her heart and soul into its rebirth, and she was suddenly reluctant to let it go.

Silly, she scolded herself. *Don't be sentimental.*

Frankie put her hand to her shorts, testing the right pocket, making sure the house keys were still safely zipped against her thigh.

She had one last repair to make, one screw to turn. Then she would trade the keys for a nice hefty check and let the mansion go.

Sucking in a resigned breath, she padded back across the boathouse roof and scrambled down the brick. Her feet were irreparably muddy. She grimaced as she pulled her socks and shoes over filthy toes.

Struggling back up the bank, through tree and hedge and vine, Frankie left the burble of College Creek behind. She stopped once to pick a handful of wild flowers. The purple flowers smelled sweet, like honeysuckle. She stuck the bunch behind her ear as she broke free of the woods. She cleaned her muddy boots on grass before she stepped onto the newly paved drive.

She straightened her shoulders as she walked slowly uphill to Edward's house. Her chin lifted. She was proud of her work.

The mansion sparkled in the sunlight, smooth red brick shining as though oiled. The trim was traditional cream, but she'd painted the front door a deep green. The windows were beveled glass between crosshatched frames—very expensive and very beautiful. Four chimney stacks sprouted from the roof. The detached garage sported two wide doors and a living space above.

A new brass mailbox stood on a pedestal by the front door, and on the stoop Frankie had placed a pot of happy pansies. The entire impression was charming and cheerful.

She'd left her telescopic ladder on the drive in front of the garage, along with her bucket of nails, her toolbox, and an iron weather vane. The weather vane was handcrafted, a replica of one that adorned the Wren Building at the nearby College of William and Mary. Frankie wanted to have it in place before her client arrived.

She set the ladder up against the garage and secured it with ropes and weights. Then she hefted the weather vane over her shoulder and stuck a screwdriver into her pocket. She climbed the ladder carefully, afraid of scraping the recently shingled roof.

Frankie had chosen the exact place for her weather vane: at the very peak of the roof, just between the garage doors. She bent her knees, balancing against the slope, and walked steadily along the roof to the spot. Setting the weather vane in place, she began securing the iron base to the peak.

Eyes fixed on her hands and tools, Frankie worked automatically, ignoring the world around her. She didn't feel the sweat that trickled between her shoulder blades, and she didn't notice time as it passed.

She'd just positioned the last screw when the rumble of a distant motor broke her concentration. A car growled up the long drive. It could only be her client—nobody without business came so far along the creek. She frowned at her watch and saw that she'd lost time in her work.

She spun the screw one last time before she straightened. Then she grabbed her tools and walked to the edge of the roof. Wind cooled the damp on her brow. In the garden below, pink tulips danced, nodding as if in welcome.

The car slowed, rounding the last curve before the house. A sports car, European. Frankie should have guessed. Any person who would spend $2.5 million on a house, sight unseen, would drive a flashy car.

The car gunned before it pulled to a precise stop in front of the garage. A shiny black door sprang open, and the driver unfolded herself. Hair black as a crow's wing, cut in a blunt bob, a little too short for the latest fashion. Lennon-style sunglasses balanced on a sharp nose, blue lenses reflecting light. A neat pantsuit the color of the morning sky, and shoes with heels that had to be at least four inches.

As Frankie watched, the woman squatted in the driveway before the left front tire, apparently examining the treads.

She ran a careful hand over the black rubber, searching. After a moment, apparently satisfied, she rose again and turned her attention to the house.

Rounding the hood of the car, she skirted the garage, stopping twice to touch the brick before pausing to stare down at a bed of daffodils and tulips. Finally, she turned away from the flowers and looked up at the front porch. Then she froze, head tilted.

Frankie held her breath. She'd hoped the woman couldn't see her past the edge of the roof. She could. She took two easy steps back, turned, and looked right at her.

Her mouth—deliciously full and painted a subtle pink—quirked as she examined Frankie with the same consideration she'd given the garden. She stuck one hand into the pocket of her slacks, jingling change or keys, and used the other to pull away her shades.

She had wide green eyes, clear and dark as the creek. Her cheek-bones were as sharp as her nose; a dimple softened the planes of her face. Her smile turned from surprised to self-mocking, and Frankie found herself grinning in return.

"Why, Francis," she said in a husky Virginian drawl, "you still trying to grow wings?"

Shock turned Frankie's knees to Jell-O. She teetered, the shingles suddenly slippery beneath the muddy soles of her boots.

FROM TWO STORIES BELOW, GWEN WATCHED FRANKIE SWAY. IN A flash she was a teenager again, frozen in place, watching her best friend fall from the boathouse, heart pounding as Frankie crashed into the creek. She'd gone under twice before Gwen had managed to grab her arm and pull her from the water. Then she'd slumped so still in the bottom of the boat, so limp and lifeless, Gwen had been sure she was dead.

She'd only been concussed and half-drowned, but it meant the end of their summers together, the end of Gwen's youth.

"Don't you dare fall on me again, Francis!" she called up at the woman posed on the roof of her new home. "My heart might not survive the shock."

But Frankie had already righted herself. Gwen's breath caught as she squatted at the very lip of the roof.

"Gwen?"

"Who else?" Gwen wished she wouldn't stand so near the edge.

"But I thought . . ." Frankie trailed off and began again. "What are you doing here?"

"It's my house," Gwen said mildly. "I've come to have a peek." She replaced her sunglasses to hide her eyes and stuck both hands into her pockets to keep them from trembling. Frankie had driven Gwen mad that final summer, climbing everything in sight: trees, buildings, bridges. Always trying to reach the clouds.

"Come down from there, Francis."

"All right. Sure. Just let me get my things." She disappeared from view. Gwen could hear her scrambling about on the shingles. "Okay, be right down. Don't go anywhere."

And where would I go? Gwen thought, regarding the garage through narrowed eyes. *Come all this way just to do a runner at the last moment?* It was tempting.

A ladder stood slanted against the bricks. As Gwen watched, slim brown legs appeared over the lip of the shingle, and then Frankie slithered into view. She dropped two stories, barely touching the ladder rungs, and hit the ground with a smile.

Gwen studied her through her blue lenses as she crossed the drive. She was still small. Tiny but mighty, they'd said as children, and that hadn't changed. Her long hair was gathered back from her face in a messy ponytail. Gwen recognized the look in her wide dark eyes: determined good humor.

Frankie held out a delicate, grimy hand. "Gwen Cook! Imagine that. I thought you were somewhere west. Seattle?"

"Seattle," Gwen said. She took Frankie's hand with a practiced smile. She remembered those same sturdy hands, cool and wet against her skin as they wrestled together in the creek.

That last summer their water battles had started over possession of Gwen's little boat and ended in a bout of heavy breathing, overactive teenage hormones boiling. Gwen had dreamed nightly of Frankie's body and their kisses. Their mostly innocent encounters had been sweetness and freedom when Gwen had spent all of that summer trapped in the dark.

Gwen realized she was staring at Frankie's mouth. Embarrassed, she released her hand. "I've taken some time off. Come back to revisit my roots, see the old place."

Frankie frowned. "Gwen, I'm so sorry, but the house is off the market. In fact, it just sold—"

"To me." Gwen made a show of studying the manicured yard and pointed bricks. "And I'm pleasantly surprised. It hardly looks like the same place."

Frankie frowned. "But I thought—I mean, a Mr. Windsor from the Pinnacle Group—"

"My personal assistant. I'm Pinnacle. And I like to do business quietly when I can." She waved a hand. "The money's cleared, I assume."

"Yes." Frankie's assessing stare made Gwen want to twitch. She held herself still. No need for Frankie to know Gwen had been fighting an anxious snakes' nest behind her ribs all the way down from DC. Apparently, Frankie couldn't read Gwen like she used to, because she only shrugged. "Well, would you like a tour?"

"That won't be necessary." She wasn't sure she was ready yet to step through the front door. Seeing Frankie again was more of an emotional shock than she'd expected. More than a decade spent trying to escape James Creek, but Frankie's warm smile made Gwen feel like she'd never left.

"Let me at least show you the fuses. You'll need to know where they are." Without waiting for an answer, Frankie climbed the front steps, glanced over her shoulder. "The locks are funny. You have to jiggle a little. I kept Edward's old door handles; just cleaned them up some. Historically accurate and all that."

Gwen eyed the gleaming lockset. The handles were certainly much shinier than she remembered. "Remarkable."

Frankie opened the front door and stepped over the threshold. Gwen followed. The interior was cool and smelled of beeswax and lemon. During Gwen's childhood the walls had stunk of booze and sweat and fear.

"I refinished the entry floors," continued Frankie. "They're good hardwood. A few of the boards needed replacing, and the banisters."

Gwen trailed Frankie through the entryway. She remembered the spacious rooms and the high, wide fireplaces—of course she did. She didn't remember the large windows or the color of the afternoon across the wood floors. The old man had kept the shades drawn and shag carpets over the wood.

Frankie led Gwen down a bright hallway and into a shining kitchen. While Gwen stood blinking, she opened a small cupboard.

"Fuses are in here. Box used to be just bare on the wall, but of course you know that. I had the shelving built around to hide it."

Gwen fought unwelcome appreciation. "Jesus. The counters are new, and the appliances. And did you cut a new window here?"

Frankie flushed, nodding. Gwen watched the pink creep into her cheeks. She'd always been an easy blusher, had hated that tell. Gwen wondered if she still smelled of spring and wildflowers.

"It must have taken quite a bit of time and money to fix this place up," Gwen said after a pause, turning in place to see every corner of the kitchen. "Last I recall, it was a rat trap."

"You're not wrong. But the place has good bones. And I've made the money back five times over, thanks to the sale. Thanks to you, I guess." She grinned, but it faded quickly. "I didn't realize you were so attached. Maybe . . . I suppose you were surprised it wasn't part of your inheritance."

"My inheritance? What, nightmares and a healthy dose of undiag- nosed PTSD?" Gwen regretted the words as soon as they were said. They felt like a confession, and she wasn't in the habit of confessing anything to anyone anymore. "I didn't expect to get the house. I figured it was going to pay off the old man's debts. So, yes, I was surprised when I heard he'd left it to you. Guess I shouldn't have been. We both know about my father and his women."

Fuck. That hadn't come out at all the way she meant. But before Gwen could backpedal, Frankie's palm flashed up and out. She had a solid right arm—the slap stung. Gwen rocked back on her heels. She supposed she deserved it.

No, wait. She *didn't* deserve it. She'd spent years in therapy before she understood no one deserved to be hit.

"Please don't do that again." She rubbed her throbbing cheek. "I only meant . . . he formed attachments. We both know that." Usually the old man's attachments had been of the sexual variety, but not always. Sometimes the bastard had just wanted a caretaker to supply the booze and clean the toilets.

"You don't know what you're talking about," Frankie replied coldly. Her gorgeous mouth was a straight line of anger and embarrassment. "You've been away for a long time, Gwen. People change."

Not Edward. But Gwen nodded. "You're right. And really, it's none of my business. It's good to see you again, Frankie, but let's just get this done. Keys?"

They clattered across the countertop, metal on stone. "I'm sorry I hit you," Frankie said stiffly. Her cheeks burned bright red. "I don't usually . . . I mean, I never . . . But it felt like you were calling me one of your father's girlfriends. *Me*, Gwen. Of all people. 'Two halves of a whole,' remember? You're supposed to know better. Fuck you for not."

Gwen winced. Frankie was already across the kitchen and down the hall. Gwen chased after, heels clicking on refinished hardwood.

"Francis."

"Enjoy the house, Gwen. Have fun revisiting your roots." She marched outside, slammed the front door at her back. Leaving Gwen alone in the old man's house, alone with the ghosts of her past.

Rain fell in sheets. Water pounded cracked walls, turning the already-stifling basement air as humid as a hot shower. Gwen leaned her elbows against the sill of the single window and peered up and out at the world beyond her father's kingdom. In the summer cloudbursts came like clockwork. This shower was right on schedule: five o'clock, by Gwen's battered Timex—almost suppertime.

In a moment, she would climb the wood plank stairs up from the basement to the kitchen and scrounge up something edible. The old man was probably already snarling with hunger.

If he hadn't already passed out in front of the boob tube, beer can slipping from lax fingers, adding another stain to the mildewing shag carpet.

In a moment, Gwen would go up. In a moment. For now, it was soothing to watch the rain fall gray across the creek woods. Wildflowers nodded their heads against the onslaught, and birds fluttered under dripping shrubs. Down below, the creek would be swollen, the air cooler. It was a perfect evening for a swim or a sail.

Gwen guessed Frankie was probably already down on the bank, absurd and eager in a bathing suit two sizes too small. She wondered how long she would wait. Maybe, if Edward was out before the TV, Gwen would steal a snack and sneak down to the water.

Thunder rolled overhead—not the natural rumble of the storm, but the rumble of heavy feet on old floorboards. Then the rattle of glass as the fridge door was thrown open and slammed shut again.

"Gwen!"

No time for a swim, then. Maybe she would escape after dark, sail the creek by moonlight. Maybe the old man would forget to lock her in.

"Gwen, dammit! Get your ass up here!" The rain was slowing up, but the thunder overhead grew closer. "Have you got a joint down there?"

His cowboy boots hammered to a stop at the top of the basement steps.

"No, Dad! Coming!" Gwen moved away from the window. Edward rarely descended into the depths of the house, but it wouldn't do to give him reason.

"What're you doing down there?" The old man's voice was slurred and piti-ful. "Lookin' at those dyke girlie magazines?"

Gwen felt rage and shame creep up the back of her neck.

"No, Dad." Slowly, she started up the steps.

"You know your mother wouldn't approve." Edward's whine deepened dangerously. "You lookin' to chase her away again? You with your drugs and magazines. You think I don't know? You think she don't know? Come up and apologize to your mother, girl."

Gwen stood very still on the warped wood. She gazed up into the square of kitchen light, regarding her father's shadow uneasily. If there was a woman up there in Edward's territory, she wasn't Gwen's mother. One of the old man's meth-head girlfriends, maybe, or a college girl who hadn't learned any better.

Gwen's stomach turned. She swallowed hard to keep the sour taste down.

"Gwen!" Edward roared, sticking his head into the stairwell. "Now, girl!"

Chapter Three

"Now!"

The shout echoed in the empty house. Gwen sat upright, gasping. Her mouth was dry, her shirt soaked with sweat. The sound and scent of Edward vanished with waking, but the better part of the rain and wind remained, solid and real against fading memories.

Groaning, she rubbed the back of her neck. She'd fallen asleep without meaning to, stretched out for just a moment in a spot of sunlight on the living room floor, tried to will the tension out of her body.

And fallen asleep.

Not surprising, really. The drive from DC had been arduous, and the emotional shock of seeing Frankie was equally draining. The sun-warmed floorboards and the view through the newly repaned windows had been irresistible.

But she hadn't meant to fall asleep. Not here, not yet—not until she'd regrouped and gathered her defenses.

Gwen didn't often dream of the old man anymore. She'd chosen Seattle because it was worlds away from Virginia. She'd purposefully kept life busy, made a point of forgetting her past, her roots, her traumas. And she'd done a good job of making a new life.

Until Mike Windsor, always vigilant, had brought Gwen a press clipping. Mike knew which details were important enough to bring to her attention and which were not. The small real estate ad had been very important. The Cook homestead was on the market at last, and Gwen discovered—to her immense surprise and dismay—that she wanted it.

For most of her adult life, Gwen had made a concerted effort not to wonder where the old man's legacy had gone. She'd schooled herself not to care, just as she'd schooled the nightmares away.

But now that the old house was on the market, something had changed. Gwen collected Louboutin shoes and Hermès bags to remind herself how far she'd come up in the world. Maybe she wanted the house for the same reason—a trophy to add to her collection, a symbolic middle finger to Edward's ghost.

She'd told Mike to make it happen, no matter the cost. And when at closing the money had been transferred to Chesapeake Renovations, LLC, Gwen—insatiably curious when it came to all things business related—had done a little googling, reached out to a few contacts, and ended up with a name she recognized.

Frankie Porter. At the head of a nice little start-up company and doing surprisingly well considering the local economy.

The temptation had been impossible to resist. Gwen had had to see for herself.

She'd told herself it was simple curiosity, but now she wondered if it was jealousy that had had her traveling across country. Had she wanted to make sure her childhood friend was happy and healthy, living her best life? Or had she picked up in the middle of the busy season and flown to Williamsburg just to spit in Frankie's eye, throw accusations in her face?

"Two halves of a whole, two sides of the same coin." That had been Gwen's romantic notion the day they'd entered middle school together, as they hung out in the parking lot, trying to gather the courage to go into the building. She'd held up a scuffed dime she'd found in her pocket as evidence.

"Which am I?" Frankie had asked, frowning doubtfully. *"Roosevelt or the funny trees?"*

"You're the sun, and I'm the moon," Gwen had replied, trying again. *"We don't need to be scared of anything because even though we're opposites, we'll always have each other's backs. We* complement *each other. Right?"*

"Okay." Reassured, Frankie had nodded firmly. *"Two halves of the same coin."*

Now Gwen touched the bruise on her cheek. "Damn." She could have handled things much better. She thought of herself as coolheaded —the moon to Frankie's sun—and she was disappointed in herself for letting emotion get the best of her.

She thought she'd been prepared.

Gwen climbed to her feet and crossed the living room. On the east wall, huge bay windows looked out across an expanse of new lawn. Twelve years ago, the lawn had been a sludge of mud and weeds. Now grass gleamed emerald in the evening shadows. The sun had disappeared behind the trees, and the clouds were beginning to shred away —right on time.

"Welcome to Virginia," Gwen muttered, pressing her forehead against the cool glass.

Beyond the edge of the lawn, pink and yellow tulips bobbed alongside a white gazebo. The creek woods looked almost inviting.

She wondered if the boathouse still slumped alongside the creek. Or had Frankie knocked it down, torn the old bricks at last from the reluctant earth? The old building had been an accident waiting to happen.

She moved away from the windows, intending to find her way out of the house and down to the water. Instead, Gwen's feet led her through the kitchen, around a sexy new stainless steel fridge, and into the little alcove that hid the basement doorway. The door was still there—repainted, brass knob polished to a shine.

She turned the knob, and the door swung open, creaking a little, as doors in old houses will, even when oiled. It was the sound of her childhood.

She didn't recall the chain that hung from the ceiling, barely visible in the gloom. It was attached to a new fixture above the stairs. She didn't need the light; her feet remembered the way.

Gwen pulled the chain anyway because she wanted to see clearly what Frankie had done.

She'd somehow erased mildew stains, painted the walls the color of eggshells, and replanked the stairs in warm honey-colored wood that matched the upstairs boards.

On one wall, at eye level, she'd installed a coatrack.

A coatrack! Gwen almost laughed aloud.

The stairs made no sound as she padded down into the depths. The notch on the wall above the second-to-last step, made one afternoon when the old man had actually ventured into Gwen's hole—and swung and missed and broken a thumb—that notch was gone, patched and repainted. Gwen touched the place on the wall where it used to be.

There was a new light switch on the wall at the foot of the stairs. Smiling grimly, Gwen flicked it on.

Frankie had carpeted the floor and put up a false ceiling to conceal the pipes. There was fresh paint and new trim around the one window —in light, bright, soft colors that made the room appear large and clean. What once had been a decrepit fireplace was now a tasteful gas insert.

And overhead, in the very center of the room, she'd installed a ceiling fan.

Frankie had made the basement into . . . what? A game room, a place for entertaining, an extra bedroom? It was warm and habitable and really quite comfortable.

Comfortable. Gwen felt sick.

She swallowed back bile and walked to her old window. She set her palms on the wall, one on each side of the glass, and watched the rain fall.

Overhead, the house was silent.

Gwen made her bed in the basement. She unrolled the sleeping bag she'd brought all the way from Seattle, spread it on an inflatable mattress she had picked up in a DC mall. They'd made the drive down stuffed in the trunk of the sweet little Porsche she'd purchased outside the city.

Furniture would come later. For now, the sleeping bag, one suitcase of clothes, and her computer would have to be enough.

The sky turned red and gold with sunset as Gwen carried her belongings from the garage to the mansion. Cicadas roared in the trees. She caught the fertile scent of summer in Virginia.

Above the peak of the garage, something glinted: the weather vane, still shiny with rain.

Frankie Porter, in the old man's house, making it into a home. Gwen gritted her teeth. Leaving the suitcase in the front entry, she strode past windows and into the kitchen. She knew without question that Frankie, who had worried so much about hunger as a child, would have stocked the refrigerator in welcome.

She found milk, cheese, and fruit. The door held flavored soda water and bottled beer. Tortillas and orange juice and bread up above. Cold cuts and mayo and Dijon mustard and a fancy salad down below. And in the freezer: ice cream and Popsicles.

She must have been expecting an army, or a family. Gwen understood the impulse; the old man's house was big enough to hold an entire clan.

She tossed bread and roast beef and an apple onto the kitchen counter, then snagged a beer. The chilled bottle felt pleasantly cool in her hand. She rummaged in vain through drawers filled with utensils and then through cabinets harboring pots and pans and paper plates.

Thoughtful Frankie had provided napkins and salad bowls and even a cheese grater. But she'd forgotten a bottle opener.

For some reason the oversight lightened Gwen's heart.

Humming absently, she popped the bottle cap free with the blunt edge of a knife, then took a healthy swig of beer before she began to build lunch out of sliced bread and cold cuts.

FRANKIE WAS LATE. THE SCHOOL BUSES HAD ALREADY LEFT, AND most of the cars were disappearing into the dusk. She wrenched her mom's old Mercedes into the first open parking spot she could find, set the parking brake, and hopped out.

She took the school's front steps at a run, then burst into the main office. Emma looked up from her computer and rolled her eyes.

"Is he furious?" Frankie asked, breathless.

"For about the first thirty minutes." The secretary's lips twitched. She tilted her head toward the office couch. "Then he got caught up in his book. What was it this time?"

"Anxious client." Frankie sighed. "Wanted to go over a thousand details about a hundred times." Digging into the canvas tote bag she carried to every meeting, Frankie freed a foil-wrapped candy bar and tossed it onto Emma's desk.

"What's this?"

"Client markets candy. These are her newest. Toffee crunch or something. She gave me about twenty. Haven't tried one, but they must be good; she's making enough money to fuel a remodel."

"Another historic mansion?"

"Houseboat." Frankie grinned. "It'll be a project. Worth every minute, though." She dug out a second candy bar and eyed the couch. "Wish me luck."

"You'll need it," Emma said, unwrapping the foil.

The office couch sagged in places, worn down by years of rowdy students. The cushions were faded but clean; the two sneakers resting defiantly on one padded arm were less so. Frankie followed feet and long legs into the sagging furniture and found her son.

"Hi, Mom." He didn't glance up from his book. This afternoon it was John Grisham's *The Firm*. A classic. "You're late."

"But not too late. We can still make it." She wanted to reach over and ruffle the sweaty thatch of dark hair that hung in his eyes. She didn't, because he was eleven, and she remembered what it felt like to be almost twelve. "Good book?"

"Not as good as *Pelican Brief*." Reluctantly, Chris edged a Rick Riordan bookmark into place and closed the paperback. "What took you so long?"

"Very enthusiastic lady who wants me to redo her boat." She watched, hiding a smile, as he straightened his sweatshirt with slender fingers before shoving the book into his backpack.

"A boat?" He considered. "Cool. Where is it?"

"For now, she's got it docked on the James." Because they really were late and because he didn't seem to be in any hurry to get off the couch, Frankie reached down and urged her son upright. "It'll take some work."

"Pay good?" His blue eyes were serious. He nibbled a little on his lower lip as he rose. Only eleven, and already he'd overtaken her by half an inch.

"Pay's great. And there are treats." She handed him a candy bar and watched while he unwrapped it. "Ready?"

"Yeah." He followed her through the office, munching on the toffee.

Emma waved as they passed. "Good night, kids. Don't forget the math quiz in Mr. Johnson's class, Christopher."

"'Night, Emma," Frankie and her son responded, almost in unison, almost matched in height—but to Frankie, different as night and day.

Chris rode shotgun, resting his sneakered feed on Frankie's tote. He cranked down the window. Sunset dappled his pale skin to orange.

"What's the debate tonight?" Frankie watched her son out of the corner of her eye as she urged the car ahead through evening traffic.

His moods had been difficult lately, and she'd yet to pin down the problem. She'd begun to think the root of the trouble was at school, although he seemed comfortable enough with both his teachers and his studies.

Over the last few weeks the quick, humorous boy who'd always been so eager to rush off to school now dragged his heels every morning and almost invariably came home in a sulk. Frankie couldn't understand what had suddenly turned her mild-mannered boy so sullen.

"We're doing the Louisiana Purchase." Chris finished the last of his candy bar and crumpled the foil. He sucked a dab of chocolate from his thumb and stared out the window, shoes scuffing lightly on her tote.

"Don't remember much debate over that one."

Chris slanted a look away from the window to see if she was serious and then rolled his eyes. "Maybe if you'd gone to school once in a while?"

"Hey, who's the parent here?"

Chris's frown stretched into a grin when he snorted. Frankie laughed. Her bright, bright son, who would go so much farther than she had. Yale, at least. Maybe Harvard, because she could dream. Six years of school left—six years of straight As and Advanced Placement and debate club.

Six years to whip Chesapeake Renovations into shape and make it provide for every bit of her son's college education.

Six years was a long time. Six years was the blink of an eye.

Swallowing a sigh, Frankie rolled down her own window. The air outside was thick with the remnants of rain. "Which side are you on?"

"For." He stuck his balled-up wrapper into the car's ashtray. "We'll win."

"Glad to hear it. Sorry I was late."

"You said so already," he replied, unconcerned. "They'll wait for me. Did you close on the mansion?"

"Sure did." And hadn't that been a kick in the ass. She was still racked with shame every time she remembered the graze of her knuckles against Gwen's face.

Frankie had been free enough with her fists as a child. She'd had to be to protect herself from schoolyard bullies and, later, from a high school date or three who'd gotten too handsy. Growing up, everyone had known who her mother was and exactly how far she would go for a shiny bauble, a secondhand car, the double-wide trailer out in the woods.

Some folks expected Frankie would be the same, and some people only listened when you made your point with your fists.

But she hadn't had to defend herself for years now. And she'd never, ever raised a fist to Gwen. Because God knew Edward's daughter had gotten enough of that at home.

It was a decade of hurt and loss venting itself in the worst possible way, Frankie decided, and she would cut off her own hand before she let it happen again.

"So, what were they like?" Chris prompted. Frankie and Chris had imagined a family for the old house—a middle-aged couple with four or even five kids, come to take over Edward's legacy and make it loud and cheerful. Chris had hoped for new young faces in the neighborhood, and Frankie had simply wished for people who would love the place as much as she did.

"You know," she said at last, trying to sound casual, "it wasn't a family after all. Just one person."

"Really?" Chris turned from the window in surprise. "One person wanted all that room?"

"Well, it is a pretty cool house."

Chris didn't look convinced. "Maybe. But wouldn't it be totally lonely?"

Frankie knew he was remembering Edward and the old man's despair as he lurked alone in one room of the empty mansion. "Maybe."

"No kids or anything?" Her son sounded baffled.

"No. I don't know." She realized she didn't. "Not with her, anyway."

"Huh." Chris grunted. "Sounds stupid to me."

For a brief moment Frankie saw Gwen, standing in front of her flashy car, hands shoved into her pockets, looking up at her as Frankie balanced on the edge of the garage. Gwen's eyes had been exactly as Frankie remembered, like the creek on a still day, but full of a new emotion she didn't recognize.

"She said she wanted to revisit her roots."

"Her roots?"

Frankie hesitated, eyeing her young son. Then shrugged. "Yeah, her roots. Thing is, the house used to be hers."

Chris gaped. "What?"

"She used to live there," Frankie clarified. "Her name's Gwen. She's Edward's daughter."

"Edward had a kid?"

Frankie nodded. "He and Gwen didn't get along so well. Gwen moved out to Seattle a long time ago."

"Gwen," Chris repeated. "Did you know her?"

"When I was a kid." *Two sides of a coin.*

"Can I meet her?"

Frankie shook her head before she thought.

"Why not?" her son demanded, instantly aggrieved.

"I'm sure Gwen is very busy."

"Doing what?"

Frankie shrugged. "Business stuff, I think. She was in the paper a few years back. Buys up struggling business, turns them profitable." The paper, she recalled, had proclaimed in huge font, "Midas Touch! Young Venture Capitalist Spins Gold Out of Thin Air: Everyone Wants a Piece."

"From Seattle? All the cool things happen in Seattle. Not like here."

"I'm sure cool things happen here, too. I mean, we *do* live in the Historic Triangle."

"Jeez, Mom. You do know our colonial history isn't something to be proud of, right?"

"Sorry." She muffled a sigh.

They drove in silence until the thump of Chris's sneakers against her tote grew angry.

"Chris. Stop that."

Chris folded his arms over his chest. "I wonder if she has the newest iPad? I bet she does. Nobody in this hick town has even seen the newest release."

The bitterness in her son's voice made Frankie glance away from the road in surprise. "Williamsburg is not a hick town. It's college central; plenty of things going on that are not related to colonial history."

"Mom!"

"Chris!" Frankie whined back, mimicking her son's wounded tone. When he refused to smile, she sighed. "Most of the buildings even have electricity."

He softened a little, hid a crooked smile. "Not most. Not on the Royal Mile."

"Maybe next century." She took one hand from the wheel and touched his shoulder. "Now, tell me about the Louisiana Purchase."

At last he relented and began to chatter. Frankie relaxed and listened to her son's lecture, determined to focus on the moment, on his enthusiasm. She did her best to push Gwen Cook to the back of her mind, and almost succeeded.

Chapter Four

GWEN WOKE JUST BEFORE NOON, startled from deep sleep by the squeaks of Virginia's thriving bird population. She sat very still, briefly confused by the sounds of her childhood, expecting the thump of Edward's boots overhead.

Then she smelled new paint and heard the murmur of the ceiling fan rotating above her head. Her pulse slowed. She blinked at the square of sunlight on fresh carpet, then up at the basement window and the morning outside.

She'd slept soundly, muddled by time zones and stuffed with food, specifically cold cuts and chocolate pie. The pie had been on a cake plate at the very back of the fridge. She'd laughed when she found it.

That last summer, Frankie had been determined to become a famous pastry chef. She'd planned to move to New York and work in an elite restaurant. They had talked endlessly of the big-city adventures they would have together as Frankie had baked pie after pie on her ma's old wood-burning stove.

Each attempt had ended in disaster. Gwen still remembered her tears when crust refused to set and filling burned. Not long after she reduced her final pie to ashes, Frankie stopped talking about New York.

Gwen decided Frankie must have finally mastered the oven, because the pie she'd found in the new fridge looked homemade and tasted of heaven. She'd downed a good portion of the treat before finally descending into the basement to sleep.

Anticipating another slice for breakfast, Gwen rolled off the mattress and wandered barefoot across the carpet to her window. Beyond the glass the clouds had disappeared, leaving blue sky with the promise of heat. She could feel the sticky warmth even through the pane.

All at once, she wanted a swim. A dip in the creek and a look at the boathouse, and after that chocolate pie and a beer for breakfast. Then some time to play with the massive TV she'd glimpsed earlier in the living room.

Feeling as rebellious as the teenager who'd fled Edward and his house, Gwen ran upstairs to her suitcase, rummaging around until she found the Chanel swimsuit she'd almost forgotten to pack. She stripped without embarrassment in front of the bay windows, pleased by the privacy the long driveway provided. Not a neighbor in sight—nothing but trees and water to every side.

She decided then that she would never put up a single curtain. She liked the way sunlight filled the house.

Because her gurgling stomach decided it wouldn't wait for breakfast, Gwen took the beer and pie down across the back lawn, munching contentedly as she walked. The midday heat felt good for a handful of minutes before she began to sweat. By the time she stepped into the woods, she was more than ready for the chill of the creek.

Plate balanced in one hand, bottle dangling from her fingers, she paused, listening. And she could hear it: the faint rush of water from below.

Gwen began the careful climb down the hill, wincing as her bare feet met twigs and stickers. She'd always gone barefoot through the woods, and she didn't intend to wimp out so late in the game, even if her toes had lost every callus she'd ever earned as a child.

She slid a little down the last few yards of the bank. Then she caught sight of the boathouse. It looked just as she remembered:

crumbling at the edges, solid at the core. Twelve years and it was still standing, unbothered by man or nature.

What a colossal joke.

Gwen set her bottle and plate at the base of the foundation and ran her fingers over the weathered brick. She had never been able to work out where Frankie saw the finger- and toeholds she used to scale the thing. She wondered why Frankie hadn't bothered to at least shore up the old building. Did she hope—as Gwen had—that the boathouse would crumble away and eventually disappear?

She turned her back on the bricks and walked to the edge of the creek. The water ran high, almost lapping against the front of the boathouse. At its center the creek appeared deep and green. Trees and vines had grown up to hang over the water.

She would have to find time to cut the growth back, maybe make herself a small stretch of sandy beach. She waded into the clear water a few steps before diving neatly into the center of the current. The water whirlpooled around her, washing the sweat from her skin. She surfaced, sputtering, and brushed wet hair back from her face.

Treading water, Gwen blinked away drops of moisture and looked around. The boathouse loomed, its sagging roof mottled. Leaves rustled overhead, dropping here and there to the surface of the water, where they swirled in widening circles. She could hear the chirrups of startled sparrows and the buzz of a solitary mosquito. Deep in the green water, beneath her rapidly numbing toes, the current dragged.

It hit Gwen at last that she had come home, and the realization made her briefly dizzy.

She spent a good hour in the water, relearning the creek's old secrets and discovering new bends in the waterway. By the time she emerged onto dry land, she was shivering and ready for the heat of the air.

She sat on a moss-covered rock and sucked on her beer. The drink had gone warm and stale. She finished it anyway.

When the bottle was drained, she stood and collected her plate. Glancing over her shoulder one last time, mentally calculating the expense and energy it would take to strip away some of the vegetation, she paused when a flash of light caught her attention. She turned, squinting at the far bank, and realized immediately what she'd found.

She dove again into the water, swimming quickly to the opposite shore. There the bank was high and uneven, mostly shaded. She had to climb out from the water on hands and knees, gripping the high weeds.

Feeling absurd and awkward, Gwen used a gnarled branch to pull herself upright, balancing alongside the overhang of a large willow. The thin, drooping branches sheltered the aft side of the little boat. Gwen cleared the branches away, pulled vines free. Patches of rotted wood fell from the stern as she scraped away moss.

Beneath twelve years' growth, the skiff was mostly whole. It would need repair—patching the fore and aft, sanding and repainting and varnishing—and both the oars had fallen to almost nothing in the soil, but Gwen thought she could save it.

"But will it still float?"

The willow had no answer. Gwen smiled. She sent sandpipers fluttering for cover when she pulled the skiff from the mud. It was lighter than she remembered, stinking of the wet earth. She dragged it behind her as she swam slowly back across the creek. Cold water washed debris from the boat's shell. The dry wood absorbed moisture quickly, until Gwen was swearing over the weight of it as she reached the bank.

Once on dry land, she propped the skiff against the boathouse wall. Washed somewhat cleaner, the wood looked to be in better condition than she would have guessed. Even so, it would take time and muscle to get her floating again. A tempting project—one she definitely didn't have time for.

Gwen had found the skiff in the marshes along the Colonial Parkway in the spring just before she turned eight. She'd wandered endlessly that year, skipping school, riding to imaginary destinations on the brand-new bike that had been a gift from her mother. It had allowed her some freedom—to get away from the house, to explore.

The skiff had been too heavy for a kid to lift when she'd found it in the marsh grass, but Gwen flagged down a passing motorist for help. People expected to see odd things on the parkway, and the middle-aged man in his fancy pick-up truck hadn't blinked twice. He'd helped

Gwen drag the boat free, and then he drove Gwen and the skiff and her bike back to Williamsburg. Gwen had been afraid she would be caught hitchhiking and that Edward would beat her for it.

Nowadays it's pedophiles kids have to worry about, Gwen thought sourly now. *Or serial killers. Or worse.*

Once safely home, young Gwen had concealed the boat in the weeds along the creek. The next year, Gwen's mother died in a car crash, and she outgrew the bike. Instead, the skiff occupied her time. It had taken her from May to June to fix the boat up, make it ship-shape again. She'd done all the work herself.

She could certainly fix her up a second time. Patch a few holes, find a new set of oars. Maybe she would feel the same pride she had as a child.

Gwen rolled the skiff over, dumped the pie plate and beer bottle into its curved belly, and lugged her up the bank, cursing again when she slipped on grass and stepped on briars.

She would find supplies in town, she decided, spend the afternoon sanding and stripping paint, replace some of the boards on the fore, patch that hole in the stern with something more aesthetic than plywood. New purpose lightening her step, Gwen left the skiff in the sunlight against the gazebo and headed for the house, determined to change out of her wet swimsuit and drive directly into town.

THE STREETS OF WILLIAMSBURG WERE NARROW AND COBBLED IN places. Gwen drove along the creek toward the center of town, her hand light on the Spyder's wheel. The air-conditioning was on blast, the radio turned up until the Stones shook the windshield. In the rearview mirror, Edward's mansion disappeared, swallowed up by trees. Other homes were hidden in the green on the outskirts of town. Within the forest Gwen glimpsed driveways and brick gables.

She passed a tiny park set at the mouth of the creek near the college docks, and around another bend, a crowded cemetery hidden behind a low wall. Gwen remembered the park and the cemetery. As a child she'd played in the park, chasing ducks, and as an adolescent she'd spent her evenings hiding on the edges of the cemetery, smoking pilfered cigarettes on the eighteenth-century tombstones.

Past the cemetery rose the Marshall Wythe School of Law, and the speed limit dropped to twenty. Gwen took her foot off the gas and coasted past the law school—newly renovated—past the brick court-house, through one intersection, and into Colonial Williamsburg. The hardware store Gwen meant to visit was at the far end of town, just on the other side of the Historic District. She'd planned to cut through the district and save time. She hadn't realized how much the living museum had grown during her absence.

Tourists were everywhere, dodging across streets and surging out of buses. Children in shorts and baseball caps raced here and there, oblivious to oncoming traffic. Parents staggered after, weighted down by water bottles and backpacks and paper shopping bags. Men and women in historic garb marched with purpose along the cobbled streets, interpreting another life, paid to be in character for as long as they wore their costumes.

Trapped between a smoking Greyhound and a crowded station wagon, Gwen sat in the Spyder and stared. She stabbed a finger at the stereo, shutting off the music. The clamor of tourists rolled into the car.

"Holy Christ."

A toddler wielding pink cotton candy like a weapon darted between the hood of her car and the back of the bus. A flustered-looking woman chased after her, flashing Gwen a panicked look as she raced by. The Greyhound inched forward, bouncing on cobblestones. Gwen recognized Duke of Gloucester Street. Craning her neck to the right, she could see down the Royal Mile and pick out the spire of the Capitol Building in the distance. Streams of people flooded the Mile, damming up here and there as they waited to visit museums. Reproductions of the original historic homes and shops lined either side of the street, picturesque in the afternoon light.

On the next block, a man dressed in a red coat and black boots drove a horse and carriage for eager tourists. The cobblestones were bright in the heat, and the row of trees did little to shade the street. The very end of the Royal Mile, just before the street reached the College of William and Mary, was cluttered with shops and restaurants. Gwen remembered the Scottish shop, and the silversmith, and the cafeteria that sold burgers and ice cream to visitors from around the world. She didn't remember the women's clothing shop or the bright-green awning of a bookstore.

The bus growled forward again. Gwen followed closely, eager to escape the madness. A woman sporting a hooped skirt walked alongside the Porsche as the car meandered over the last yard of cobblestone and onto asphalt. Gwen heaved a sigh of relief, then had to slam on the brake as the bus ground to a halt just a block past the Royal Mile. The Greyhound disgorged another herd of tourists. They pressed around Gwen's car.

Idly, she noted a second cluster of shops had grown up behind the original Merchants Square. Separated from Duke of Gloucester Street by a parking lot, the stores looked just as crowded as those on the Mile. Another ice cream store, she saw, and a jeweler's, an art gallery . . . and Chesapeake Renovations.

Gwen wrenched the steering wheel, sending her car swerving out from behind the bus and into the nearby parking lot, almost running over a family wearing matching Lakers T-shirts in the process.

"Jesus!" Gwen scowled at the shop front. "How the hell did she afford this prime piece?"

She swung the Spyder into an empty parking space and slid out from behind the wheel, slamming the door shut. Keys clenched in one fist, she crossed the lot and regarded Chesapeake Renovations grimly from behind her shades.

The shop was hardly more than a closet—a hole in the wall, compared to its larger neighbors—but the sidewalk had recently been hosed down, and the sign hanging over the shop's front window was beautifully lettered. A small placard in the window indicated that the store was open.

Gwen ducked inside. Music played, something soft and classical that spoke of strings. Oriental rugs warmed the floor, and framed photographs covered the walls. A man leaning on a square oak kiosk regarded Gwen with friendly interest.

"Can I help you?"

"No."

Restless for no reason she could quite put a finger on, Gwen stalked across the rugs to the nearest wall and glared at the first row of photographs.

"Two of our latest," the man said, undeterred. He stepped out from behind the kiosk and joined Gwen at the wall. "The smaller one is down near Jamestown, and the mansion is actually up here along the Creek."

Gwen grunted wordlessly. She stared at the neatly framed "before" and "after" photos of Edward's mansion.

"Do you have a home that needs some work?" the clerk asked. He smelled lightly of apples. His clothing said "salesclerk," but Gwen noticed that his hands were rough and stained, his fingernails bitten down to the quick.

"No." Gwen turned her attention from the old man's house to the photos of a smaller two story. The "before" and "after" shots were astonishing. The lovely little saltbox in the second frame was little more than a slant-roofed shack in the first.

"Could be you're looking for furnishings? We have catalogs," the clerk suggested hopefully.

"Really? Furniture?" Gwen eyed the man.

He arched one brow and smiled. "Some. Mostly eighteenth-century reproductions. And we do have a cabinetmaker on-site. We're a unique full-service firm."

"You don't say." Gwen paced along the walls, glancing from one set of photographs to the next, unable to believe her eyes. Restored garages, storefronts, apartment buildings, gas stations—even, displayed in a whimsical red-and-green frame, a doghouse.

"All this?" She studied a snapshot of a local restaurant. "She does all this?"

The clerk had returned to his kiosk but was still watching her with the not-so-subtle interest of a shark scenting blood in the water. Probably it was the stack of Cartier bracelets on Gwen's wrist that had attracted his attention, or maybe her icon Fendi miniskirt.

"Do you know Ms. Porter?" he asked.

"We go way back. How long has this shop been open, anyway?"

"About eight months. It's our first shop front."

"A business like this would cost a pretty penny to get started." And Frankie had never had two pennies of her own to rub together.

The man narrowed his eyes at Gwen. He was built like a redwood, had hands the size of dinner plates, and he was definitely not the sort of man Gwen wanted to anger. "If you'd like to leave your name, I can let Ms. Porter know you stopped by."

"No," Gwen said. She pressed her keys into the palm of her hand until they bit into her skin. "No. I'll tell her myself."

"MOM! WE'RE OUT OF PEANUT BUTTER!"

Frankie looked up from a sheaf of architect specs and focused her weary eyes on the kitchen door.

"Try the cupboard."

"I did!" She could hear Chris rummaging through drawers. "I only see your chunky! Gross."

"There's some creamy in there somewhere." Sighing, Frankie abandoned the specs. She rose from her desk. Bending backward and then sideways, she stretched the kinks out of her back. Her bones ached from sitting too long.

Chris popped his head around the swinging door.

"Found it!" he said, flashing a rare smile. "There was a jar behind the M&Ms."

"Peanut butter and toast sounds good." Frankie trailed her son back into the tiny kitchen. "Aren't you home early?" Somehow she'd lost track of time.

He shook his head as he shoved bread into their ancient toaster. "Soccer practice was just sign-up today; nothing real. We don't start until next week." He unscrewed the jar and sorted through a drawer for a knife. "Think it will be cooler on Monday?"

Frankie glanced out at the sunny afternoon. "Dunno, kid. I don't see any sign of fall."

"But it's almost October," Chris complained, stirring the peanut butter. "And A/C's still out at school. Emma said the main unit's, like, totally melted or something."

"Emma would know." Frankie grabbed her own stash of peanut butter from the cupboard. She grinned at her son. "Don't worry; you'll be complaining about the cold soon enough. I remember someone whining all winter long."

"That's because it didn't snow more than an inch, and it rained all December."

"Winter in Williamsburg." Unimpressed by her son's dramatic sighs, Frankie licked peanut butter off her knife. "Maybe this year you should see if you could get one of those dress-up jobs during break. The Historic District's always looking for kids your age."

Chris wasn't enthused. "They're called interpreters, Mom. And you have to wear tights. And be nice to tourists."

"I hear the pay's good." *A little extra money for the college savings account? Yes, please.* "You'd make some spending money. You could pick up a few new paperbacks. And you could put some of it away in—"

"The college fund," Chris said, supremely bored. "I know, Mom."

"Christopher." Frankie knocked gently on her son's forehead with sticky peanut butter knuckles. "You'll thank me when you get that acceptance letter from Virginia Tech."

"That's years away." Chris's mouth turned down at the edges. "And I thought it was MIT."

Frankie rolled her eyes. She freed a piece of singed bread from the toaster with her knife. It stuck. When she tried to drag the bit of crisp bread free, she stung her fingers on the edge of the toaster.

"Mom."

"Yeah?" The burnt toast was sticking to the grill and putting up a good fight. Muttering, Frankie scraped at the black edges with her knife.

"Mom, there's a sports car coming up the drive. I think it's a Porsche."

Frankie immediately forgot the toast. She stood on her toes to peer out the kitchen window. A familiar, very shiny vehicle wound its way up the dirt road that served as their driveway.

"Look at that." Chris couldn't keep the awe from his face. Frankie recognized the glazed look in her son's eyes. The sinking feeling in the depths of her stomach completely banished hunger pangs.

"Stay here, hon, and finish your snack." She wiped her smarting fingers on a dishrag. "I'll see who it is."

Damn Gwen, what was she doing all the way out there? Frankie hadn't worked up a sufficient apology yet. She stalked through the house and out the front door.

The car eased to a stop behind Frankie's ancient Mercedes. Dust settled, dulling the Porsche's fresh-from-the-factory sheen.

Now she'll have to get it washed, Frankie thought with a great deal of petty satisfaction. *Serves her right for driving a car like that up here. She knows how bad the roads are.*

Or maybe Gwen didn't. Frankie felt her stomach dip again as Gwen stepped out into the heat. Maybe she'd forgotten. Briefly Frankie was ashamed of the rutted dirt drive and embarrassed by the shoebox-size house that crouched bravely in the dust. She crossed her arms more tightly across her chest, reminded herself that she had reason to be proud.

Nobody, especially not Gwen Cook, had the right to make her feel ashamed. Not Gwen, who'd taken most of her meals at Frankie's table, done her homework on their front porch. Why, hadn't Frankie patched Gwen's torn trousers, cut down a few of Ma's shirts when Gwen had grown out of her own?

Only, Gwen wasn't wearing patched trousers and hand-me-downs anymore. Her skirt was short and tailored, showing off legs a mile long. She wore a crisp white blouse and gold bangles on her wrists. A spray of diamonds sparkled in her earlobes. The shoes on her feet looked like they had cost a fortune.

She was as out of place in Frankie's front yard as a hybrid rose in a field of summer weeds.

In one hand, she carried a bouquet of white daisies.

"Francis," Gwen drawled. Only a few days back in town, and her southern accent was sneaking in beneath polished city syllables. She paused in front of the porch steps, tilting her head in Frankie's direction. "You've given your ma's place a facelift."

"Just some paint and new boards." It had been her first real project, and she was absurdly proud that Gwen had noticed. "It'll do us for now."

"It looks good. Still smaller than a breadbox, but now much prettier. Ma must be happy."

"Ma's dead." Frankie tried to ignore the lump that formed in the back of her throat whenever she thought of her mother. "Dead and buried more than a year now."

"I'm sorry."

Frankie knew Gwen meant it. Some of the tension went out of her spine.

Gwen seemed to recall the flowers in her hand. "These are for you. An apology."

"I'm the one who should be apologizing." The fading bruise on Gwen's face was an accusation. It horrified Frankie that *she* had put it there. "I should never have—I'm sorry, Gwen. I'm not like that. I don't know what I was thinking."

"You weren't. You were reacting." Gwen held out the flowers. "I suppose I was a shock, after all this time. So you get this one pass. Just the one, mind."

Frankie didn't want to take the offering, but white daisies were her favorite—always had been—and the expression on Gwen's face was hopeful. It had been so long since anyone had brought Frankie flowers.

She had the flowers in her arms before she could stop herself. They smelled of spring and youth and shade beneath the hot sun. Frankie cradled the offering gently, resisting the urge to bury her face in the soft petals.

Gwen nodded, apparently satisfied. "We both acted inexcusably. I'm hoping . . . Frankie, can we begin again?"

Frankie frowned. "I don't know." They'd been good for each other once, but there was too much water gone under the bridge now, too many dangerous emotions close to the surface. At least, on her side. She couldn't tell for certain what Gwen was thinking, and that was distressing. She'd always known before.

Gwen looked away, then back again. "I'm sorry, but you know the old man, Frankie. He had a talent for manipulation and a taste for pretty women. And then he goes and leaves you his house."

Frankie felt blood rise in a flush along her chest and neck. "I know that. Who'd know it better? Or maybe you forget I was there, too."

"I don't know what to think."

Frankie's could hear her pulse thumping in her ears. "Little Frankie who never had more than two pennies to rub together, who'd kiss the boys and girls at school because they'd give her candy and pop, who always talked about the townie she'd marry and the big house they'd have. So I guess *some* people might make assumptions. But not you, Gwen. You knew me better than that."

"I thought I did." Gwen cleared her throat. "I do." She took the steps up the porch, hands spread in surrender. "Like I said, we got off to a bad start. There's just . . . it's a lot. More than I expected."

Frankie could see the faint tick of pulse in the hollow of Gwen's throat. She thought she could smell James Creek on her skin. Gwen had smelled just the same, like earth and tree and wet loam, decades ago when they'd spent hours together on the creek. Frankie remembered drifting in the deep-green current on the summer evenings, sharing secrets, planning impossible futures. She remembered the sweet urgency of innocent kisses exchanged in the belly of Gwen's boat.

Frankie had always known she was Gwen's first. Thinking of those kisses now, fresh heat warmed the pit of her belly—a fire that had nothing to do with temper. She looked up at Gwen. Gwen looked down. Her face was very still, cool and remote and yet somehow faintly puzzled.

Then she shifted slightly, leaning down. Frankie could feel the heat of her breath on her mouth. Was she going to kiss her? Really? Here, on Ma's porch, after a decade of absolutely zero communication?

Frankie knew she should put a stop to it, but she couldn't help wondering if Gwen tasted the same. She couldn't help wanting to find out.

"Mom! The toast's burning!"

Frankie saw the flash of disbelief in Gwen's green eyes, followed by something that looked surprisingly like hurt. She turned abruptly, stepping back out of the way to make room for the eleven-year-old boy now standing just inside the door, moving as far from Frankie as she possibly could on the small porch. Frankie could practically see the dismay vibrating beneath Gwen's fancy clothes and stiff smile.

Shit.

Chapter Five

"MOM," Chris repeated when Frankie didn't respond. He stared at Gwen as he spoke. "My toast's burning."

He wasn't wrong. Frankie could smell the dry scent of smoke and charred bread, could see the smoke through the door.

"Shit!" She brushed past her son and into the house. Smoke filled the kitchen, issuing in billows from the oven. "Were you trying to make toast in the *oven?*" Frankie grabbed a hot pad from a hook on the wall, trying to free the smoldering rack from inside the oven. It made an angry grinding sound as it came free. Three pieces of withered toast burned like napalm on the rack.

"Toss them in the sink!" Chris suggested from somewhere in the smoke. "Douse 'em!"

Frankie's eyes watered. Coughing, she held the grill away from her body, feeling foolish. In the hall past the kitchen, the smoke detector began to wail, late to the party.

"Dammit!" she yelped.

"Mom!" Chris materialized at her side. "It's still burning."

Gwen, her hand wrapped in a colorful dishtowel, reached around Frankie and grabbed the grill. Heels clicking efficiently over the linoleum, she carried the rack to the kitchen sink and turned it upside down. Over the angry alarm Frankie heard the crackling sound of burnt toast hitting the bottom of her enamel sink, then the groan of pipes as the tap ran. More smoke billowed, making Chris sneeze.

"Chris, the window—" Frankie began, but Gwen interrupted.

"I've got it. Turn on the fan over the range."

Frankie fumbled until she found the switch on the oven. She heaved a sigh of relief when the fan whirred into life. The smoke cleared almost immediately. The detector in the hall went blessedly silent. Ears ringing, Frankie wiped her eyes and looked around. Her son stood next to the oven, contrite.

"Careful; it's still hot," she warned. She glanced over at the sink, watching as Gwen unwrapped the dishtowel from her hand. She stood with one hip propped against Frankie's counter, skirt riding up just a little too high, body language just a shade too relaxed.

Shamming, Frankie thought. Gwen had always been good at hiding her emotions.

"I think Grandma's oven's dead, Mom." Chris announced. "It's all black inside."

"It's not dead; it just needs a cleaning. Did you even google 'how to make toast in an oven' before turning it to broil?"

Chris's expression turned mournful. Frankie relented, ruffling his hair with gentle affection. "It's fine. No harm no foul. Unless"—she turned toward Gwen—"did you burn your hand?"

"Manicure's a bit worse for wear." Gwen's expression was remote, guarded. "But no. I'm afraid your towel is a lost cause." She held up the square of red, and Frankie saw two baseball-size holes seared into the fabric.

"Bad day for the kitchen," Frankie said lightly, then resigned herself to introductions. "Chris, I told you about Ms. Cook."

"Gwen," she corrected.

"Christopher." Manfully he held out a hand. Gwen shook it silently.

"Thanks for the help," Chris added. "How'd you know about the fan above the range?"

"Your mom tried to bake a pie in this kitchen years ago. Practically burned the house to ashes. I saved her butt and helped her clean up the mess before her ma got home."

Chris snorted. Frankie felt her own lips curl in response.

"If I remember it rightly," she said, quirking a brow, "*you* were the one who wanted the pie in the first place."

The landline shrilled, cutting off Gwen's reply.

"I'll get it." Chris dashed from the kitchen with an energy that made Frankie sigh. She stood for a moment without moving, listening to the wordless murmur of her son's voice in the next room.

"Really, Francis? You kept the old number?"

Frankie heard the dry amusement beneath in Gwen's drawl. She shrugged it off. "Ma never could get the hang of cell phones. Besides, it still comes in handy. The reception out here isn't the greatest."

"Boy's a sharp one." Gwen hadn't moved from her slouch against the counter. Frankie was pinned by her stare.

"He is something," Frankie said. "One day he'll be president." She tried to make it a joke but couldn't quite hide the quiver of pride in her throat.

"He yours?"

"Yes. Not that it's any of your business." But she said it gently. She grabbed a clean rag. "You've got burnt toast on you. Let me get it off before it ruins your blouse." Wetting a corner of the rag, she crossed the kitchen and dabbed at the smear on Gwen's forearm. Gwen twitched but didn't pull away.

Goose bumps popped up on the flesh beneath Frankie's hand, and tiny hairs stood up along Gwen's arm. Heart racing, Frankie peeked sideways at her face from beneath her lashes. Then she froze.

Gwen's mouth was drawn tight, her nostrils pinched. "You might have warned me," she said coldly, accent sharpened to a blade. "His daddy lurking around here somewhere, too?" She dropped her gaze pointedly to Frankie's left hand. "Or maybe not. Don't see a wedding ring."

Frankie dropped the towel into the sink. Disappointment and regret washed over her in a flood. "I appreciate you coming all the way out here, Gwen. But if don't pick your words carefully, you'll need to go buy a second bunch of flowers." She aimed a level stare at the other woman. "That poison in your eye looks a lot like jealousy, and the way I recall it, you were the one who ran all the way to the West Coast like a hound with its tail between its legs. So you've got no right."

"Jealous?" Gwen made a show of looking around the small kitchen. "Of what? I don't see anything to be jealous of. You can dress up Ma's old house all you want, Francis, but underneath it's still shitty double-wide squatting on government land."

Fury fizzled orange behind Frankie's eyes. Her groping fingers found the round canister she used to store flour. She heaved the cylinder with all her strength. It crashed against the counter three feet from Gwen, spilling flour in a waterfall onto linoleum.

Gwen laughed out loud. She was across the room in a heartbeat, breath blowing quick and hot against Frankie's ear. "Still got your share of the Porter temper, I see. Thanks for aiming wide. Flour's a bitch to get out of good wool."

"Get out." She turned her head, lifted her chin, glared fire. Gwen shook her head, twisted to nudge Frankie back up against the oven. Even through her own jeans and T-shirt, Frankie could feel the warmth of her skin. Gwen had always radiated heat.

"Maybe I *am* jealous," Gwen whispered. "Maybe I didn't realize what I'd lost until I saw you up there on the roof like it didn't matter to you at all you were thirty feet off the ground." The anger drained from her eyes. Instead, tension etched across Gwen's brow in tiny lines, and the corners of her mouth creased downward, as if in pain.

"Gwen," Frankie said sadly. Under the woman's carefully polished exterior, she glimpsed a flash of the wounded girl.

"No. I don't want your pity," Gwen said, and kissed her.

Frankie remembered sweet, fumbling kisses and questing hands. This was different. There was nothing of sweetness in possession. Gwen took her mouth as if she meant to claim it, scalding with her tongue, pressing closer. A spark of arousal started low in Frankie's belly, a fire that quickly spread. She stretched up onto her tiptoes for more. Gwen sighed against her mouth. Her hands, soft and warm, found their way beneath Frankie's T-shirt, stroking. Frankie heard tiny whimpers and realized the helpless noises were her own.

And then, as though from very far away, she heard another sound—a sharp click and followed by the hiss of gas. She stiffened. "Gwen."

Gwen was too busy exploring the lines of Frankie's bra to pay attention. While Frankie appreciated the effort, circumstances had changed.

"Gwen!"

Gwen's mouth left hers, and her searching hands retreated, immediately missed. Breathing heavily, she regarded Frankie with lazy assurance, eyelids at half mast. "What?"

"The range," she said, squirming away. "You turned it on again."

"I turned it on?" Gwen stepped back but kept one hand clasped around Frankie's wrist. Her smile grew faintly mocking. Frankie blushed and was furious with herself when Gwen's grin widened.

"Fine. *We* turned it on. Move away." She swooshed a hand. "Let me switch it off before we start another fire." Gwen's breath danced across the back of Frankie's head as she fiddled with the knobs on the ancient appliance. She shivered in reaction.

"You're still a danger in the kitchen." Gwen nuzzled the curve of Frankie's ear. She sounded so very southern and so very pleased with herself. Frankie bit down on a smile.

"Usually I let Chris do the cooking. Despite evidence to the contrary, he's less destructive." She meant to make Gwen smile, but it was the wrong thing to say. Gwen retreated, deliberately putting space between them.

"I'm late," she said, wiping her hands neatly on Frankie's crumpled dishrag. "For a thing. A phone call. Business."

"Okay."

"Listen." Gwen shook her head, making her sleek bob shimmer. The diamonds on her wrist caught the light. "We'll talk. Later, all right? Just not now."

Frankie's heart squeezed, but she wasn't going to defend her life choices. "Okay. Later."

Gwen walked past Frankie into the evening. She didn't look around as she stepped off the porch.

Frankie shut the door so she wouldn't have to watch her oldest friend drive away. Grabbing the towel off the counter, she began to clean up the flour. She wiped, she rinsed, she wiped again. As she rinsed out the towel for the last time, she glanced dully out the window and caught her breath. Gwen was still there, curved over the sweet little car, her back to the house, elbows on the roof, forehead on her fists. Frankie took a deep breath, chased unwelcome tears from her eyes with the tips of her fingers, and went to get the broom. She didn't look out the window again until she heard the rumble of tires on the dirt road. Then she stood in the kitchen and watched Gwen's car until it disappeared around the bend.

GWEN PULLED INTO THE EMPTY PARK, STASHING THE SPYDER sideways across two shady parking spots. She left the windows open to let in the dusk, then stepped across asphalt and onto grass. Pulling off her shoes, she groaned at the feel of cool grass between her toes. Good heels were a power play, an important part of her repertoire, and she wore them like a champ; she could probably run a half marathon in her Louboutins without complaint.

But bare feet on grass was better than caviar on toast.

At the bottom of a gentle slope, James Creek turned sluggish and pooled into swampy marshland. Reeds and tall grasses drooped in the heat, tips almost touching the muddy water. A white heron fished along the shore. Farther out the wetlands widened again, and the water began to flow more quickly. Up and down tree-covered banks, old docks cut into the water and sagged with the weight of years. Many were attached to houses hidden behind the greenery. One or two of the piers belonged to the college and were used by the rowing team.

Gwen paced back and forth along the bank, trying to walk off the knot in her chest. When she could breathe again, she made her way up and over to the arched wooden bridge that was the park's main attraction. The boards trembled slightly beneath the soles of her feet, but the bridge was still sturdy. Here and there, initials had been carved into the rail.

Gwen walked until she stood at the very center of the arch. She leaned out over the water, watching eddies shake the reeds. When she was a kid there had been ducks, swarms of them, and sometimes geese. Now the waters were empty, except for the lone heron waiting in the shallows on the far bank.

She wondered if the ducks had already moved off for the winter. If so, they'd been premature. Even in the twilight sweat prickled the back of her neck. She shut her eyes and listened to the gurgle of the water, hoping the soothing sound would bring peace, but faces materialized on the backs of her eyelids: the old man's scowl, Christopher's wary curiosity, Frankie's grin.

The shock and hurt and then fury on her face when Gwen had mocked the sagging double-wide. As if she hadn't spent half her child-hood there, living off Ma's kindness.

"Hell!" Gwen brought the flat of her palm down against the railing.

They'd all been poor as church mice back then; Frankie's ma was no different from the rest. But Juliet Porter had been different from most of the meth addicts and pot farmers living back in the woods. She'd been soft at the core and hard around the edges, with a rare dramatic temper that burned hard and quick. Unlike Edward's cruel, cold tide, Ma's temper was all bark and no bite.

The way Frankie told it, Ma had always known exactly what she'd wanted out of life. She'd grown up in the backcountry of West Virginia, ducked out on any attempt at schooling, and spent the first quarter of her life on street corners and at country fairs, hawking the lawn ornaments her dad had carved. At nineteen she'd grown bored of the hills and found her way to Williamsburg in a long-haul trucker's cab.

Ma had never wanted money for money's sake. But she had always loved things—things and men. And because she was a pretty piece—all long dark hair and wide black eyes and the sort of curves that made a man's body tighten—she'd soon discovered that the easiest way to acquire things was by way of a lover's wallet.

And more power to her, I suppose. Better than anyone, Gwen under-stood about looking out for herself first. She'd spent her time on the streets of Seattle, done things she didn't like to think about to put food in her mouth and a roof over her head.

She'd seen the photographs of a young Juliet in Frankie's living room and heard stories of her youth from Edward, but the Ma she remembered from childhood had begun to go gray, begun to bend a little at the spine. She'd worn slacks and frilly blouses and spent the days clerking in a gift shop on the Royal Mile. Ma had learned to be discreet, but she never gave up her men, or her things. Her single bright-eyed daughter grew up surrounded by the—frankly tacky, in Gwen's opinion—gifts of local suitors.

Once, when Frankie was six and Gwen seven, a snub-nosed boy on the school playground had called Ma a slut. Gwen had watched with a group of classmates as the little girl he'd been tormenting retaliated with a fist to the nose. Gwen had added a kick to the boy's gut for good measure. They were both sent to the principal. And that was how Gwen Cook met fiery Frankie Porter, the one kid who wasn't afraid to give the school bully hell.

After that, they became fast playmates and conspirators. Whenever Gwen visited the house at the end of the dirt road, she always spoke politely and respectfully to Frankie's ma. And Ma had always returned the favor, pretending not to know Gwen was the daughter of the creek's most-infamous drunk.

Gwen sighed. Overhead, the sky had turned to indigo, the color of her father's angry gaze. And the same dark-blue eyes had looked out at her from Christopher's thin face.

Gwen felt sick. Blue eyes were a dime a dozen. Of course the kid wasn't Edward's spawn. She knew that. It was just hurt—and, yes, jealousy—turning Gwen's thoughts in a dark direction.

She could have said something. Like, "Hey, Gwen, great to see you. Here are the keys to your new/old house, and by the way I'm a mom now, so stop staring at my ass like it's a tall drink of water and you're desperate for a swallow."

Gwen groaned. It did matter, even if it shouldn't. It felt like a betrayal, which was nonsense. Because Frankie was right. It was Gwen who had cut all ties and run, Gwen who had locked Frankie away in a box in the back of her head with all the other bits and pieces of life on James Creek. She'd barely thought of Frankie at all. Of course Frankie had grown up and moved on.

Gwen turned abruptly and left the bridge to the gathering darkness. Out over the water and on the far bank, she could see the fluorescent glow of fireflies; tiny flickering stars come down to Earth. She sat in her car for a long time, watching until they faded away, before slowly driving back to Edward's house.

Chapter Six

"Pedestal sink's no good, Frankie. Threading's completely shot, and there's a crack running straight center down the middle."

Frankie paused over a bucket of teak oil. She craned her neck around, peering under her elbow. "Tina knew we'd probably need to pick up a new one."

The metal bucket rattled between her work boots as a particularly fierce swell caused the boat deck to bump and sway. The man standing half in and half out of the aft stairwell grimaced.

Frankie bit back a smile. "Looking a little green, Jack."

Her partner groaned. "You couldn't have asked for dry dock?"

Frankie grinned and dipped a paintbrush into the oil, sloshing with happy enthusiasm. "It's faster this way, and cheaper, which should make you want to sing hymns of praise."

"The books thank you, but my stomach won't. The James smells like an armpit in the summer." He leaned against the tilt of the boat, impatiently slicking sweaty curls from his forehead. Built like a tank and as reliable as an alarm clock, Jackson Pierce was Frankie's most valuable asset. And he knew it.

"It's not so bad." Frankie shot a glance down at the river. Here near the shore the James was not as deep as James Creek, and reeds grew up out of the shallows. But at least the water was clear. She glanced over at the faded pier lined with houseboats of various character. "People here keep the water clean. Though I never did understand why anyone would want to pay good money to live so far out."

"A long way from Baja." Jack took a shallow breath. "Antique or repro for the replacement sink?"

"Tina wants as close to the original as possible," Frankie told him. "Antique's better, if you can find one."

"I've got a man in Richmond. Likely he'll have one close enough. I'll drive out on Wednesday."

"Wednesday should be perfect." Frankie considered this a moment. "We'll yank the old one tomorrow."

"And won't that be fun." But he smiled as he looked around the deck. "She's coming together faster than I expected."

"You and me both." When the boat rocked again and he winced, Frankie snorted. "Get back on dry land before you puke all over my hard work."

"Aye, aye, Captain. Dinner still on tonight?"

"Are you kidding? Pizza night at Chez Pierce? Chris is chomping at the bit."

"I'll see about streaming something with swords and trolls, then. Appropriately bloody, but no decapitation." Frankie laughed as her friend beat a hasty retreat. Even battling the rocking boat, he moved with the sureness of man who knew and trusted the strength of his body.

Left alone, Frankie unlaced her work boots, walked barefoot across the deck, and took the narrow stairs down into the bottom of the boat. The living quarters below were carpeted with a thick cream Berber. The carpet had cost a pretty penny, and Frankie, who spent most her day among paints and caulking and sawdust, never ventured across it in her work boots. Tina Princeton had dashed off to Zurich for three months, leaving Frankie with explicit instructions and an almost-unlimited restoration budget. She'd also left behind an ancient fax machine and the loudly expressed hope that the boat would be ready for habitation by the time she returned.

The fax machine lived on a small table in the single bedroom.

Frankie checked the tray and found it surprisingly empty. Usually Tina dashed out four or five faxes before lunch when she'd changed her mind about this shade of paint or that color of fabric.

Skirting a rolled-up tarp and a bundle of swatches, Frankie crossed through the tiny living room and into the galley. The kitchen floors were hardwood and deeply scratched. Every board would need refinishing. The teak cabinets were still in good condition but would need a lot of hard work before they were beautiful again. Luckily, Jack had a magical touch when it came to carpentry.

The refrigerator was new, chrome, and shiny. Frankie didn't think it belonged in a 1920s houseboat, but Tina had wanted to keep it, and the client was always right, even when astoundingly uneducated in the ways of restoration. Frankie opened the fridge and dug around until she found the gallon of orange juice she'd buried there earlier in the morning. Standing in the galley, she gulped the cold juice directly from the jug while eyeing the cabinets. Tina's deadline of three months was beginning to look doable. Sticking the OJ back into the fridge, Frankie plucked a banana from the bowl of fruit she kept on the kitchen counter. Munching thoughtfully, she crossed back and forth along the galley floor, estimating work time and supply availability. She finished the banana quickly, dumped the peel into a plastic bag she kept in one corner for stray trash, and headed back to work.

On the way up to the stairs, she passed again through the bedroom and stopped, frowning. The room was mostly as Tina had left it. A teak platform bed, a dresser, and two Craftsman-style standing lamps took up most of the space. The cotton sheets on the bed were smooth and unwrinkled, waiting for the client's return. But the white daisies in the pottery vase were beginning to droop. Frankie sighed. She hadn't been able to leave the flowers in the dust after Gwen's angry departure. But she hadn't wanted them in her house, either, where Chris would wonder, and she would have to face them every morning when she woke up and every evening before she climbed into bed.

She hadn't wanted to think of Gwen at all. So she'd dropped the flowers into a spare vase and carried them to Tina's houseboat, where she could ignore them for most of the day and enjoy them exactly when she wanted to. Only, it hadn't worked quite that way because every time she came in for a snack or a break or a trip to the head, there the flowers were, faintly accusatory. And now, three days old, they were beginning to wilt. Not enough sunlight in the depths of the boat, Frankie supposed—or maybe the darn things were trying to make her feel guilty.

"Go ahead and die on me," she muttered, glaring at the vase. "See if I care. Go on; I dare you."

But when she climbed out into daylight, Frankie carried the flowers with her. She set the vase smack on the middle of the deck—where she knew they would get enough light—laced up her boots, and went back to work. Painting oil onto teak was an easy-enough job, even if the combination of heat and fumes made her head swim, but today Frankie couldn't seem to make the work come together. Twice she dropped the brush sideways into the bucket, submerging it completely, and once she spattered drops of oil onto the freshly painted white wheelhouse. The oil wouldn't hurt the paint, but Frankie didn't want to chance a stain, so she took several minutes out to swear, clean up the mess, and swear some more.

Frankie kept seeing, over and over again, the back of Gwen's neck as she bent over the dusty Spyder. She kept feeling, over and over again, the urgency of Gwen's mouth on her own.

She shivered. More oil splattered. Infuriated, she tossed the brush back into the bucket and reached for a mop-up rag. When she turned back the paintbrush had sunk to the bottom of her bucket. She almost kicked the bucket, brush, and oil clear across the deck and into the James River.

"Too much sun, Frankie," she told herself, fists clenched. "Never get a thing done if you carry on like this." The fumes were making her head throb.

She glanced at her watch. Almost half past four. The sun would be easing up soon. She would get another good two hours in before Chris needed a ride home from school. Two hours closer to completion, and she really didn't have time to waste. She needed to get back to work.

Fuck.

She cleaned up quickly but efficiently, then checked twice to make sure the boat was locked before she left.

❧

Fʀᴀɴᴋɪᴇ ʜᴇᴀʀᴅ ᴛʜᴇ ᴍᴏᴡᴇʀ ᴛʜʀᴏᴜɢʜ ᴛʜᴇ ᴏᴘᴇɴ ᴄᴀʀ ᴡɪɴᴅᴏᴡ before she turned onto the drive even though she couldn't make out the lawn through the trees until her Mercedes was halfway up the drive. Then she saw Gwen, dressed in a pair of sweats cut off at the knees, a blue tank top, and ratty tennis shoes. The shoes had definitely seen better days. The tank top was tight in all the right places, showing off her curves.

Gwen in sweats and sneakers was a very different creature from Gwen in couture with gold bangles on her wrists. The first was familiar —the Gwen Frankie had grown up with. The second, despite—or maybe because of—the arrogant looks and the flash of diamonds, was equally intriguing.

Gwen stopped the mower when she heard the car. Leaning on the handle, she watched Frankie as she climbed out onto the pavement, expression shuttered.

"Looks like hot work," Frankie said in greeting. Sweat slicked Gwen's brow and collarbone. Frankie barely managed not to lick her lips. "Guess I supposed you'd hire someone to do the yard."

Gwen shrugged. "I like my privacy. And I like that I now have a lawn of my own to mow."

"Yeah, well. You've got one front and back, and they're both huge. I should know." She crossed her arms, tucking her fists under her elbows to squash a nervous urge to crack her knuckles. "Where'd you get the mower? It looks like a relic."

"Hardware store in town." Gwen regarded her with veiled impatience. "Didn't expect to see you here, Francis."

"I came looking for you," Frankie confessed.

"Obviously."

Frankie gritted her teeth and pasted on a pleasant smile. "Got a minute?"

Gwen hesitated, then nodded. "Let me finish up here." She indicated toward the house. "Go inside, get us something cold to drink? I'll be up in a moment."

Unaccountably pleased, Frankie started up the drive. Her tulips were doing well, and the climbing rose she'd planted alongside the chimney was already starting to lean against the bricks.

"Frankie?" Gwen called, distracting her from the heartening maroon shoots on her rose. "Take off your boots before you go inside. Leave them on the porch. Looks like you've been tramping through a pigsty."

"They're my work boots!" But Gwen had already turned around and started the mower.

Frankie couldn't look away. Gwen had grown into a woman in the last twelve years. Of course she would have—Frankie knew that. But the beauty in that change surprised her. Lean cords of sinew and tendon moved whip-tight along Gwen's spine as she pushed the mower over the grass. More muscle bunched along her shoulders and knotted in her calves. Gwen was, Frankie deduced, no stranger to the gym.

Perspiration glistened at the small of her back, stained the waist-band of her sweats, left crescent moons in cotton under her breasts. Frankie had to pinch herself to keep from drooling.

"Get yourself under control, Porter," she warned herself. "Jesus, it's been a long dry spell." She shook herself hard and clunked up the front steps. She shed her boots on the doormat, rolling up the soiled cuffs of her jeans for good measure. Then she pushed open the front door and stepped into the house.

She had almost managed to forget how much she loved the old building. Sunlight spilled across the walls onto curving banisters that still smelled of lemon polish. She'd labored hard to keep many of the old lead-glass windows and all the period light fixtures. The house had been a pain to work on, but the result made her heart sing. Swallowing a nostalgic sigh, she walked slowly down the front hall, taking a side door through the butler's pantry and into the kitchen.

She didn't see any sign of habitation. She guessed Gwen must have dumped her belongings in the upstairs master bedroom. Even the kitchen was spotless, which was surprising. She'd never known Gwen to pick up after herself so thoroughly. When she wiped a finger along the counter, it came away clean. Maybe Gwen had been eating out every night or ordering pizza in.

Frankie felt a pang of regret. She wanted the gorgeous kitchen she'd so lovingly restored used daily and with passion. When she opened the fridge, searching for a cold drink, she saw evidence of an uneducated stomach. Cold cuts, potato salad, and a mangled chunk of ham waited on an uncovered plate. Her pride was soothed when she noticed the mostly eaten pie. Gwen had replaced the beer Frankie had stocked with a brand of her own—craft beer, a step up from the cheap stuff they'd snuck as kids—and way back behind the ham, on an oval platter she didn't recognize, she found sliced watermelon. The thick pieces made her smile. You could take the woman out of Virginia, but Virginia always stuck with the woman. Frankie didn't know a house in the state without fresh watermelon in the summer.

She grabbed a beer, then dragged the platter of watermelon from the fridge and carried both with her onto the back porch. Gwen had watered the potted plants arranged around the deck and swept up after the rapidly growing honeysuckle vine Frankie had coaxed along the railing, but the white Adirondack chairs appeared unused. Kernels of dried honeysuckle blossom drifted across the seats, nudged by a sluggish breeze. Frankie brushed the petals free and settled into the nearest chair.

The sun was dipping lower on the horizon, and the air felt cooler, pleasant. The beer chilled her tongue, and she let go a long sigh, beginning to relax. She helped herself greedily to the watermelon while studying the lawn at the back of the house. She noted where the plantings were doing well and where they were not, and she considered the pile of tools and the canvas tarp piled next to the gazebo. In the distance she could still hear the faint rumble of the mower.

She was almost dozing by the time Gwen came through the kitchen and onto the porch. She grunted with pleasure when she saw the melon, stole a slice, and then dropped into a chair. When Frankie offered up her beer, Gwen shook her head. Sweat sculpted runnels on her cheeks and painted the prow of her nose. She ate her watermelon with a fastidiousness that was close to obsessive. That was new.

Frankie caught herself staring. Gwen turned her head and met her eyes, and what Frankie saw there made her look down and away.

"Didn't expect to see you again," Gwen said at last. She sounded indifferent, but Frankie felt the heat of her gaze on the top of her head and tried not to squirm as a frisson of reaction sped along her spine.

"I don't know," Frankie replied after a moment. She swallowed a mouthful of beer. "You were rude, and out of line, and about as rational as my preteen son."

"So you've come for more?"

Frankie thought she detected reluctant humor in her tone. Surprised, she lifted her head. But Gwen was watching the woods, licking watermelon juice from her thumb. "We always used to drive each other nuts. I'm not sure we were ever kind to each other, sometimes." She cocked the neck of her beer bottle in Gwen's direction. "But we always made up after."

"You want to make up?" Gwen still wouldn't look at her, but Frankie saw the corners of her mouth curl upward. Then she remembered that last summer's preferred manner of "making up" and felt the blood rush from the tips of her toes to her hairline.

"I think . . . I want us to learn how to be kind to each other. And . . . I don't owe you an explanation. But maybe I want to give you one. About the house, I mean. Settle my conscious."

Gwen leaned forward in her chair. She rested her forearms on her knees. "I'm not sure I want to hear it. And we both know my genetics are faulty when it comes to kindness."

Frankie squelched a sudden strong urge to stroke the scowl from her brow. She set the beer bottle at her feet and stood up, taking four steps across the deck to the porch rail. She leaned back against the slats, tenderly avoiding the honeysuckle vines, and faced Gwen down much the same way she would a confrontational client.

"I can read your mind like today's newspaper, Gwen. And I'm just going to say this once—and, for the sake of the friendship we had, without raising my voice—Chris is not Edward's child."

"Boy's a dead ringer, Francis."

"That's your daddy issues talking. Or your anxiety. And God knows it's not your fault." Frankie added, more gently, "There are many blue-eyed men in this town, you idiot. Twenty, thirty, maybe hundreds. Most of them are about three million times more desirable than Edward ever was."

"I want to believe you. I do believe you. But I can see the old man looking right back at me."

"Only because you see his ghost everywhere. You always did, even when he was alive. I'm not surprised coming home again has stirred it up. Come on, Gwen; you know better."

Please tell me you know better.

Gwen made a frustrated noise. She rose in a fluid motion and paced to Frankie's side, and then away again. Frankie watched her retreat to the far corner of the porch. She wanted to go after her but kept still. Gwen had never enjoyed anyone's sympathy.

"I know you're right. And I thought I *had* let him go."

The growing breeze stirred the honeysuckle. Frankie inhaled the sweet scent, closing her eyes.

"All I'm saying is that Chris is not Edward's son. He's mine." And that's all that mattered in the entire world.

"What about his daddy?"

"Lives in Richmond," Frankie said, eyes still shut. "He's an investment banker." She heard Gwen's smothered cough and smiled. "Sounds too straitlaced and upstanding for me, I know. He wasn't that way when I met him. He was wild and funny and a great fuck, the one time we had sex."

The air shifted again. Frankie opened her eyes. Gwen stood at her side, hands curled around the porch railing.

"Where did you—" Gwen broke off, clearing her throat in annoyance. "Sorry. Stupid question."

Frankie answered without embarrassment, "In the back seat of Ma's Mercedes, three weeks after you ran away. He played varsity football. He was a senior. He had a fantastic body, and he knew how to sweet-talk a girl." She shrugged. "I was mad at you, Gwen. Sad and lonely. You ran off on me, and you didn't even bother to say goodbye."

"It was the best thing I could do at the time. You knew that. I thought you knew it."

"I can see you think so." Frankie looked out at the creek so she wouldn't witness Gwen's misery. "Anyway, all it took was the one time. I got pregnant. The football hero went to college on a scholarship, and became an investment banker, and married an Amazon-tall blonde with long legs, and eventually decided it would be best to forget he'd ever had a son or a past on the creek. It was fine; it was what I expected. People do what they can to find their way out." She smiled gamely, furious with herself that it still stung. "He had very blue eyes, by the way. And muscles you wouldn't believe. Everyone knew he could press his own weight."

"I've never seen the appeal of a muscular man—or any man, in general. They tend to take up too much room and are stupid beyond belief, as your football hero proved by leaving you behind."

Frank's heart turned over. Gwen was smiling, and it was the old self-deprecating smile she remembered, promising mischief, half a dare. She reached along the railing, tugging gently on the end of Frankie's ponytail. Her touch and the perfume of the honeysuckle made Frankie pleasantly dizzy.

"It wasn't like that; not really."

"No? How was it, then?"

"It was just sex in the back of the car, an itch scratched. It felt good, and I enjoyed it. I never bothered to wonder what he thought of me or even what he thought of anything."

"Sex in the back of your ma's car." Exasperation deepened her drawl. "Francis, you have any idea what I would have given to get you in the back seat of any car?" Her fingers wandered over to cup Frankie's chin. Frankie couldn't breathe. She opened her mouth on a snappy reply but managed only a wordless murmur.

Gwen's eyes were as wide and green as the creek. She smelled of sweat and summer, and she made Frankie remember lust.

"I'm going to kiss you," Gwen said, calm and matter-of-fact as you please, but Frankie saw the shuddering rise and fall of her rib cage.

"Okay. Yes, please."

This time the kiss was long and slow. Gwen took Frankie's mouth gently, tasting, exploring. Teasing until she opened further. Frankie felt longing start low in her stomach and spread through her veins, blossoming into wildfire. A sharp, sweet stab of need took her behind the knees, pitching her forward. Gwen shored her up, held her beneath the honeysuckle, and let her taste the flavor of desire.

"Jesus Christ." When Gwen broke away, she was breathing like she'd just run the Colonial 10K. "Christ, Frankie. Come inside?"

Frankie knew where that would lead: to the big antique bed she'd installed in the master bedroom, to the linen sheets and the cloud-soft duvet. She saw the intent in Gwen's fierce expression and in the trembling of her hands where they gripped her shoulders.

"No," Frankie said, although her insides had gone liquid at the thought of what Gwen might do to her in the embrace of that antique bed. "Not yet." Gently, she detached herself from Gwen's embrace. Her body throbbed in protest. "Remember that bit I said about being kind to each other?"

"Remember when I said I'm genetically deficient?"

"That's not a thing. You're not your father. And life shouldn't only be all about making up, no matter how good it is." That much Frankie knew. She'd seen how her mother had broken her heart over and over again against a string of careless lovers. "Or hiding bruises. The kind that leave marks and the kind that don't. Right?"

Gwen looked painfully baffled. "You're asking the wrong person, Francis. All I know is I want to see if you still wear little scraps of lace under your clothes."

Frankie's cheeks caught fire. She shoved her fists under her armpits so she wouldn't give in and reach out. "Not yet," she repeated. "It's been twelve years. Maybe we should spend some time getting to know each other again."

Gwen breathed out through her nose in frustration. "Fine. Jesus. What do normal people do when they're getting to know each other? Again. Dinner? Dinner. Tonight. Let me take you to dinner." She sounded pleased with herself, like Chris when he'd solved a particularly difficult math problem.

"Chris and I already have plans tonight."

"Tomorrow night, then. You owe me that much."

"I *owe* you?" She stiffened.

"Hell yes, Francis. You owe me. I know you remember how badly I wanted to get you in the back of your ma's car. And you gave that honor to some selfish jock." But Gwen was grinning and so obviously at ease with herself that Frankie wanted to freeze the moment and keep it forever.

"Don't tease!"

"And now I've come back, and you owe me dinner, at the very least." Gwen's eyebrows quirked upward, self-mocking and expectant. Frankie laughed.

"You've still got an ego the size of an elephant." Secretly, she was glad of it, comforted to know some things remained exactly the same.

Gwen followed her onto the front stoop. Retrieving Frankie's dirty work boots, she set them at her feet with a tiny flourish.

"Dinner," she prompted. "Tomorrow night. I'll pick you up at seven."

"I'll have to check with my sitter."

"Sure. Maybe see if you can book the gig until morning."

That stopped her laughter. "I can't." But it was tempting enough to make her wonder.

"Why not?" A hint of vulnerability flickered behind Gwen's self-satisfied mask. "Seems like an excellent idea to me. A whole night to talk, right? And . . . other things."

Frankie knew she was blushing. For once she didn't care.

"We'll see," she said. "We'll just see.

Chapter Seven

"FUCK MY LIFE!"

"Christopher!" Horrified, Frankie shoved breakfast dishes into the kitchen sink and turned to stare at her son. Unrepentant, Chris glared into the backpack he'd dropped on the counter.

"I forgot to make lunch last night. Now it's too late, and I'll have to go without."

"That's no excuse for a filthy mouth." Frankie tried her best to look stern. *Stern* was something she'd only had to learn in the last few weeks, as Chris's tantrums grew more frequent, and she hadn't quite got the hang of it. *Stern* made her feel like she was sucking on a lemon.

"Grandma used to say you had the filthiest mouth of them all when you were a kid."

"Grandma was right. I did have a dirty mouth, until she got tired of my sassing and rinsed my tongue with detergent. You know better. Eleven-year-old boys don't use cuss words."

"I'm almost twelve," Chris pointed out. He scraped a thumbnail across the kitchen counter, tracing the pits and tracks in the worn tile.

"Twelve-year-old boys shouldn't cuss, either."

"Roddy Green does. He says 'fuck' and 'shit' all the time. Just last week he called Mrs. Johnson a real b—"

"Chris!" Frankie barked. Apparently when push came to shove, she could do *stern* just fine.

Her son stuck his hands in his back pockets and rolled his eyes. Frankie took a firm grip on her temper, silently reminding herself that although she would never win Mother of the Year, she'd done a tolerable job so far and would learn to handle this new stage.

"You are not Roddy Green. And if I hear another cuss coming from your direction, Christopher, I'm going for the detergent."

Chris didn't look impressed. "You wouldn't; not really."

Frankie smothered a sigh. She could feel the prickling of the sensitive flesh on the back of her neck that meant a headache was coming on, and the day had barely begun. It had started out badly. After dallying too long in the shower, Chris had complained loudly when the hot water ran low. He'd sulked through breakfast because they were out of blueberry syrup, and then he'd moved so slowly to clear away dishes that Frankie had to bite her lip to keep from nagging.

As usual, they were running late. She had an important client probably already waiting at the office on her arrival, and her angry son appeared rooted to the kitchen floor. Pressing fingers again along the nape of her neck, she silently studied her child and wondered how exactly he'd turned from a sweetheart into a tyrant between one month and the next.

"You're right," she admitted when the silence stretched to an uncomfortable length. Chris lifted his gaze from the linoleum to her face. "I wouldn't really wash your mouth out. I'd probably just ground you until Christmas; and I'd hate to do that because then you'd miss debate finals." Chris winced and worked his jaw. Frankie held on to her courage with both hands, plunging ahead before he could interrupt: "And then you'd be miserable. But you're already making me miserable, Chris, and that's not fair."

She expected one of the sarcastic replies he'd become so adept at throwing her way, or even another curse word. She steeled herself against exasperation and hurt. Instead, tears glittered on his lashes. Frankie felt as though she'd been punched in the gut. She wrapped her arm around his shoulders. A pang of guilt stung her own eyes.

"What is it, hon? Can you tell me?"

"I did tell you!" Chris shrugged off her arm. "I forgot to make lunch, and now I'll starve all day!"

Frankie didn't know whether to laugh or shout. Several of Roddy Green's filthy words came to mind. "Nothing else?"

"Nope." Defiant again, he zipped up the backpack and slung it across his back.

"School's fine?" Frankie tried. "Grades are good?"

"Mom." He made the word into one long groan. "I've got straight As in every class, okay?"

"Sometimes grades aren't everything." She surprised herself by the admission.

"Mom." Chris rolled his eyes again. "We're already way late. I'll probably miss PE. Shouldn't we be going?" As if he hadn't spent the last two hours trying to delay departure.

Frankie shook her head. It felt like her already-topsy-turvy world had just spun off its axis. "What about lunch?"

"I'll just go without. It won't be so bad."

Frankie tried very, very hard not to give in. She'd been a backyard con artist in her own day, the snottiest of the little snots. She knew the game, she knew the rules, and she could see that her intelligent son was learning how to walk the walk. But the slump of those thin shoulders and the way he dragged the soles of his shoes across the kitchen floor made her break out in a sweat. She promised herself she wouldn't give in. She knew better.

She reached for her tote anyway.

"Here." She dug through the clutter until she found the five-dollar bill she'd set aside for lunch. "Take this. Get something in the cafeteria."

It was their long-standing rule: no cafeteria lunches. Brown bagging saved money and was healthier. For five years Chris had packed his own lunch and been happy. Now, he accepted her offering as though it were the most natural thing in the world.

"Fine." He sighed. "Can we go now?"

Frankie shut her eyes and counted to ten—to twenty, to fifty—and then, when she thought she could possibly face the rest of the world without breaking anything, she grabbed the keys from the counter and followed her scowling son out into the morning.

SHE WAS IN THE MIDDLE OF A MUCH-NEEDED BREAK, HALF DOZING IN the heavy sunlight, when she heard Gwen's tread on the creaky steps that led up from Chesapeake Renovation's rented storefront to the empty attic space above. Nobody else would take the staircase with such single-minded purpose and careful regard for life and limb. Jack tended to climb the steps on the balls of his feet, complaining loudly about broken bones, and her troupe of messenger boys always seemed to be running a race.

And even though she hated to admit it to herself, she still remembered the keyless tune Gwen whistled under her breath when she was in an especially tricky mood.

Still afraid of heights, Gwen? Frankie tried to dredge up an ounce of sympathy, but she really wasn't in the mood.

The whistling wound to a halt as Gwen reached the landing, picked up again as she found her way through dust and shadows to the balcony, cut off abruptly when she discovered just exactly what the balcony entailed. Hardly more than a concrete ledge and an iron railing, the balcony looked out kitty corner over peaked roof, treetop, and asphalt lane to Duke of Gloucester Street. Only two feet wide, the space had barely enough room for the clay pot of geraniums and barstool.

The barstool had been abandoned by a client. It was ugly as sin and steady as a rock. It was also taller than the balcony rail by a good two inches, leaving Frankie feeling as if she were floating on nothing but leather and southern breezes.

Knowing Gwen would need time to adjust to the height and lack of solid ground, Frankie waited in silence while those sparse southern breezes tickled the crown of her head and tossed tendrils of hair into her face. Then she brushed the tussled hair behind one ear and opened her eyes.

"You're about seven hours early," she pointed out, fixing Gwen with her best prickly stare. "And I'm busy."

"I can see that," Gwen drawled. Ignoring Frankie's glare, she dragged her own green gaze from the tip of Frankie's mussed bun, down across the thin silk shirt and short wraparound skirt she'd worn to beat the heat, and over bare legs and bare feet to the sandals she'd abandoned beneath her stool.

"I have been busy. Very busy," Frankie snapped, furious with herself because the casual study drew her body taut, as though she were sixteen again and not a grown woman who hadn't yet decided what she wanted. "The phones haven't stopped ringing since we opened, and I've got a client furious because I had to reschedule this morning's meeting." She tried not to remember the feel of Gwen's mouth on her own. "What are you doing here, anyway?"

"Your clerk told me you were up here, having lunch. What's on the menu today, air and sunlight?"

"He's my partner, not a clerk." Frankie's empty stomach made her think of Chris. She'd spent most of her lunch break fretting uselessly, and as a result she was tired and grumpy and ready for a good spat. Because she remembered precisely how to push Gwen's buttons, Frankie turned from the Historic District and smiled sweetly. "Why don't you come on out? The view's incredible."

"I can see that from here." Gwen cocked one brow. She remained exactly in place, on the threshold between balcony and attic, lounging against the doorjamb, looking much too relaxed and comfortable in tailored slacks and a crisp linen tunic. The wilting heat didn't appear to touch her. Frankie's sour mood grew.

"You're taking me to dinner, not lunch. I told you I had to work. What are you doing here?"

"Thought I'd check in." Gwen turned her attention to the tourists. "And maybe I wanted to see you at work. You can almost read their lips from up here."

"I'm not going to chicken out, if that's what you're thinking. You said seven o'clock. I'll be ready."

"Good." Gwen replied mildly. And then: "Look at that. Kid's got a bazillion guns."

In spite of herself, Frankie turned back to the Royal Mile, locating the boy in question. Loaded up with toy rifles and pistols, the cheerful toddler staggered in his sneakers. Frankie could almost hear the child's gurgle of mirth when he dropped a tiny musket.

"Brit," Frankie diagnosed, watching as a man in a baseball cap hoisted the boy onto his shoulders.

"What?"

"The British kids always go for the guns. The Canucks like the pan whistles and Paul Revere hats. And kids from the good ol' U-S-of-A prefer candy and ice cream." Gwen's mouth creased a little in amusement. Frankie's heart flopped. She'd forgotten how, even on the worst days, she'd always been willing to share a joke.

"And you know this how?"

"I watch." Frankie wiggled her bare toes in the sunlight. "You pick up things if you pay attention to details. During the early-summer months most of the tourists are local. After July, they're generally from overseas. Even before I rented this place"—she waved a hand at the building behind her—"I used to take walks through CW in the afternoons and just watch. Listen. Wonder what it's like to come from so far away, to just pick up and travel wherever and whenever you want."

She slid from the stool and walked across the tiny balcony to run restless fingers through brilliant geranium buds. "But I suppose you know all about that. I imagine you've done your own share of traveling."

If Gwen heard her bitterness, she didn't react. "Some."

"Go wherever you want and then whisk right away again when things get hairy. Right, Gwen?"

"You looking for a fight, Francis?" She sounded amused. Frankie shook her head and sighed.

"Ugly morning."

"I can see that. Want to tell me about it?" She'd always been ready to share a joke, and she'd always been willing to listen. That was something else Frankie had forgotten—maybe on purpose. She leaned back against the side of the building, tilted her chin, and considered the lines of the roof.

"Chris was a terror all morning. In fact, he's been a terror for the last few months. I can't figure what's up with him. He's always been the sweetest kid. And lately it's like he's completely on edge of . . . something. Some sort of Dr. Jekyll complex."

"I always preferred Mr. Hyde." Linen whispered as Gwen shifted on the threshold. "Being a single mom must be hard," she added grudgingly.

Frankie tried not to smile. "Triter words, I've never heard."

"Thank you."

"Thing is," she continued, trying in vain to ignore the zing of mirth that threatened to lighten her mood, "I've always been a great mom."

"A great mom, and modest, too."

A bubble of laughter escaped Frankie before she could stop it. Defeated, she turned from the roof and contemplated the woman on the threshold. She wanted to resent Gwen for making her troubles humorous. Instead, she felt the old fascination rise and an easing of the constriction around her heart.

"Pot and kettle," Frankie accused, smiling.

"I've never been called modest," Gwen agreed. The corners of her mouth lifted.

"Any kids?" Frankie asked, although she knew there weren't. Google was her friend, and although over the years the tabloids had caught Gwen here and there with a companion on her arm, the girlfriends seemed to change as often as her shoes. Certainly there had been no talk of family.

"Nope. Pinnacle is my baby."

"Married? Girlfriend?" Heat blossomed over her cheeks, and she bent again over the geraniums to hide it.

Gwen answered easily, "No. No time."

Frankie broke a bud from the plant, crushed the stem between her fingers, and brought it to her nose. The pungent scent helped to clear her head.

"What's it like, anyway?"

"What?"

"Seattle?"

"Wet. Green. Busy." Gwen shrugged. "Good."

"But here you are again."

"Sometimes even a world traveler finds herself in search of a little peace."

"Living in Edward's house?" She wrinkled her nose in deliberate disbelief. Gwen nodded, eyes narrowing. The intensity of her regard made Frankie quiver.

"I guess I'm glad you're back, after all. I mean, if it makes you happy," she said, coolly polite, so she wouldn't have to face this new surge of old desires.

"'Happy'?" Gwen echoed as though the word was foreign.

She shifted in the doorway, stretched out a hand, and trailed her thumb across Frankie's chin, through the trickle of pollen the geranium had left behind. Frankie froze. And then, because it felt right, she closed her eyes and leaned into Gwen's touch. The ball of her Gwen's thumb nudged at her lower lip. A spike of pure undiluted lust made Frankie gasp. Gwen bent, brushed a disappointingly chaste kiss against Frankie's forehead, then stepped away, moving out of the heat and back into the shelter of the attic.

"Your phones are ringing," she said quietly.

Through the pounding of her pulse in her ears, Frankie could hear the distant shrilling that meant break time was over and clients were impatient. "I should get back." But her legs were rooted in place.

"I'll see you this evening," Gwen replied. Casually, she dug her car keys and shades out from a pocket.

"This evening," Frankie repeated. How could one single gentle kiss chase every working thought from her traitorous brain? *Careful, Frankie.* But her body wanted what it wanted. "Gwen?"

Gwen tilted her head in silent inquiry.

"Thanks for listening."

"Don't worry so much, Francis. The kid will turn out fine. You did." Gwen smiled but didn't reach out to touch her again.

She was halfway across the dusty attic floor before Frankie called after, "Wait. You never said why you'd come." She grabbed her abandoned sandals and left the balcony.

Gwen paused in a swirl of dancing dust motes, still smiling. "I did say. Just to check in."

Frankie stood, mute, listening to the tap of heels on the old staircase as Gwen left. She heard Jack call out a question. Curious, Frankie leaned into the stairwell, but she couldn't hear what answer, if any, Gwen made.

Just to check in. She'd stopped by just to check in. Frankie didn't know what to think. The Gwen she'd grown up alongside, although both nosy and overprotective, would never have admitted such a thing.

She'd said she'd moved into her father's house in search of peace. Gwen at seventeen hadn't believed the luxury of peace existed, especially not in Edward's territory.

And she'd made Frankie laugh instead of giving in to the fight her bitter mood wanted. Gwen had known—remembered—exactly how to make her smile, how to lighten her heart, if just for the moment.

Still leaning into the stairwell, Frankie grinned. Dinner with the new grown-up Gwen just might be more than bearable.

Chapter Eight

"I THINK YOU'RE MAKING A MISTAKE."

"It's just a date, Jack." Frankie rummaged through the bathroom drawer. "How can I not own even one tube of lipstick?"

"You don't wear lipstick," Jack pointed out. "And I was referring to my dinner, not yours."

"It's pizza." Just in case she'd somehow buried a tube in with the toothpaste and Tylenol, Frankie peered into the medicine cabinet. "You like pizza."

"It's vegetarian on whole-wheat crust. What kind of mom orders vegetarian on wheat crust for her babysitter?"

"I'm on a health kick. And Chris likes vegetarian. The babysitter will have to adapt."

Giving up on the faint hope of lipstick, Frankie snatched an ancient bottle of hair spray and considered it through narrowed eyes. Jack plucked it from her hand.

"You don't wear that stuff, either, and it's not too late to change your mind."

Frankie rolled her eyes. It was like having two preteens in the house instead of just one. "I already phoned in the order."

"I meant about your dinner. You sure you want to do this? I mean, the way you tell it, she broke your heart into about a thousand pieces."

"It's just dinner. Dinner's fine. Dinner's good." Frankie studied herself in the medicine cabinet mirror. The butterflies in her stomach didn't seem to show on her face.

"It's the after-dinner bit I'm worried about, the 'book the babysitter all night' part. I promise Gwen's sorting through her bedside drawer right about now, and it's not hair spray she's looking for. It's . . . whatever you ladies use instead of condoms."

Frankie groaned. "You're a shitty wingman, Jack."

"Too bad you're stuck with me." He followed Frankie into the back hall. "But while I can't help you pick out your shoes, I am handy with a router, I'm always on call for emergency babysitting, and I've got a packet of lube in my wallet if you haven't got your own in that envelope you call a purse."

"Jesus. Please just shut up. Where's Chris?"

"Setting up dirty Scrabble in the parlor."

"Very funny." She found Chris in the kitchen at work over the microwave. "Popcorn?"

"Hi, Mom." He smiled, and it was genuine. "Jack said he was hungry, and he didn't want to wait for the healthy pizza. We're going to play Scrabble before movies."

Frankie raised her eyebrows. "Sounds like fun. Don't stay up too late."

"We're going to stay up until dawn." Jack ruffled Chris's hair. "And have ice cream for breakfast."

"We're out of ice cream." Chris's shoulders slumped.

"I came prepared for anything. When your mom called, I stocked the truck with triple-brownie fudge." He glanced at Frankie. "I'll go get it now. Give you two a moment to say good night."

He left them to the sound of popping corn. Chris stared down at the toes of his sneakers. Frankie crossed the kitchen and slung an arm around his waist. "Okay with this?"

"It's just a date, Mom. You've had one or two before."

"One, maybe." Frankie poked his ribs until he squirmed. "Don't let Jack stay up all night, or he'll be cranky in the morning."

Chris scoffed. "He'll be snoring by ten."

"I will not!" Jack ducked back into the kitchen, ice cream in hand. "Quick, it's melting. Your lady's here, Frankie. Nice car, if you like them overpriced."

Frankie shot him a final look before kissing her son goodbye.

"Good night, boys. Behave."

"Good night, Mom," they replied as one, and then immediately forgot her for the beeping microwave.

"You said dinner," Frankie grumbled. She glared through the window of Gwen's little car and out at the crowded parking lot. "You didn't say anything about the Trellis."

"I believe they serve dinner at the Trellis," Gwen replied, amused by the uneasy tapping of Frankie's foot against the Porsche's floor mat.

"I thought you meant a steakhouse or Chinese or even fast food." The rhythm of her foot increased. She wore clunky black wedges that made her look taller and turned the curve of her slim ankles elegant. Gwen couldn't seem to pull her gaze from those ankles.

"Gwen?"

Gwen closed her fingers hard on the wheel. "Fast food. Your dates usually court you in drive-throughs, Francis?"

"I don't have time for dates." Frankie glared across the stick shift. "We can't go to the Trellis, Gwen. I'm not dressed for it. Look at you! Is that pantsuit even off the rack? It looks like a million dollars."

"You look fine." She looked perfect. The simple black sheath she wore hugged every gentle swell, bared her collarbone and her thighs. It was enough to make Gwen salivate. She'd even done something with her hair, pinned it back from her eyes, emphasizing the delicate bones in her face. And she smelled like gardenias.

"People wear silk to the Trellis," Frankie argued, "not secondhand clothes and discount shoes."

"I like those shoes." Because Gwen caught the gleam of panic in Frankie's eyes and understood, she captured one small hand and squeezed reassuringly. "They've got the best corn chowder in the state. One taste and you'll forget anything else."

"Easy for you to say," Frankie muttered. "My feet are killing me. I don't know how you do it."

Gwen laughed, gave her fingers a quick kiss, and then hopped out into the evening. Frankie followed more slowly. Once out onto the asphalt, she hesitated, eyeing the lights of Merchants Square with distrust.

"You sure?"

"Positive." Gwen took her hand again, urging her gently across the parking lot. Frankie huffed but didn't struggle, although once or twice it looked as though she wanted to turn stubborn and dig in those heels. "Their bread has won awards," Gwen coaxed, outwardly calm, although the sway of Frankie's hips in that dress made her want to pull her behind the nearest shrub and kiss her breathless.

Ever since she'd left Frankie in the empty attic rooms above her shop, Gwen had been dizzy with arousal. All afternoon she'd been able to think of nothing but the silken brush of Frankie's mouth against her thumb.

"And dessert," she murmured. "I know you've heard of their famous chocolate desserts."

Frankie glanced over, suspicious. "How many times have you eaten here?"

"Once or twice. When I first got into town, after I ran out of pie and before I had time to shop for groceries." They crossed the cobblestones into Merchants Square. "There it is. Looks nice, doesn't it? Little white lights and all."

Frankie slowed to take it all in. "It is pretty," she admitted grudgingly. "Look how they weave the vines up the lattice above the door."

"The Trellis," Gwen replied lightly, though anxiety was beginning to knot in her stomach. It was important she did this right. "You want to eat out on the patio or in?"

"In," Frankie replied without hesitation. "It'll be cooler in."

"As the lady commands."

She guided Frankie beneath white fairy lights into the restaurant. The hostess met them with a smile and led them through a busy dining room to a table against one large window. Gwen heard Frankie draw a breath as she craned her neck from side to side, trying to see everything at once.

"Look at how they match the floor and the tiles on the hearth," she said after the hostess had seated them and drifted discreetly away. "And look at the paintings on the wall. Local. I recognize the artist. Someone has good taste."

"I brought you here to eat, not assess the decor." But the animation on Frankie's face made Gwen grin. She smiled back over the squat white candle flickering at the center of their table.

"I can't help it. It's beautiful." Frankie's eyes were as wide as a kid's at Christmas, her lips slightly parted. Gwen was foolishly, painfully, glad to see she'd lost none of the innate wonder she'd had as a child.

"Told you so. And here comes the bread." Gwen watched as Frankie carefully chose a piece of Irish soda bread from the basket. She took a bite and closed her eyes in bliss, and Gwen had to stop herself from taking her hand again. She wanted to touch her to reassure herself that she was actually there.

She was afraid if she moved too fast, she would scare her away.

"Gwen. We're here only two minutes, and you're practically vibrating." Frankie deftly buttered her slice of bread, all the while pinning Gwen with her frown. "You can ask me about the house. I know you want to."

Gwen shook her head. Edward's house was the last thing on her mind. "We're here to eat. Take a look at the menu."

Frankie's gaze didn't waver. "That's the real reason you stopped by my office this morning, isn't it? To finish our conversation. Now you've thought about it, you have questions, but you're too polite to ask." She nudged the breadbasket with her pinkie finger, sliding it over the tablecloth. "It's okay. Of course you'd have questions. Go ahead and ask, Gwen. Heavens, you're nervous as a long-tailed cat."

Gwen chose a breadstick. She looked for the waiter, wanting a drink. Wine, or maybe a whiskey. Frankie wasn't wrong. Almost as much as she wanted to strip the distracting little black dress from her curves, Gwen wanted to know how Frankie Porter had ended up with the Cook estate. Because Christ knew the old man never gave anything away for free.

And if he'd somehow taken advantage of Frankie, Gwen would dig him up and kill him all over again.

"Seriously?" Frankie sounded mildly disappointed. "You always did prefer suffering in silence to doing."

She stiffened. "I've spent the last decade working my ass off. I didn't have time to brood."

"Could be that's the problem. Fine, then." Frankie crossed her arms on the table. "I'll go first. Level the playing field or whatever. Because I have questions, too."

"I don't know what you mean." But she was afraid she did. Thankfully the waiter chose that moment to appear at her elbow. Gwen gratefully ordered a bottle of merlot, then pretended to study the menu as soon as he left, hoping Frankie would do the same.

She didn't. Seemed like neither of them know how to let well enough alone.

"What happened that night, Gwen? Why did you run away? Was it because of me?" Frankie cleared her throat. "The fall?"

"You didn't fall," Frankie retorted sharply. "You jumped."

Frankie's mouth tightened. "Sure. Maybe. I don't really remember."

"You. Jumped!" Gwen repeated. This time she let all the horror of that night show on her face.

Frankie turned pale. Luckily the waiter returned to their table before Gwen could say something regrettable. She stiffly ordered a salad and a steak to fill the ache in her stomach. Frankie took her time with the menu, probably trying to recover her nerve. Afterward they sat in silence as the waiter poured their wine.

Frankie, being Frankie, tried again: "So . . . it *did* have something to do with that day. With my birthday."

"You were an idiot." Strange that after so many years, the bitterness hadn't eased one iota.

"I guess I was. Didn't bother you before."

"You were the one stupid enough to jump, but I was the one got blamed for it."

The candle on the table flickered. Frankie's face seemed to blur in the soft light.

"Blamed?"

Gwen shrugged, stared down into her wine. "Once Ma saw you settled in that night, she came storming over. Gave the old man what for. Said it was me who dared you to take the leap."

"She did? Fuck. And of course *he* took it out on you after." Her voice was rough with sympathy. Gwen hated to hear it.

She shrugged again. "Beat me bloody, no surprise. Broke a tooth, my wrist, a few ribs. So instead of suffering in silence"—Gwen shot Frankie a dry look—"I decided enough was enough and packed a bag, stole the booze money from under his mattress. Took off."

"But it wasn't your fault."

"No shit. You were the stupid idiot who thought she could fly. I should have let you drown." They both knew she didn't mean it.

"Is that why you didn't say goodbye?"

Gwen looked up. Frankie's fingers were wrapped around the stem of her wineglass, the corners of her mouth turned down. Gwen's conscience prodded.

"No, Francis. I told you: he beat me bloody. I was a mess. I didn't want you to see me that way. Helpless and broken. You'll probably recall"—she grimaced—"even back then, I had a lot of pride."

Frankie bowed her head. The waiter popped up again, this time placing huge leafy salads on the table.

"Eat," Gwen said gently. Frankie grabbed her fork and took a hasty bite. Even in the dim light Gwen could see the face she made. "Arugula," she volunteered, amused in spite of the crack in her heart. "You'll get used to it."

It was the right thing to say. Frankie's chin came up. "Seattle doesn't have a monopoly on arugula. I know what it tastes like." Her mouth curved. "Like sweat."

Gwen choked on her wine. Frankie winked and speared another forkful of greens.

"Hush. You're disturbing the tourists." Her soft, rueful laughter melted Gwen's heart and made her shudder with the terror of so much *want*.

"Francis." She leaned forward, dared to capture Frankie's hand, brushed a kiss across her knuckles. "I've missed you. You have no idea how much. *I* had no idea how much."

Frankie paused, fork suspended. She sighed. "I can't afford to make a mistake right now, Gwen. You need to know that."

"I get it. But you and I . . . you and I were always meant for each other. You know that." She had to know that.

"Do I? Things weren't easy with us, even when we were kids."

"Yeah, well. We're adults now. We'll do better." In that moment, Gwen believed they could. Frankie rolled her eyes, but she squeezed Gwen's fingers.

"I'm passing on the arugula. Can we skip to dessert?"

Gwen laughed and brought the palm of Frankie's hand to her lips. She laughed again when Frankie quivered under her mouth. "You never could resist chocolate."

"Me?" She grinned back. "You're the one with the addiction to sweets."

Gwen nuzzled Frankie's wrist and felt the flutter of her pulse against her mouth. A small sigh slipped Frankie's lips, and Gwen's body burned at the sound. "Maybe we should take dinner home."

Frankie snatched her hand back so quickly the silverware chimed. "No way. We're staying. This is the Trellis. Besides," her smile grew bright with secret amusement, "there's no hurry. I booked the sitter for the night."

"Jesus, Frankie." Gwen took a long swallow of wine. "Eat. Eat quickly."

THEY TOOK DESSERT TO GO, WRAPPED PRETTILY IN TINFOIL TWISTED to resemble a swan. Frankie sat silently, the swan in her lap, and stared straight out the front window as Gwen sent the car zinging through Colonial Williamsburg and up Creek Lane. A light rain pattered on the windows, leaving gray streaks across the glass.

"Cops love this corner," Frankie warned as they blazed past an upscale gated community.

Gwen didn't reply. Somehow Frankie's hand had come to rest on Gwen's knee. The scent of her was enough to drive anyone wild, and the weight of the wrapped chocolate dessert in her lap caused the hem of her skirt to edge up above her thigh, baring a delicious expanse of skin.

"And there are deer around."

Out of the corner of her eye, Gwen saw Frankie wet her lips in a quick nervous gesture. She slammed on the brake. The Porsche slipped on the wet pavement and then came to a purring halt in the middle of the road.

Frankie's eyes grew huge. "What is it?"

Gwen silenced her with a kiss, leaning across the front seat and claiming her mouth. Frankie stiffened in surprise and then relaxed with a sigh. Her fingers reached out to tangle in Gwen's hair, and Gwen knew with a thrill of relief that they were both on the same page. She pulled away, breathing heavily, and sent the car speeding back into the night.

Frankie didn't say a word. Her fingertips left divots in the tinfoil swan.

They almost didn't make it up the drive. Gwen stopped again to taste Frankie as she helped her out of the car. The rain curled her ponytail and tightened the dress about her body. Her body was a work of art, soft and hard in all the right places. Gwen ran her hands up and down Frankie's spine as she nibbled along the curve of her neck and then reached down to cup the tight swell of her perfect ass.

Frankie's fingers danced along the waistband of Gwen's slacks, drifted upward, trailing wet fire beneath her shirt, making goose bumps explode. Her eyes were slanted and full of moonlight.

"Frankie." It took all of Gwen's resolve to pull her mouth from the hollow of Frankie's throat. "Inside." But Frankie didn't seem to hear. Her fingers walked along Gwen's rib cage, found the edge of her bra, then trailed more fire down Gwen's front toward her belly button.

"Gwen," she whispered.

"Come up to the house." Warm rain and cool moonlight turned Frankie's shadow to silver. Gwen could see the high peaks of her nipples through clinging rayon. She swallowed a groan. "I can't wait—"

"Then don't." Frankie bent to unstrap her heels, tossed the shoes onto the lawn. "Here. Now." She settled slowly onto the wet grass, pulling Gwen after. Her grin was dazzling. "The night is beautiful."

"You," Gwen said between breaths, "are beautiful."

She knelt in front of Frankie on the grass, caressing her breasts through wet fabric, stroking the flat plane of her belly, longing to explore every inch. Then her hand reached the juncture of Frankie's thigh, fingers slipping beneath that short skirt, sliding behind a scant lacy barrier. She was so warm—*the sun to my moon*—and gorgeously slick with arousal.

Gwen's control evaporated at last. Frankie laughed breathlessly when Gwen pushed aside her panties.

"And here I thought you weren't hungry." She gasped, arching against Gwen's fingers. "You didn't touch a thing at dinner."

"I wanted you, Frankie. Always only you."

Chapter Nine

Frankie opened her eyes to opaque light and the distant squeak of gossiping birds.

She blinked, stirring beneath warm sheets. Yawning, she reached across a mound of pillows for her alarm clock.

No alarm clock.

Her hand bumped carpet and jarred the sleep from her head. Memories returned in a rush that sent a sweet, burning ache through her bones. Brushing the hair from her eyes, she sat up.

The sheets were the kind of cotton her best clients preferred, blue as the ocean, and they still smelled new. The mattress was thin and low to the ground, and when Frankie took a peek under the fitted sheet, her suspicions were confirmed: an air mattress. Not that she had noticed the entire night through, between quick catnaps and the relentless, incredible flights of passion Gwen had stirred within her. They'd both been insatiable, insistent, demanding. Like the teenage lovers they'd never had a chance to be.

Only with dawn had the desperate edges soothed to something more tender. Then they had taken each other slowly, gently exploring with mouths and hands.

Frankie sighed, stretching. Dawn was long gone. The sun shone through the basement window, collecting in a rectangle on the carpet, and she was alone between the sheets.

She slid reluctantly out of bed, looking for her clothes. Her shoes were in a sodden pile at the foot of the mattress. She had no idea where exactly her dress had ended up. Her body felt languid and liquid and well used—and already, despite stiffening muscles and several small bruises on one thigh, she wanted more.

"Get a grip," she scolded herself. She stalked naked through the sunlight to Gwen's suitcase abandoned in one corner of the room. Unzipping the bag, she dug around until she found sweatpants and a hoodie sporting the Seattle Mariners logo. She pulled the hoodie over her head, then struggled into the sweatpants. They bagged at her ankles, several inches too long.

She rolled the pants up, pulled on a pair of fluffy white socks, and ran her fingers through her hair. Frankie remembered wearing her watch to bed, but when she looked for the time, her wrist was bare. She spent several minutes digging through rumpled sheets, managing to unearth Gwen's discarded bra—Wacoal, camouflage, no underwire—before she found the watch. It read half past noon.

"Holy shit." Frankie couldn't believe it. She hadn't slept past eight in years, if ever. Even as a child she'd preferred to rise with the sun. Feeling a motherly pang of guilt because the last thing her son needed at the moment was a perpetually tardy mother, Frankie strapped the watch back onto her wrist and shot up the basement stairs.

The door to the kitchen was open. As she hopped up the last two steps, she smelled bacon.

No fucking way.

Frankie had renovated Edward's dark kitchen with sunlight in mind, widening the windows and choosing light marble for the countertops. Jack had used a pale stain on the cabinets, and they'd chosen stainless steel whenever possible. The result was worth the effort. The countertops gleamed, and the cabinets reflected warmth in splashes across the floor. The windows sparkled. Through the glass she could see the deep-green swatch of the back lawn. The kitchen was perfect, lovely.

She adored it.

"Quite a change you managed. The old man kept it dark as a tomb."

It took a second for Frankie to find Gwen through the glare, and when she did her throat went dry. She stood in front of the industrial range Frankie had installed herself, tending the griddle. Her hand on the spatula was deft as she flipped bacon and sausage. Scrambled eggs sizzled on a second frying pan, and a platter of toast steamed on the counter.

"Eat." Gwen pointed at the toast with the tip of the spatula. Obviously not long from the shower, her hair was damp, black as it had been in the rain but drying here and there to chestnut. Her pajamas were pink silk, visibly expensive. She smelled lightly of citrus and cinnamon.

Body lotion, Frankie supposed, drifting closer. Gwen Cook had grown into a woman who used body lotion and wore pink Louis Vuitton pajamas. Frankie might have smiled at the joke if she hadn't been so unnerved by the way her body responded to the homey sight of Gwen tending spitting bacon. Gwen, who had stripped away Frankie's every reserve in bed and was still a mystery in so many ways.

Typical. Skipped most the talking and went straight to the kissing. That was a mistake, Frankie knew, but she couldn't regret it. Not when Gwen looked so happy and relaxed in front of the range, and Frankie's body was still thrumming like a well-tuned guitar string.

"It's late. You shouldn't have let me oversleep. Chris will be worried."

Gwen shook her head. "I called your babysitter, explained you were off schedule." She looked up from the griddle. "He said to tell you he'd get your kid off to school right on time."

"Jack's worth his weight in gold."

Gwen flipped a sausage. "Partner and babysitter, I take it. He asked me to remind you to pick up varnish on your way in to work, by the way. Seems a pretty cozy arrangement to me."

"I told you, he's my partner. Jack and I go way back, and I owe him for more than babysitting favors."

She watched as Gwen sorted that out, braced herself for a snide remark. But Gwen only shrugged and transferred sausages to a paper towel. "He told me there'd be hell to pay if I treated you badly. Pancake?"

The heat of her stare gave lie to her lazy smile. Frankie's stomach forgot hunger and tied itself into knots. "How about a shower first?"

"If you like. Use the bathroom upstairs in the master suite. Extra towel on the counter." Gwen set the spatula down and crossed the kitchen tiles with a grace that made Frankie want to sigh in appreciation. Gwen kissed her lightly. "But when you've showered, you'll eat. I don't cook for just anybody."

WHEN FRANKIE RETURNED A DELIBERATELY QUICK FIVE MINUTES later, Gwen had set the bacon to warm beside the toast and was dishing up scrambled eggs. The tinfoil swan from the night before had been dissected and a huge piece of chocolate cake revealed.

"You usually sleep in the basement and shower upstairs?" Frankie asked.

Gwen turned from the range, and when Frankie saw her face, she realized she'd stepped on guarded territory. "I like the basement. I feel comfortable there."

"There's a perfectly comfortable and very expensive antique bed waiting upstairs. With linen sheets and a down comforter."

Gwen smiled. "Is that an invitation?"

"An observation." Frankie snagged a piece of bacon and took a bite. Her taste buds kicked into overdrive. "I'm starving."

"Good." Gwen passed her a plate of eggs and a fork. Frankie ate three pieces of bacon and then gathered up the chocolate cake and took the entire feast over to the kitchen window. She settled on one of the high barstools she'd hunted down one weekend in Richmond, pleased at how well the stool fit the counter height. Much better than the accident waiting to happen on the balcony of her shop. She took a mouthful of eggs and arched her brows.

"You really can cook."

Gwen shrugged as she served herself breakfast. "I got tired of burgers and pizza and premade salads. Also, I can't sit down in a restaurant without drawing attention."

Frankie considered that as she ate, remembering the newspaper headlines. *Everyone wants a piece.* "So you spend time in the kitchen instead?"

"It's relaxing. And it turns out I'm good at it. Unlike some people, I've yet to set a kitchen on fire."

"Ouch." Frankie took the hit as earned, sucking bacon grease from her fingers as she glanced around the kitchen. None of her furnishings had been changed, and it didn't look as though anything had been added to the necessities she'd provided. "I'm flattered that you seem to like my interior design, but maybe you should think about doing a little shopping. You know, add something here or there, make it less of a showpiece and more of a home."

Gwen leaned against the counter in the sunlight. "I haven't really thought about it. Maybe next summer."

"You're going to eat in the kitchen for an entire year? A nice dining-room table wouldn't set you back too much."

Gwen paused over a mouthful of eggs. She swallowed. "A year? I bought the house, but I haven't left Seattle."

At first Frankie thought she hadn't heard right. Then her stomach lurched. She set a buttery piece of toast back onto her plate. "You said you were moving into the house."

"I am." Gwen set her own plate down on the counter, frowning. "But not year-round. A month or two here and there, in the summer. Francis. I thought you understood that." Worry made her vowels sharp.

It wasn't hurt that lumped in the back of Frankie's throat and turned the taste of eggs to ashes. It couldn't be, because she refused to let Gwen break her heart a second time. "Oh." She set her food aside. "Well."

"I've got work to get back to. I can't leave Seattle indefinitely." Gwen crossed over to Frankie's side, searched her face. Frankie did her best to keep it expressionless.

"You blew a shitload of dough on a house you only plan to visit?"

Gwen said gently, "You know why I wanted the house."

"I guess I do." Frankie set her breakfast plate carefully on the counter, fisted her hands in her lap. She couldn't make herself meet Gwen's eyes. "A regular blast from the past, is it? You got your daddy's house and, as a nice little bonus, you finally got your childhood sweetheart in the sack. Wow. You really are great at acquisitions." She slid from the stool. "I've work of my own to get back to."

"Frankie. It's not like that at all. Come on, now." Gwen practically stepped on Frankie's shadow. "Don't run out on me."

"Fuck, Gwen. You promised me. I told you I couldn't afford any mistakes, and you said we were meant for each other." She wouldn't make it a plea. "I need to go."

"We are meant for each other." As if to prove it, Gwen bent down and took her lips with lazy assurance. She tasted of eggs and bacon and tenderness, and when Gwen's tongue traced her lips, Frankie shivered. Gwen pulled back, stared earnestly down. "I never lied to you. We *are* meant for each other. We can make this work."

Anger evaporated like an evening summer storm-burst, softening to anguish. "Can we? How? How long are you staying?"

"I don't know." Gwen's fingers stroked Frankie's wet hair back, soothing. "Two weeks here, maybe three. Summer's almost over, and there's a lot of work waiting for me on the coast. I can't just pretend I don't have responsibilities there."

Tears pricked the corners of Frankie's eyes. She squeezed them back. "Maybe this time you'll say goodbye before you run off."

Gwen brought her hand to her mouth and pressed a kiss to Frankie's palm. Her expression was pained. "I'm sorry. I thought you understood."

"Don't be sorry. Last night was a gift." She wouldn't lie, even when hurt made her want to lash out.

"Yes." She exhaled, then said abruptly: "Move in with me, Francis. Spend your days and nights with me, every moment until I have to fly back west."

"Every moment?" Frankie teased while her heart cracked a little more. "We'd be at each other tooth and nail before the first hour was gone."

"And spend the rest of the day making up." Frankie saw the careful gleam of hope on Gwen's face. She smiled gently as she turned to clean up the breakfast dishes, shook her head.

"Francis."

"I can't. You know that." She dumped the dishes into the sink, squirted soap, ran the hot water. All so she wouldn't have to look Gwen in the face.

"Is it the kid? Fine. We'll move you both in here. It's a big empty house, you said so yourself. He can sleep upstairs in that bed you're so fond of."

"While you and I suck tonsils on an inflatable mattress in the basement?" Any other time, Frankie might have laughed. "It's not just Chris, Gwen. There are things we still need to talk about: your father, this house. We should have done so last night." She gestured at Gwen, back at herself. "Maybe we could have avoided this . . . misunderstanding."

"Fuck the old man. He can go to hell."

Frankie frowned. "You want to be a child again, Gwen? Hiding in the creek all summer long, us against the world, hoping real life won't intrude?"

"Would it be so bad? Just for a little while." Gwen scrubbed her fingers through her hair, mouth petulant. Frankie resisted the urge to wipe that pout away with a kiss.

Instead, she shook her head. "I've grown up, Gwen. *Real life* is what I do, and it makes me happy. Seems to me maybe you're still running from your ghosts, and you're no good to me running."

"I'll always make my way back to you, Frankie." There was real pain beneath the frustration in her voice. Frankie hurt for both of them.

"That's not enough." *I need more out of life, Gwen. I* deserve *more.* Defeated, she wiped her fingers on her borrowed sweatpants. "I want you to take me home, please."

"That's it?" Gwen threw her hands in the air and turned in a circle, pink silk fluttering around her ankles. "Come on, Francis. You can't give up on us now, not now that I've finally—" She stopped, bit her lip, took a deep breath. "There's something I want to show you."

Be strong, Frankie. "I'm not interested."

"It'll only take a minute. Then I'll drive you home." Gwen held out her hand, and when Frankie hesitated her mouth went flat. "Trust me."

It was a low blow. Frankie had always trusted Gwen. Trusted Gwen to keep her secrets, trusted Gwen to shield her from trouble, trusted Gwen to have her back when she slipped up.

That, at least, hadn't changed; Frankie wasn't sure it ever would. Bracing herself, she clasped Gwen's hand.

Gwen led her out of the kitchen and across the back lawn. The grass was still wet and cold. Water dripped slowly from the roof, collecting in the flowerbeds around the house.

"You're making me ruin a pair of your socks." Frankie glanced down at the wet cotton on her feet.

Gwen didn't break stride. "I've got others."

"Where are we going?"

"The gazebo."

"Why?"

"You'll see."

"I don't like surprises."

Gwen made an inelegant sound. "You love surprises. Stop complaining, Francis. It will only take a minute."

Frankie huffed. Gwen made her feel sixteen again: always slightly off balance and more than half in love with her best friend. She wanted to shout, she wanted to cry, she wanted Gwen to kiss her until she couldn't stand.

And the worst part was, Gwen was right. Frankie loved surprises. Anticipation could almost make her forget the bruise on her heart. By the time they reached the gazebo, she was in the lead, tugging Gwen along behind.

"This?" Frankie peered doubtfully at the pile of tools and the heap of white canvas tarp. The roof of the gazebo shielded the clutter from rain but only barely. She wondered if Gwen realized how quickly those shiny new tools would rust.

"This," Gwen agreed, pulling away the canvas with a flourish.

Frankie gulped a breath and held it until her lungs began to hurt. Then she let it out in a slow exhale, watching Gwen out of the corner of her eye. "Wow. You've been working hard."

"Off and on." Gwen tugged more of the tarp back, revealing the whole skiff.

It was easy to see how much time and effort had gone into refurbishing the little boat. Gwen had sanded it down, removing old paint and mildew. Several new boards gleamed among the old, and Frankie knew as well as anyone how much care it took to work wood around the skeleton of a boat. The original anchor was gone; a newer version lay propped against the gazebo, waiting.

"It's wonderful."

Gwen didn't seem to hear. She blurted, "I've ordered new oars. And I thought I'd put in a small bench seat. Paint, obviously. Something bright. Blue, maybe."

"Blue would be perfect. I didn't know . . . how did you learn how to do all this?" It would have taken trial and error, and a lot of patience. The Gwen of Frankie's childhood had never had much patience to spare.

"YouTube. Same way I learned how to cook." Gwen picked up a hammer, turning it in her hand. "I found the boat in the weeds. More than half-buried. At first, I thought I'd just patch it up, wait until next summer to really work on the job. I guess I changed my mind."

"Because you just couldn't wait to get back out on the water and search for pirate treasure?"

Gwen set the hammer carefully on the gazebo floor, out of the damp. She smiled, wry. "Tempting as it sounds, no. Actually, I had your kid in mind. I got to thinking—a boy that age probably has too much energy, and time to waste. We did, right?"

Baffled, Frankie nodded.

Gwen rushed on: "Maybe your Chris needs something to do, to keep his hands busy, to keep him from thinking too hard. God knows this boat was a blessing when I needed it."

Frankie couldn't help herself. Her resolve melted like ice cream on a hot summer afternoon. "You're right. He'll love it."

"If he and I put our minds to it, we could get it out on the water before summer's over." Gwen began stacking the other tools alongside the hammer. "I'm handy enough with the basics, but if we run into any trouble . . . Well, I'm sure you've free advice to give."

"I've always got plenty of free advice."

Gwen glanced up, brows raised. "Are you crying?"

"Of course not." Frankie sniffled, wiping at the traitorous moisture. "It's the rain."

"I never thought to see you cry, Francis. A childhood of scrapes and bruises, and never a single tear." She leaned down, pressed her forehead against Frankie's. "I thought it would be a good thing."

"It is a good thing." She let herself lean in briefly before pulling away. "It's a very good thing. Chris will be crazy about the idea." She swiped at the last of her tears and let her heart warm at the thought of her son and her best friend working together over the little boat. "He was continuously asking to swim in the creek when I worked on the house."

"He can swim all he wants."

"Thank you. But you should know this doesn't change my mind, Gwen. We won't move into your house, and I won't be asking Jack to babysit overnight again. At least not anytime soon." *I won't let you hurt me again, Gwen. No matter how blatantly sexy you look in rumpled pink silk pajamas.*

Gwen nodded. "You're the best thing that ever happened to me," she said quietly. "I'm not going to let a second chance slip away. You can trust me. I promise."

"We'll see. But for now, how about we try friends?" Frankie suggested. "Just like old times."

"If that's what you want." Gwen didn't sound disappointed, or irritated, or insulted. Or any of the other noisy emotions Frankie expected. *Hoped for?* And she certainly didn't sound brokenhearted. She just sounded . . . resigned. "I can do friends. For now."

Chapter Ten

RAIN CAME AGAIN in the night, rushed by the wind into slanting show-ers. Gwen stood in front of the windows in her spacious new living room, watching tiny rivers cascade over the edge of the roof. Clouds obscured the moon. Only the deck lights kept back the dark; in their silver glow the woods appeared eerie, unnatural.

The house had once leaked like a sieve. Gwen remembered damp patches on the ceiling and the steady ooze of wet along the windowsills. In the basement, during the worst of the summer monsoons, water would run through cinder blocks and make tiny lakes on the floor. The house had always rattled against even the lightest wind gusts. It still rattled.

Even Frankie's talented hands couldn't make old bones into new, but somehow the vibrations seemed more cozy than desperate. As far as Gwen could tell, Chesapeake Renovations had managed to banish every drip and leak. Frankie still had the power to lighten the darkest patches of Gwen's life.

She rubbed a hand over her face, trying to chase away a headache. In the windows her reflection mirrored the action. She leaned closer. The face in the window was her own. No matter how many times she searched her reflection, she could see nothing of her parents. *And thank God for small mercies.*

Lightning flickered in the distance above the gray hump of the woods. It lit up the inside of the house like the flash of a camera, and Gwen's reflection vanished. Narrowing her eyes against the throb in her skull, Gwen climbed the staircase to the second floor. She didn't bother to turn on the lights. Even restored, the house was still her own, and she knew it from floor to ceiling, could probably walk it from front to back with her eyes closed and never stumble or stub a toe.

She paused on the threshold of the master bedroom. Porch light suffused the windows from below, illuminating the bed at the center of the room. Smooth, carved oak rose in swirls and knobs over a high mattress. The edges of the headboard had been worked to resemble climbing ivy. More carved vines spread their leaves up four tall posts. Frankie had chosen white sheets and a white duvet. Even in the dim light, the bed looked tempting.

For a second, leaning against the doorframe, Gwen allowed herself to imagine Frankie on the mattress: Frankie naked in the sunlight, long hair spread across white sheets, skin flushed in the aftermath of passion. Frankie quietly languid, open and welcoming. Frankie wild, hot, and wet as a summer storm.

Gwen tore her eyes from the bed. She was pretty sure it was bad manners to fantasize about fucking a friend. She was also 100 percent sure that she would never get the addictive taste of Frankie's body out of her head. She'd wanted Frankie for as long as she could remember. That wasn't going to chance no matter what label Frankie wanted to put on their relationship.

The master bedroom had once been Edward's—dingy and musty. Rank with beer and smoke and sweat. The carpet gray with age. The old man had slept on a sagging mattress under a soiled wool blanket, year-round, summer or winter. Now, as the house rattled against the wind, Gwen inhaled only the lingering scent of honeysuckle. Frankie was wrong. There were no ghosts left behind to haunt Gwen.

Frankie had chased them all away.

HEAT AND HUMIDITY STRUCK AGAIN JUST BEFORE LUNCH. BOUNCING along a rutted road toward the James, Gwen kept the air-conditioning at full blast and said a vicious prayer every time the car hit a pothole. If she'd known she would be chasing away her vacation on Virginia's back roads, she would have ignored the Spyder's sexy temptation and picked up a used truck instead. It would have been more practical, and cheaper to boot. Weeds scraped the underside of the car as Gwen turned off dirt and onto gravel.

Battery Pier might be Newport News's hippest place to dock a boat, but nobody had thought to pave the road. Then again, maybe that was supposed to be part of the charm. Gwen gunned the car up over a steep rise. Gravel splattered. The rise turned into a plateau, flat and brown, weeds and marshland to either side. Farther along the road she finally saw a sign for Battery.

Even through the rush of the air-conditioning, she could smell the James. The James River was, in places, the widest stretch of flowing water on US soil. Wider even than the famous Mississippi, or so Edward had claimed when Gwen was a child. Sluggish and never clear, the muddy river water was almost as full of salt as the ocean it flowed into. The navy used the river to ferry carriers and destroyers. Beyond one of the deepest bends, just off Carter's Grove, the government kept a graveyard of military ships, anchored and forgotten.

But along Battery Pier, the James was little more than a deep marsh. The pier itself was lopsided, old logs sinking here and there into the water. The boats in their slips were varied and colorful. Gwen parked her car in a turnaround near the back of the pier. When she climbed out, heat struck like a blanket across her shoulders. Squinting through her Gucci shades, she crossed over the gravel and stepped onto waterlogged cedar.

Battery Pier rocked on the water, but Gwen found her balance easily. She'd given in to common sense and dressed for adventure: jeans, a vintage Pink Jones T-shirt, and a pair of comfy trainers. Dressing down felt like shedding the armor she'd collected for herself over the years—expensive, understated fashion as a display of power in an uncertain world—but she wasn't such an idiot that she would, as one of her Seattle-socialite ex-girlfriends used to say, "wear Prada to a pig roast."

Gwen walked faster as a flash of neon swimming trunks caught her eye at the end of the pier. Jamming both hands into her pockets, jingling change, she watched as Chris jumped off the edge of the pier. The kid's form was good, which was reassuring. He could probably hold his own swimming in the creek.

A lazy breeze blew off the water, cooling the sweat on the back of Gwen's neck. She reached the last square of cedar logs just as the boy cannoned a second time into the water. She stood, waiting, until Chris resurfaced.

"Water cold?" she asked as the kid snorted river from his nose and mouth and brushed hair out of his eyes. He looked up at her, treading water, blue eyes hooded against bright sunlight.

"Not really." Chris spat more water into the James. "Shallow enough to be warm."

"Need a hand up?"

"No." Chris slithered up and out of the water until he sat on the pier. Flicking a string of marsh weed from his knee, he eyed Gwen with reluctant curiosity. "What are you doing here?"

"Looking for you." Gwen crouched so she could look the kid in the face. "I need an extra pair of hands to help me with a project."

"Mom mentioned it," Chris said slowly, "She said you've got an old boat you wanted to fix up and that if I helped you, I could borrow it sometimes."

"It's only a little boat, but if you help me fix it up, you can use it anytime you want."

"Why?" The poignant mix of disdain and hope in that one word made Gwen want to reach out and squeeze the boy's shoulder in reassurance. Huh. Like she'd told Frankie, but she hadn't expected the urge to comfort. She just wasn't the nurturing type.

Gwen said, "Honestly? I've grown too big for her, and I want her to go to someone I know."

Chris looked doubtful. "Why me?"

"You seem like a kid who needs a boat."

Gwen waited. Chris chewed his lower lip and swirled his feet in the water. Out over the river a gull screeched and swooped. "I have a pretty busy schedule," he said after a moment. "Soccer on Saturdays and Thursdays, and debate on Mondays and Wednesdays. Pizza night at Jack's every Tuesday. Every Tuesday." A flash of defiance brought pink spots to the kid's cheeks. He was definitely his mother's child.

"Okay." Gwen refused to acknowledge a quick burn of jealousy. Jack seemed to have made himself a fixture in Frankie's life. "How about Friday afternoon and part of the weekend?"

Chris shrugged. "I could do that. How long would it take?"

"I'm not sure. It's my first time, too. Two weekends, maybe three. A couple of hours every weekend. I think we might get it finished up pretty quickly."

"We'd work at Edward's place?"

"My place," Gwen corrected. She added, "I've got it up on dry land under the gazebo."

"Okay." The kid's expression grew grudgingly eager. "Where did you find it? How small is it, really?"

"Out along James Creek, right where I left it when I was a kid. Small, but not too small for someone your age. It'll catch speed if you treat it right. The current's strong in front of the house."

"Really? How fast?"

"I clocked in once at thirty seconds from the boathouse to the big bend. And that was with your mom as added weight." What an afternoon that had been—the wind in their hair, stolen beers in a paper bag at their feet.

"No way." A slow smile stretched across Chris's face. "I know that bend. Thirty seconds?"

Gwen grinned at the boy's enthusiasm. "Could have been a deal faster without a passenger squirming around."

Chris snorted. He hopped to his feet. "Can we start this Friday?"

"Sure. Your mom could drop you off after school."

The kid's face fell. "I forgot. She's got a client meeting on Friday. Those usually run late."

Gwen shrugged. "Then I'll pick you up."

The kid's jaw dropped. "In your Porsche?"

"Sure." If the car upped Chris's street cred, Gwen was happy to help.

"Cool. Yeah. That would be . . . cool." He was almost dancing in excitement. "Just let me ask my mom." He dashed back along the pier, leaving a trail of wet footprints. The prints were long and wide, a man's feet on a boy's body. Soon enough, Gwen marveled, Frankie's son would grow to fit them.

Chris stopped halfway along the pier and scrambled up a crooked slip. Gwen watched as the kid hailed a large houseboat. Frankie's head popped up over the stern. Gwen made her way slowly along the slip. The kid was chattering up a storm. Frankie didn't glance at Gwen until she stood alongside the boat. Then her eyes widened, and her expression became guarded.

Gwen played with the change in her pocket, waiting.

"It's all right, isn't it, Mom?" Chris repeated with an air of impatience. "I mean, you already said I could."

"I didn't mean for Gwen to have to shuttle you from school." Frankie frowned and leaned out farther along the rail of the boat. She wore stained dungarees over a thin blue T-shirt. Gwen guessed the dungarees were some sort of work uniform. The thin T-shirt didn't leave a whole lot to Gwen's overeager imagination.

"Gwen said it wasn't a problem. She said she'd pick me up—in her Porsche. *Mom.*"

Frankie laughed. The low chuckle sent a spear of longing straight through Gwen. She balled her fists in her pockets. "How can any mother deny her boy a ride in a Porsche? If you're sure Gwen doesn't mind."

"Gwen doesn't mind," Gwen promised. "I'll be there after school on Friday."

"At three," Chris said.

"At three." Gwen matched Frankie's smile. "You want to join us after your meeting?"

Frankie's smile wavered. "I think I'll let the two of you handle it."

"Invitation's open." Gwen rocked on her heels. "We could always use an extra pair of hands. Tacos and pie after."

"Tacos and pie?" Frankie tilted her head. "You drive a hard bargain. We'll see."

Gwen closed her eyes and let the heat and humidity wash over her skin. She could hear the creak of cedar logs, the scuff of Chris's bare feet on the pier, and the slosh of water against the houseboat. And Frankie's breathing, quick and light in the sodden afternoon. It felt peaceful. She couldn't remember the last time *peaceful* had been a word in her vocabulary.

She opened her eyes. "Speaking of food, how about lunch?"

"Lunch?" Chris straightened, eager. "I'm starving."

"I've got work to do—" Frankie began.

"That's a shame because I've gone and hauled a picnic all the way out here over every wretched road in the county, and I'm not hauling it back."

"A picnic?" Frankie echoed.

Gwen grinned. "Ham sandwiches and potato salad, and chocolate ice cream for dessert."

"Ice cream? In this heat?"

"Haven't you ever heard of a blue ice pack and a cooler, Francis?"

"Man!" Chris crowed. "Chocolate ice cream. Come on, Mom. I'm so hungry I'm going to die."

Frankie brushed the damp hair from her cheeks, exasperated. "You just had breakfast."

"Hours ago!" The kid heaved a long-suffering sigh. "Come on, Mom; please?"

"Yeah, Mom," Gwen murmured under her breath. "Please?"

Frankie flushed to the roots of her bangs. She shot Gwen a quick glare before succumbing: "All right. Fine. But we're eating on the pier. I don't want to risk getting ice cream all over Tina's boat."

"Come on down, then." Gwen hoped her shades hid the thrill of triumph she felt when Frankie winked playfully at her son. She dug into her pockets, retrieved her keys, and offered them to Chris. "Cooler's behind the seat. It's not heavy."

"No worries." Chris grabbed the keys. "I'll be back in a sec."

Frankie watched from her perch on the boat as Chris raced back along the pier. Gwen noted the faint curl of pleasure on her lips, heard her chuckle as her son slipped on the damp logs and then scrambled to regain his balance.

"Kid seems good," Gwen offered.

The breeze blew chin-length blonde tendrils around Frankie's eyes and ears. She looked down, suspicious. "What are you doing here? I thought we were going to . . . take some time."

"It's lunch, Francis," Gwen drawled. "A chance for two friends to get to know each other better. That's what you wanted, isn't it? Besides," she continued, "I came for the boy. To see if he wanted me to help me with boat."

"How did you know we were here?"

"Picked up the phone and asked some questions. Your clerk was very helpful." And that was the overstatement of the year because it had been like pulling teeth to get the man to talk. Luckily, Gwen was used to dealing with difficult clients.

"I told you, he's my partner, not a clerk. A *friend*."

"You have standing weekly date nights with all your friends? Fantastic. I'll mark my calendar. Wednesdays work for you?" Gwen didn't think of herself as a jealous person. She hated to admit that Frankie's friendship with Jackson stung like a bitch.

She'd been naive—stupid—to assume Frankie's life would be exactly as they'd left it more than a decade earlier. Frankie was a human being, not a treasure frozen in amber. Of course she'd moved on, made new friends. Built a business. Had a kid. Become an adult.

"It's not a date," Frankie retorted easily. "And it's none of your business."

"You're right," Gwen agreed, because she was an adult, too. "It's none of my business. Are you coming down?"

"For chocolate ice cream? Of course." Frankie swung herself up and over the boat rail. The pier rocked when she dropped down. Gwen held out a steadying hand. Frankie batted it away. "I'm not going to break."

"I know it. Here comes lunch." They stood side by side, watching as Chris lugged Gwen's cooler from the shore. The breeze off the James tossed Frankie's scent into the air. The hair on Gwen's forearms prickled in reaction. She had to stuff her hands back into her pockets to keep from reaching for her again.

"You've made his day," Frankie admitted as Chris made a goofy face across the logs. "I don't think I've seen a grin like that since at least July."

"I'm glad. I'd like to make yours, too."

"Well, bless your heart." The Virginia in Frankie was strong when she wanted it to be. "You and your sweet surprises." She watched Gwen from under lowered lashes. "It's almost like you're showing off. Guess you didn't grow out of *that*."

"Go bold or go home." Because she desperately wanted to kiss that smug look away, Gwen left Frankie standing on the pier while she went to help Chris with the cooler. Together they set their burden in a spot of shade at the end of the slip and, under Frankie's direction, began laying out food.

"The sandwiches are huge," Chris marveled as he passed out napkins.

"There's a shop in Merchants Square," Gwen said, digging a six-pack of cola from beneath the ice pack. "They specialize in sandwiches. They have a secret house dressing. It's still the best I've ever tasted." She heard Frankie laugh and glanced over. She stood on the edge of sunlight and shade, relaxed and smiling as she unwrapped a turkey-on-rye. Gwen wished she dared dig out her phone and snap a photo to keep for the long, dark nights.

"Gwen and the Cheese Shoppe are old friends," Frankie said. "I think the bread ends and dressing kept her alive when we were kids. It was an addiction."

"Says the woman who can't resist dessert. The savory and the sweet —we make a good pair." Gwen rummaged in the cooler and fished out a small cardboard box. "Luckily, the Trellis does desserts to go."

Frankie groaned. The sound was frankly sexual. Gwen bit her lip to keep from squirming.

"Not more cake?" Frankie demanded.

"No. Sour cream fruit tart." Gwen distracted herself by winking at Chris. "Fruit's healthy, right?"

"Totally."

"Give me that." Frankie reached for the container, but Gwen shook her head. "Savory first, Francis. Don't want to set a bad example," she said, deadpan, while Chris whooped with laughter.

Frankie tried to snatch the cardboard box. Gwen caught her grasping fingers and squeezed. Frankie froze but didn't pull away as expected. Her eyes were wide, her lips slightly parted as she met Gwen's stare.

"Sit," Gwen coaxed. Gently, she tugged Frankie down onto the logs. "Try a sandwich; you'll be glad you did. Cola or lemonade?"

A small frown creased Frankie's brow. She looked at Gwen as if trying to solve a puzzle, which was silly because Gwen was the least-enigmatic person she'd ever met. But Gwen let her look her fill.

"Lemonade, please," Frankie said at last, then took a large bite of her sandwich.

They took their time with lunch, lingering in the shade as the afternoon heated up, licking crumbs from fingers and swallowing every sweet drop of soda. Chris ate two of the gigantic sandwiches and helped Frankie devour half of the tart, all the while running on about the skiff and how best to get the boat shipshape and seaworthy.

"Does it have a name?" he asked, separating bits of strawberry from crust.

Gwen shook her head. "Never christened her; but you're right, she could probably do with a name. Why don't you think about it and let me know what you come up with?"

Chris licked pastry crumbs from his finger and stared out over the water, obviously deep in thought. Gwen watched the boy with veiled interest. She didn't know much about kids, but Frankie's son had a liveliness about him, a sharpness of attention, and a dry wit she found intriguing. She wondered how much of that intelligence was innate and how much came from growing up under Frankie's care.

The breeze shifted. Gwen grabbed for her fluttering napkin. Chris pounced on a wayward piece of plastic wrap, then yelped as a sudden gust sent an empty paper cup spinning into the water.

"Go get it," Frankie said, smiling. Chris handed Gwen scrunched plastic wrap and then ran easily along the pier, jumping gracefully into the river.

"What happened to the 'don't swim until you've digested' rule?" Gwen asked mildly. Out in the water Chris made a dramatic show of capturing the errant cup.

"It's not very deep here. Besides, we never paid any attention to rules, either," Frankie pointed out. The bridge of her nose had turned pink in the sun. Gwen caught herself staring and cleared her throat.

"You're burning."

"I always do," Frankie agreed. She began sorting the remnants of her lunch into the cooler. "Bring your suit?"

"I planned on lunch, not a dip," Gwen said. "Besides, the river here is full of silt." She shuddered dramatically. "And probably turtles."

Frankie snorted. "Lunch was nice," she admitted gruffly. "Dessert was a low blow. But you get extra credit for making Chris laugh. He hasn't smiled so often in weeks."

"What are friends for? And you're welcome." Gwen hated to put an end to their afternoon, but she also knew better than to overstay her welcome. "Tell Chris I'll pick him up on Friday."

To Gwen's surprise, Frankie's smile blossomed to brilliant.

"What?" Whatever she'd done, she wanted to do it again, just to see that grin.

"Nothing." But she laid her hand over Gwen's fingers where they gripped the edge of the cooler. "Let me help you with that. It's the least I can do."

&

GWEN HAD BEEN EXPECTING THE VISIT. TRUTH WAS, SHE'D BEEN considering a little reconnaissance of her own.

Best to get it over with quickly, Gwen thought as she parked her Porsche alongside the Chevy parked in front of the garage. *Threaten to kick him in the balls if he hurts Frankie and then offer him a brew after.*

"Afternoon," Jack said from where he sat on Gwen's front steps. He didn't bother to stand up, which was not a point in his mama's favor. "Pretty ride."

"Does the job." She leaned casually against the hood, scrutinized the man through her shades.

"Got half the town talking. Rich tourists usually come in on buses."

"I'm not a tourist."

"Could argue that." He rose then, and just kept unfolding. Gwen resisted the urge to crane her neck. Damn if he didn't top six feet by a mile. "I guess we haven't been introduced properly. Name's Jack Pierce."

"Frankie's told me all about you." Which wasn't really a lie because there didn't seem to be all that much to tell about Pierce. Gwen's assistant hadn't been able to dig up much of interest about the itinerant carpenter who'd finally decided to settle in southern Virginia. He seemed squeaky clean, which only made Gwen suspicious. *No one* was squeaky clean. "What do you want?"

"Well, then, if you know who I am, I'm supposing you know that, too."

"You're blocking my steps."

"You're keeping me from a good night's sleep."

Gwen took a slow breath. She showed him her phone. "911 on speed dial, asshat. There's nothing worse than a man who thinks he can intimidate a woman with his body."

He opened his mouth. Shut it again with a click. He looked like a fish out of water, and maybe his mama really didn't pass down a lick of good sense.

"There's no need for the cops." He spread his hands and sat down again, as if getting low would deflect her temper. "Listen. I don't mean any harm. I'm just here about my family."

"And by family you mean Frankie and Chris." It was the obvious deduction to make.

He nodded. "Listen." And now he looked as earnest as a choirboy, damn him. "It's no sweat off my back that Frankie's got a thing for boys *and* girls—"

"She's bisexual," Gwen confirmed dryly.

"I know what bisexual is," he retorted. "And I've done some googling, and you sure aren't hiding that you're a . . ." He trailed off.

Choirboys. Jesus.

"Lesbian."

"Right. I don't like to out people like it's the Sunday-morning news, and Christ knows you can't believe everything you read in the tabloids." He clasped his hand over one knee. "None of my business, really. Only it is. Because I'm Frankie's best friend." And wasn't that a punch in the gut. "And Christopher's godfather. And I can see Frankie's got heart eyes for you, Ms. Cook. I'm just wondering, have you thought about the fallout? This isn't Seattle. You and Frankie start a thing, well . . . she's not one to hide her light under a bushel—it won't be a secret for long. I guarantee some folks will look sideways. I'm just not sure Chris won't get teased at school. And what about Frankie's business? She's just barely got it off the ground. We're in the Bible Belt. Some people are right idiots, and not kind about it."

Pierce looked so sincerely pained that she wondered if he was speaking from experience. Her gaydar was usually excellent, but the man was a cipher. She sighed and put away her phone. Any man Frankie chose to be her son's godfather probably couldn't hurt a fly.

"You've got nothing to worry about. A: Seattle's my home, and B: I've been known to eat homophobes for breakfast." When Pierce continued to look doubtful, Gwen groaned. "Fuck it. Come inside. I've got a couple of brews in the fridge. Let me convince you there's nothing to worry about."

Chapter Eleven

FALL HIT all at once with a whoop and a holler. Humid summer breezes turned to driving blusters, snatching leaves from trees and stripping faded summer blossoms from the wildflowers that grew up along every roadway. New colors ripened overnight. The yellows, oranges, and reds of the season tinted myrtle and maple. The air smelled of woodsmoke and spice. In Colonial Williamsburg tourists jammed the roadways, marveling at the seasonal decorations and sampling spiced cider and mulled wines.

Lincoln Middle School was done up for the season—dried corn husks rattled in the wind over the front doors, bales of hay alternated with pumpkins up and down cracked concrete steps. Gwen, remembering similar decorations from her own schooldays, knew that the gourds wouldn't last more than a week. Pumpkin smashing never went out of style.

As she pulled into a turnaround outside the school, Gwen saw that the profusion of fall decorations wasn't the only tradition that hadn't changed. Students sat in clumps on the concrete steps, divided into groups by boundaries as simple as dress and hairstyle, as complicated as economic class and academic standing. The jocks and cheerleaders ruled the top steps, the band club the bottom, and a handful of tiny synthetic worlds rotated between.

Gwen had spent her afternoon hours behind the gym with a pack of stolen cigarettes and borrowed comic books. She'd never bothered to find a place on the school's front steps, but even from a distance she had been aware of the unspoken rules and the inner workings.

Frankie's son, Gwen was mildly surprised to see, had a place on the steps closer to the top than the bottom. Not bad for a skinny kid. And the boy's crowd looked wholesome enough: Dockers and jeans and one pair of fatigues, and not a vape pen anywhere in sight. No girls, either, Gwen noticed with a good deal of amusement. Six gawky boys—too old for the playground, too young yet to bother with the promise of a short skirt or tight sweater. But not too young to appreciate a flashy car.

As one the six boys trooped down the stairs, eddying to avoid their huddled classmates, and then log-jammed against the Spyder. Gwen lowered the windows as curious eyes admired the hood and rims and tail fin. Only the kid in the fatigues seemed to have any real courage. Narrowing his skeptical brown eyes, he peered over Chris's shoulder and into the car, studying Gwen with guarded curiosity.

Gwen ignored him.

"Ready?" Gwen asked Chris.

"Yeah. I guess." He hid his excitement well, but Gwen could see it lurking in the corners of his smile.

Frankie's son wore jeans and a rugby shirt. His sneakers were fashionably dirty, his backpack casually torn, and his hair flopping in the wind. He looked average and middle-class and wise with it—exactly the type of kid Gwen had once envied. She felt an unexpected jolt of pride and relief. To hide it, she popped the lock and waved a hand. "Get in."

Chris tossed his backpack into the car and slid into the passenger seat. Fatigues leaned through the open door, daring to stroke one freckled hand over the dash.

"What's she like on the straightaways?"

"Like lightning." This close to the car, Fatigues smelled heavily of weed. Even though she knew she was being a terrible hypocrite, Gwen revised her opinion of Chris's crowd one notch lower.

"Pick her up in Richmond?" Fatigues pressed, leaning in farther.

"Alexandria." Gwen turned to Chris. "Ready?"

Chris nodded and grabbed the door. Gwen sent the windows up again. Fatigues retreated, smirking. The door slammed with a satisfying crack. Undeterred, the brown-eyed boy leaned forward again until his breath smeared the glass. Gwen knew better. She was a grown woman, and she'd long ago left behind the tangled emotions of junior high. But the snot was just asking to be taken down a peg.

Gwen knew better, but she couldn't help herself. She gunned the Porsche's sweet, sweet engine until it growled, and then she sent the car screaming away from the curb.

Chris gasped. "Cool." The reek of smoked tires enveloped the cab. Gwen glanced in the rearview and was pleased to see the school shrink into the distance. With a snap of her wrist and a flick of a button, she lowered every window in the car again, breathing out a sigh of relief as cool, fresh air chased away the stink of burnt rubber.

"Your mother would kill me." She stabbed a finger at the radio until Annie Lennox sang through hidden speakers.

"Yeah." Seeming unconcerned, Chris squirmed in his seat. He peeked out the back window and then ran his hand over the glove compartment. He eyed the gearbox with interest. "Take you long to learn how to drive a stick?"

"Learned first on a stick," Gwen told him. "My old man had a pickup—a Ford. Around here, in those days, manual was pretty much standard."

"I'm gonna get a manual, soon as I turn fifteen and can get my learner's. Roddy Green says his dad will sell me a secondhand Nissan, cheap. I'm gonna get a job delivering pizzas to pay for it."

"Roddy Green, the kid with the attitude and the ugly pants?"

Chris's mouth twitched in amusement, but he had a boy's deep loyalty to his friends. "Roddy's not so bad. He's just nosy. His dad runs a used-car lot and does NASCAR stuff on the side. Roddy knows a lot about cars."

"NASCAR." The bread and butter of the South. "You follow the circuit?"

"Nah." Chris scoffed. "NASCAR's not a real sport. I like soccer."

Gwen found herself smiling as she turned the car onto Creek Lane. "I'm a PSG fan, myself."

"Saint-Germain?"

The depth of disgust in the boy's sigh made Gwen laugh. "Fuck no. Brazil all the way to the top."

"We'll see."

But Gwen was pleased. She could talk professional soccer any day. NASCAR, not so much.

Leaves scattered in front of the car as they approached the house. Gwen parked near the garage, took a steadying breath. She hadn't expected nerves. She didn't know a thing about prepubescent boys, but could it really be so hard? "How about a snack before we get to work?"

"Sure!" Visibly enthused, the kid grabbed his backpack and followed Gwen to the front door. "Got any more ice cream?"

"Must be your lucky day because I make a point of never running out."

Frankie's clients lingered longer than she had expected. She couldn't complain, as most of the overtime was spent discussing the little extras that could only plump her paycheck at the end. But by the time she finally shook hands on the deal and locked up the shop, it was far later than she'd intended. She stopped at home long enough to shuck her work clothes and pull on something cozy, choosing an old pair of jeans and a rust-colored fisherman's sweater that had been a gift from Ma. The sweater's sleeves were too long, and the turtleneck bunched at her chin, but it was the warmest piece of clothing she owned. It was pretty and soft, and it reminded her of Ma's generous spirit.

Even so, as she climbed Gwen's front steps and rang the bell, the chill in the air managed to sneak through the heavy knit and make her wish she had thrown on a coat. Fall was well and truly settling in.

Nobody answered the doorbell. After two more attempts and five minutes of standing on the stoop trying not to shiver right out of her boots, Frankie gave up and wandered around the side of the house in search of her son. She found him on the back lawn on his hands and knees in the grass, applying varnish to the underbelly of Gwen's skiff with a concentration he usually reserved for his beloved books. Looking at him fondly, she stood for a moment against the house, content to watch.

A shiny red barbecue, low to the ground and wide enough to grill a small sheep, flickered happily in the fading evening. Frankie guessed it was meant more for warmth, though it was giving off more smoke than heat. Chris didn't seem bothered by the haze. He paused every few moments to stand in front of the fire before going back to work. Her son wore a pair of canvas work gloves Frankie knew she had never paid money for, and a huge green sweatshirt. The sweatshirt looked stiff, as if it had never been worn or washed, and an elaborate logo running down the left sleeve spelled out *Pinnacle* in a bold font.

And there was Gwen, crossing the lawn from the back of the house, moving with the lazy grace that reminded Frankie of a housecat well pleased with its surroundings. She bent to adjust Chris's grip on the paintbrush, saying something too low for Frankie to hear. Chris nodded. Frankie grinned at the cozy picture the two made together. When she left the shadow of the house, her boots squeaked on the damp grass.

Chris looked up. "Mom," he said with less enthusiasm than she'd expected. "You're here."

"I'm here." She stopped in front of the barbecue, held out her hands to the flames. "Looking good, my man. Need any help?"

"We're almost done for the day." Chris turned his attention back to the skiff. "After I finish this coat, the paint has to dry overnight."

"Oh." She didn't know whether to be disappointed or amused by her son's dismissal. Then Gwen caught her gaze, her eyes full of wicked green glints.

"The kid likes to do everything himself. Can't say I'm surprised. But we're glad you're here—just in time to help me rustle up some dinner.

Frankie wrinkled her nose. "That doesn't sound anywhere near as exciting as boat repair."

"Oh, come on." Gwen waggled her expertly shaped eyebrows. "Tacos are always exciting. You shred the lettuce. I'll toast the shells." She slung a companionable arm over Frankie's shoulders, gently steered her toward the house. Frankie thought about resisting, but even through several layers of clothing—today, "Gwen casual" was a cashmere lounge suit and leather slides—Gwen's body warmed her quickly and more pleasantly than the barbecue, and Chris didn't look as if he would miss her at all.

"I'm really am glad you came," Gwen said solemnly as Frankie watched the wind toss a brown leaf across the lawn. "

"That makes one of you," Frankie grumped. She pulled the ends of her sleeves over her fingers, tucking her hands into her armpits.

Gwen chuckled—a deep, rich sound that Frankie felt more than heard. "He's having fun. When's the last time he got to hang out and be a twelve-year-old?"

"I can't believe how fast this world grows them up. Feels like just yesterday he was spitting pureed carrots all over his front, and look at him now. Practically a man." She hated being maudlin, and she always tried her best not to be a mother hen, but lately she couldn't help but miss her easy toddler.

"You're telling me. Think I saw a whisker sprouting on his chin."

Frankie stopped in her tracks, craning her neck to look back at her son. "You're kidding!"

"Yes." Gwen laughed again. Frankie felt the kiss of her breath against her temple. Her arm tightened once around Frankie's shoulders as they stepped into the kitchen, then she stepped away.

Frankie stopped in the light of the kitchen, frowning at the flight of empty beer cans spread like dominos across the kitchen table. "Christ, Gwen. You know there's a perfectly good recycling bin under the sink. And tell me you haven't taken it upon yourself to teach my son how to hold his beer."

"You know better." Frankie wasn't sure, but she thought it was embarrassment making Gwen duck her head. "I had a visitor last night, that's all. We did a lot of talking, and a lot of drinking. Turns out we have a few things in common." She regarded the messy table with a scowl. "I meant to clean up; just got busy."

"Guest? What guest?" She'd never met anyone other than herself who could stand to spend a night drinking with prickly Gwen Cook.

"Well." Gwen busied herself with opening the fridge, poking about, hiding her face from Frankie. "I guess your buddy Jack's almost tolerable, once he pulls the stick out of his ass. Did you know he's got his own home brew going?"

"Yes," Frankie said slowly. "Jack stopped by? What did he want?"

"Just to talk. Wanted to make sure my intentions were good and all that. I managed to convince him he had nothing to worry about." Gwen set a package of ground turkey into Frankie's hands, nodded at the oven. "Here. Stove top runs hot. Try not to burn it."

Frankie was too busy trying to wrap her head around Gwen and Jack gossiping over a six-pack to snarl over the insult. She found a pan, a spatula, and a little olive oil, and she set the turkey to browning. She tried not to notice the ease with which Gwen moved in the kitchen. Somehow, as Frankie struggled to keep the meat from searing too quickly, Gwen managed to turn raw vegetables into salsa and toast taco shells at the very same time.

"You really *are* good at it," Frankie admitted in disbelief. "The cooking thing."

"Thank you," Gwen replied gravely. Frankie knew she was laughing at her. Hiding her own smile, she turned her attention toward the kitchen sliders and looked out over the lawn, where Chris worked in the dusk. Against the flicker of the barbecue, her son's face appeared long and thin. He had been growing so quickly lately, and it was as if his bones couldn't quite keep up. She knew the outgrown clothes and his lanky body frustrated him, but she'd assumed the restless moods were just something every boy went through—growing pains, puberty.

Lord, puberty. Maybe that was the simple explanation. She winced and hunched her shoulders. She didn't think she was ready for Chris's puberty. She'd had enough trouble with her own.

"You need to stir it." Gwen said into her ear, and she almost jumped out of her skin.

"Dammit!"

Gwen took the spatula from her hand, replacing it with a glass of white wine. "Stop worrying. Here, let me stir in the spices. Go and get your kid. Dinner's ready."

⁊❧

LATER, AFTER EVERY LAST CRUMB HAD BEEN CONSUMED, CHRIS AND Gwen retired to the living room to watch an apparently pivotal soccer game, and Frankie took herself out onto the back deck and dropped into one of the Adirondack chairs she'd been lucky enough to find at a Richmond estate sale. The wind had died, but the air was still nippy, and she pulled the collar of her sweater up over her mouth and nose and buried her hands between her knees. She loved winter—even Williamsburg winters, where nature couldn't decide whether to rain or snow or freeze—but the change of seasons always took some getting used to. And fall, so beautiful, seemed to come and go in a matter of days.

So she ignored the cold and leaned her head back on the chair and tried to count the stars. But the little pinpricks of light were as numerous as the thoughts in her head and soon began to blur. Eventually she shut her eyes, listening to the whisper of the creek instead.

"You asleep?"

"No." She didn't open her eyes. "Who's winning?"

"Barcelona," Gwen said after a disapproving sigh. "I brought you a blanket. And hot chocolate."

"Thank you." Frankie sat up. She took the steaming mug of chocolate as Gwen spread chenille over her knees. "Where's Chris?"

"Asleep in front of the TV." Cupping her own mug, Gwen settled into a second chair. "Painting can tucker a person out. Guess you know that."

"I like painting. It's relaxing." Frankie took a sip of the liquid chocolate. She groaned in pleasure. "Want a hand tomorrow?"

Gwen slanted her a look. "Maybe. We could probably use all the capable hands we can get. But I sort of think the kid would like to do this one on his own."

"Without his mama, you mean?" Frankie couldn't decide whether to be amused or touched that Gwen cared enough to think her son through.

Gwen didn't deny it. "We had a good time today." She sounded surprised.

"And you'd rather I didn't butt in." She felt a pang of something that felt too much like hurt, and she quickly chased it away. "You pick up a psychology degree along with the chef skills?"

Gwen only shook her head. She took a slow sip of her chocolate. "I remember what it's like to be his age."

Somewhere not too far away, someone was using their hearth. Frankie could smell woodsmoke in the night. She, too, could almost remember what it was like to be twelve and uncertain of her place in life.

"Scheduled another job today," she said, deciding to shift the subject to safer ground. "I'll start next month. Would have been sooner, but the guy has to fly down to Atlanta for the next two weeks. Some sort of poker convention."

Gwen must have heard the yearning in her voice, because she looked up from her drink, intent. "Still longing to fly, Francis? How long has it been?"

"Since I was about two." She smiled as she remembered the leap she'd taken from her Ma's dresser.

"Your ma always said you'd kill yourself trying to reach the stars."

Frankie liked the way Gwen grinned at her sideways, like they were sharing a secret. "And you've been grounded here your whole life."

"Grounded works for me." Gwen took her empty mug and set it on the deck. Her fingers curled around Frankie's, squeezing gently, warming. "You could fly out and see me sometime between fall and spring. Seattle's full of old houses. You'd love it."

"Probably I would. But I don't spend money on frivolous things. Got the future to think of. Got my business to think of."

"I'll buy you a ticket; you and Chris both—"

Frankie cut her off with a quick shake of her head. "Let it be, Gwen."

Gwen nodded. She chafed Frankie's cold hands between her own. Frankie could feel the caress all the way down to her toes, and her skin prickled in reaction. She shivered involuntarily, goose bumps rising up beneath her sweater. It would be so easy, she thought, to let her body take over. She was an adult, she'd had an affair or two, and she knew that the body didn't need promises.

It was the heart that complicated matters.

Gently, Frankie pulled her hands away. Crossing her arms against her chest, she spread her legs long and crossed her ankles, slouching into her chair.

"You and I," she said decidedly, meeting Gwen's green stare straight on, "are finished dancing around the subject. It's time to talk about Edward."

Chapter Twelve

GWEN TURNED HER FACE AWAY. "There's nothing to say."

"You're wrong. There's plenty. You just won't ask."

"Because it doesn't matter."

"It does matter. It should have been yours, Gwen. I've felt that way all along. Maybe if I'd known how to get in touch with you—" *Had the courage*, Frankie meant, because God knew she might have just picked up the phone and dialed Pinnacle, asked for Ms. Cook, please. "It might have made a difference."

Gwen's mouth thinned into a straight line. "He wrote me out of the will long ago. There's no reason to think you could have changed his mind."

"Maybe." Frankie folded her sleeves over her hands and tucked the makeshift gloves under her chin. "Like I said, people change. He eased up quite a bit during the last two years."

Gwen sat rigid, silent, for so long that Frankie prodded her with the toe of her boot. "Earth to Gwen."

"I'm listening."

Frankie sighed. "He got sick. Did you know?"

"I knew the drink would dissolve his liver eventually." That was cruel even for Gwen, but Frankie supposed she had the right.

She rubbed her chin against the wool of her sweater, seeking comfort. "It wasn't that; it was cancer—in his throat, in his lungs, all over. I think it spread pretty quickly." She paused, waiting for a reaction, but Gwen's attention appeared riveted on the distant trees. "Doctors wanted him in hospice. He wouldn't have it. Said hospice was for people who were dying." Frankie rolled her eyes heavenward. "Stubborn old man."

"He was a bastard," Gwen said, soft as velvet and cold as steel.

"Maybe a lot of that was the drink. Drink does bad things to people. Not that that excuses anything," she added quickly. "There's no excuse for how he treated you. I'm just saying that after he dried out, he was different.

"Is there a point to this, Francis?"

"The point is, he wouldn't let hospice help him. He scared or outmaneuvered everyone who tried. So that's where I came in." She took a deep breath and looked out into the woods, wondering what Gwen saw in the shadows. "He and Ma had been in touch off and on since you ran off. I don't really know what they talked about. I didn't care to ask. But then when Ma died he sent flowers, showed up at the funeral. Twelve years sober and closer to death's door than he liked to admit. He needed live-in care. I needed the money, badly. I knew what he was capable of, but I could see he'd changed. And, you know, nothing much scares me, especially not a bad reputation. I've grown up with one of my own." She laughed quietly, but Gwen only turned and stared at her through eyes that were more black than green. "Anyway, it worked out better than either of us expected, I think."

"So you played nurse." The sarcasm fairly dripped off Gwen's tongue. "For how long, six months? A year?"

Frankie squashed her exasperation. She'd known from the beginning it would be a difficult conversation. Where Edward was concerned, Gwen's scars ran deep, for good reason. And Gwen had always masked her hurts with thorns.

"Two years," she said. "The one doctor who managed to run some tests gave him three months to live. Edward had to prove him wrong.

"And I did more than 'play nurse.' We moved in with him, Chris and I. Took care of him twenty-four hours a day. Fed him, washed his clothes, shopped for his food, gave him baths when he was too weak to handle it himself. I'd had some experience, you know."

Gwen cocked her chin in silent query.

"Ma," Frankie explained. "Blood pressure eventually did her in but not before several strokes left her mostly helpless." She shrugged. "Sure, Edward was still full of piss and venom, but most of it was bluster. He never lifted a hand to either of us—or threatened to—or you can be sure we would have been out of there faster than a toupee in a hurricane. I think he was lonely and scared. Chris did him some good, and Jack."

"Pierce? You're kidding me. A fucking group effort, was it?"

"Oh, hush. I needed someone to help make the place livable. Most of the plumbing was down, and the electricity in the kitchen. I found Jack in the papers." She smiled faintly. "He started on the house. And if I needed help with Edward, well, he had muscle and a peaceful way that got the job done. He's a good man, Gwen."

"Let him drink my beers in my kitchen, didn't I?" Gwen drew her knees up on the chair, wrapped her arms around her ankles. "I'd fucking propose, but he's just not my type."

"Very funny." But Frankie was glad to see Gwen's faint smile. "Edward fought to the end. And he never stopped wondering about you. Read all the Seattle newspapers, looking for any mention."

"He gave up the right to wonder a long time ago." Gwen bounced out of her chair, paced in a circle, gripped the porch rail with both hands. "You were an idiot. You shouldn't have risked Chris in this house, Francis." She shivered.

"Are you cold?"

"What?" She sounded a million miles away.

"I'm freezing and that fancy lounge suit doesn't look very warm."

"I'm not cold. Is there more?"

Frankie yanked her turtleneck back up against her lower lip and exhaled warm air down her sweater before speaking. "In between looking after Edward and doing my best to keep Chris well adjusted, I learned a few things from Jack. Turns out I had a talent for reno, and I liked it—fixing things, making them better, stronger, useful. We started talking about a business. There was plenty of work to be done around town. Small fixes, bigger jobs. I cashed out the few stocks Ma left to Chris. Jack had some money put away, decided to invest. It was a gamble. But Chesapeake Renovations is still here today." She glanced at Gwen, who stood motionless. So Frankie continued softly, "Then, almost two years exactly to the day we moved in, Edward fell asleep in the living room and never woke up. It was quiet at the very end. He didn't have much pain. By that point we had hospice nurses in twice a day." Frankie tilted her head back until the stars came into focus. "Chris and I moved out, back into our shoebox on the hill. It wasn't until four months later that I found out he'd left the house and a bit of money to Chris."

"To Chris."

"Yeah. Seems there was more than a chunk of cash left over in a college fund your mother had started for you when you were born. It was enough that I could roll most of it back into the house, some of it into the business, and basically invest it toward Chris's future. I was lucky. Thanks to an eager buyer, my investment tripled." She meant it as a joke, but Gwen didn't rise to the bait. Elbows propped on the railing, she stared down at the lawn. Frankie couldn't read her expression.

"Are you angry? I know we really didn't have any right to the money. It was meant to be yours." She wasn't sure if she could explain to the new Gwen Cook how desperately she had needed that money and how determined she had been—still was—to make Chesapeake Renovations work.

"It was the old man's decision," Gwen said quietly. "I didn't need it then. I don't need it now."

"He had a soft spot for Chris."

"The old bastard didn't have a sentimental bone in his body."

"He missed you, Gwen." Frankie rose and joined Gwen at the railing.

"You're not going to convince me, Francis." At last, Gwen turned her back to the shadowy woods. "Edward's dead and gone. You managed to salvage something usable out of a wasted life. That's a good thing. Let's leave it at that."

Frankie nodded, feeling something close to relief. "Okay. I just wanted you to understand."

"There's nothing to understand. You took what you could and did well by your kid. Most people wouldn't have had the talent or the drive to manage it."

Frankie puffed out her cheeks and expelled a breath. "Thank you."

"Mmm." Gwen focused on Frankie for the first time in many long minutes. She grinned. "You *are* cold. Your nose has turned pink."

"Freezing. Let's go inside. Chris and I should be heading home." She grabbed the chenille throw and wrapped it around her shoulders. Gwen grasped her elbow before she could reach for her empty mug and tugged her gently back across the deck. Frankie froze when Gwen pulled her close, hands gentle as she wrapped the blanket around them both. Frankie started to protest, but Gwen tapped her nose with one finger.

"Don't fuss, Frankie. I'm not going to jump you." Gwen's free hand rubbed up and down Frankie's backbone, warming the goose bumps from her flesh.

"What are you doing?" Frankie knew she should put up more of a fight, but Gwen's warmth was such a comfort; and besides, what harm was there in a hug? Gwen probably needed one, though she would never admit it. Any talk of Edward was salt in partially scabbed wounds.

"Watching the stars. The skies are always clearest before the fall sets in."

"They're lovely," Frankie agreed. "Like diamonds. I tried to count them earlier, but . . ."

Gwen leaned in. "But?"

Frankie pulled her gaze from those fathomless green depths, but when she did Gwen's mouth stole her attention. She recalled its dance across her belly, soft as a butterfly. Across her belly, she remembered, and lower, until she was begging for more, and more again.

"Francis." Gwen brushed a tendril of errant hair from Frankie's brow, making her start. "Where did you go?"

Frankie hoped Gwen couldn't see her sudden blush in the dark. "I couldn't count them all before they went fuzzy."

Gwen's ribs vibrated. "Have you thought about glasses?" But when Frankie scowled, she relented: "It's easier if you start in this quarter."

She freed her arm from the blanket, pointing. "With the North Star. And if you move up there, you've got the dipper." Her finger sketched in the night sky. "And then left, and you've got—let's see, fifteen, sixteen—there's seventeen and eighteen . . ." Her hand danced like a sorcerer's, making Frankie's eyelids heavy. Stifling a yawn, she nestled closer until the back of her head rested in the crook of Gwen's arm. Gwen droned on, her voice soothing. Frankie didn't fall asleep—not exactly—but her eyes drifted shut, and she began to float, rocking weightlessly above the deck, stretching up into the stars with Gwen's voice to guide her.

"Gemini," Gwen murmured just as Frankie cupped her hands around the brightest star. The star flickered. She couldn't quite grasp the white heat. She grumbled.

"Francis."

The star burned out, and Frankie fell to the deck like a rock. Her body jerked and her eyes snapped open. "What?" she asked, alarmed. "What is it?"

"You were asleep." Gwen's chin rested against her temple. "Shall we call it a night? I'll wake Chris." She retreated, slipping out of the blanket. At the sliders she paused and looked back, frowning. "You're okay to drive? I don't want you falling asleep at the wheel. I could run you both home."

"No. I'm fine." The words tried to stick in Frankie's throat. "We'll be just fine."

THE OLD MAN LAY DYING. GWEN SAT CROSS-LEGGED ON SHAG CARPET, *listening to the wheeze and hitch of labored lungs. Outside, the last of the summer thunderstorms tossed gouts of wind and fistfuls of hail across the trees. The house shook, but even the howl of the wind couldn't drown out Edward's groans.*

"Daughter," the old man rasped in the space between one breath and the next, "bring me my bottle." He lifted one feeble hand from his dirty blankets as though he could summon the drink to his side. The bottle in question lay over-turned only a few inches from Edward's mattress. A thin stream of whiskey ran

onto the carpet. Gwen could smell the tang of alcohol even from across the room.

"My whiskey, girl. I need a drink." Edward coughed.

Gwen didn't move from her space on the floor. She thought she should feel something in her father's last moments—sorrow, relief, regret, jubilation, anything. Alcohol fumes stung her eyes, and the rattle of the storm made her heart pound but other than that . . . nothing.

Nothing.

"I'm not afraid of you anymore," she told the man who had never deserved the title "Father." "Just fucking die already."

"One last drink," Edward pleaded. His yellowed eyes rolled in desperation. "I'm not ready. I'm not ready!"

The buzz of her phone sent Gwen spinning from dream to groggy wakefulness. She sat bolt upright, gasping, and had just enough sense to realize she'd overslept and it was full daylight streaming through the basement window before she reached across the mattress, grabbing her mobile.

"What is it?" she snapped.

"Gwen?"

"Mike." She should have known. Rolling off the mattress, Gwen carried the phone across the room to the window. Beyond the glass the afternoon was bright—not a cloud in the sky. She repeated, "What is it?"

"Where are you? I've been trying to reach you all morning."

"Still in Virginia, Mike. Flight out's not until next week. You have my itinerary."

The dream had left a monster of a headache behind Gwen's eyes. She rarely slept so deeply. She hadn't dreamed of Edward since her first night back in the house. Mike rumbled on. Gwen closed her eyes, trying to concentrate.

"Fine," she said when the man paused to take a breath. "That's not a problem. It's an easy fix. We'll draw up a few papers, make sure there are no loopholes. I'll email you something before five."

"You've been away too long," her agent said, falling somewhere between mournful and stern. "Your personal touch is needed here. It's not the same without you at the table. Your shareholders are worried."

"I've been in touch with all of them." Gwen rubbed her eyes. She could still smell the ghost of old whiskey.

"So have I, more than once, and they're not happy. You're needed back here, Gwen."

"Soon, Mike. They can wait a few more days." She hung up before her assistant could list further concerns. The man was a blessing—Mike knew Pinnacle almost as well as Gwen did—but the man could be a mother hen, and Gwen didn't have the time or inclination to deal with his anxieties on top of her own.

Across the back lawn the woods were red and gold. She realized, with a tiny shock in her gut, that fall had truly arrived. Summer was gone. Time was running out. And just like the old man in her dream, Gwen wasn't ready.

&.

CHRIS AND GWEN LAUNCHED THE SKIFF ON A COLD FRIDAY afternoon as a thin September storm raced through the heavens and rain fell through the canopy of colored leaves.

"It'll float," Chris said, almost as a prayer, as he wiped raindrops from his nose and carefully edged the little boat into the creek.

"Of course it will," Gwen agreed. The kid had done a great job with the boat. Varnish made the hull shine, and the multiple patch jobs they'd put it through were almost invisible beneath layers of nautical blue. A restored anchor waited in the skiff's belly. All the vessel lacked was a name and a christening. And that was up to Chris. But after witnessing the serious attention Chris gave to the task, Gwen didn't suppose he would be making a final choice anytime soon.

The kid slipped a little on the muddy bank, and the skiff rocked wildly in the water. Chris hopped into the shallows after it.

"Shit," he spluttered. "Water's cold."

"Watch it," Gwen warned, knowing very well that the boy was supposed to keep a clean mouth. "Your mom will be here any minute." Then she waded into the frigid water, and her own choice words split the air.

Chris snorted. "Told you it's cold."

"Damn right. Jesus." And the trickle of rain through the trees didn't help much, either. "Okay, kid. I'll hold her steady while you climb in."

Waist-deep in the water, Chris hesitated. "You sure it won't sink?"

Gwen hid a smile. "If it does, you'll swim. I'm not worried; I've seen you in the James. Just stay away from the current in the middle; it drags some."

"Okay." Reassured, Chris grabbed hold of the skiff and hoisted himself over the edge.

"Careful," Gwen cautioned. "Don't swamp it."

The skiff tipped precariously before settling low in the water. Chris found his balance on one of the short benches. Then, grinning, he reached for the oars. "We're floating!"

"So you are," Gwen agreed. "Seems tight enough." She ran her hands under the waterline, checking the boards. "Take it out slow. Ready?"

"Ready." Chris settled low and gripped the oars.

"Ready. Go!" Gwen gave the boat a gentle shove. It slid smoothly from the shallows, wobbling as Chris tested his balance, and then the boy got the hang of her and let the current take hold.

"It's easy!" The kid's huge smile blinded her. "She just goes where the water takes her."

"The hard part's bringing her back in." Gwen sloshed from the shallows and sat on the muddy bank in the shadow of the boathouse. "Practice turning in the deep before you try it."

But Chris caught on quickly, hardly seeming to struggle as he guided the skiff back to shore. By then the rain had increased to a real shower, and the boy dripped from head to toe as he clambered back onto the bank and helped Gwen tow the boat onto land.

"She's great!" Chris almost hopped up and down as they pulled the little boat safely up the hill and away from the swelling creek. "I can't believe she's all mine . . ." That last bit trailed off uncertainly.

Gwen glanced at the kid's shining face. Her heart squeezed. She would miss him, and wasn't that an unexpected kick in the pants. Somehow over the last month, she'd grown more attached to Frankie's bright little man than she'd anticipated.

"It's all yours," she promised gruffly. "And as soon as you give her a name, we'll christen her in style." It wouldn't be an easy promise to keep—not all the way from Seattle—but somehow, she would manage.

Chris went still. His gaze skittered away to the treetops. "Can I name her anything I want? Really?"

"Sure. I thought we'd gone over that." Gwen ran a tarp over the open belly of the boat and then straightened. "You've got a list a mile long."

Chris shoved his hands behind his back and rolled his shoulders. "Does it have to be a girl's name?"

Surprised, Gwen shook her head. "Traditionally, but we're not sticky about etiquette. Name it what you want."

The brackets around the kid's mouth eased, and he puffed out his cheeks. "The *Richard Tilletson*," he said firmly.

"*Richard Tilletson'?*" Who the hell was Richard Tilletson?

Chris nodded, jaw set. "My dad. That's my dad. I want to name it after my dad."

Chapter Thirteen

"His dad?" Frankie paused in the front hall, muddy boots suspended in one hand.

"Is your investment banker with the muscles called Tilletson?" Gwen asked dryly.

"Richard?" Frankie's puzzled frown turned to a fully fledged scowl. She set her boots neatly outside the front door, then slumped against the wall. Gwen tried very hard not to notice the curve of damp cotton against her hips. She'd dressed for a day in the office with clients, and her black sweater was rumpled, her long skirt wrinkled. A long strand of pearls was arranged in graceful loops around her neck and along her collarbone, down her chest.

Gwen recognized the pearls. They had belonged to Frankie's ma, a gift from a navy boy. Ma had worn the set nearly every Sunday of her adult life. She remembered how determined Frankie had been to wear the pearls herself one day. Now they shone luminescent in the half light through the windows, somehow turning the girl from Gwen's childhood into something precious and grown up.

"After all these years Richard's decided to look us up?" Frankie crossed her arms. Her mouth hardened into dangerous lines, dispelling the illusion of delicacy.

Tiny but mighty.

"Other way around, I'm afraid." Gwen offered the glass of white wine she'd poured as soon as she heard Frankie's car in the drive. She'd picked up the bottle at a local winery, intrigued by the pretty label, willing to temporarily forego her favorite stout for a little elegance. "Chris found your quarterback on the internet."

"But we have parental controls." Frankie sounded aggrieved.

Hiding amusement, Gwen shrugged. "A friend's house, maybe. Seems he did his research pretty thoroughly. Kid's got brains." She was secretly proud of his ingenuity. He took initiative.

Frankie took a healthy swallow of wine and then sighed. "I know that." She left the support of the wall and took her stemware into the kitchen.

"You can't blame him for looking." Gwen followed closely at her heels. Her hair smelled of rain and woodsmoke and, in spite of the changing seasons, spring.

"I know that," Frankie repeated. She shot Gwen an irritated glance. "I just didn't think . . . I wasn't ready. I never kept anything back. I've told him everything about his father that I know. Which doesn't add up to much."

"He's naturally curious about his daddy, that's all." Not something Gwen had experience with personally, but she thought she could imagine Chris's frustration.

"Because his mother's not enough." It started out as a growl and ended in a whisper.

"Francis." It made her angry that Frankie would even think so. She took a sip of wine to keep from raising her voice. "You know that's not true."

"I know it is true." Frankie paced along the bank of windows. "Chris has his father's genes. He's been strong and smart and bursting with talent from the very first day. Just like his father, thank God. I'm the local yokel. Barely finished high school. Never bright enough or brave enough to escape the creek. Lord"—she spun around, glaring as if Gwen were the devil come up from below—"even you managed to find your way out. Even you!"

"Even me," Gwen agreed with a tiny, painful twist of her heart.

"I thought about running, once. More than once. Most seriously just after Chris was born. But where was I going to go, really?" Frankie's hands fisted around the wineglass. "At least here I had Ma to help us, to make sure we ate. And then I had to lean on Edward."

"No." Gwen's frustration grew. "You've got talent in spades, and the kid's smart enough to see it. Hell, you built a business from the ground up, and that's no easy thing; I should know."

"Chesapeake Renovations is no Pinnacle. We do okay, but it's day to day. No fancy sports car in our future." She blinked rapidly. "You know he's been acting up, lately. Sulking. Keeping his door shut. He doesn't talk to me at all. I had to learn from Jack that he picked up detention for passing notes in class."

"Little things. You and I both caught plenty of detention, or have you forgotten?"

Frankie waved a hand. "I had no idea he even thought about Richard. But, look, he had no trouble talking to you about it! You've spent, what, three whole afternoons with him?"

Somehow Gwen had become the one at fault. She took another healthy swig of wine, wishing she'd gone for beer instead. The elegant, cozy scene she'd been imagining at the winery was obviously not in the cards. Carefully she said, "I really just think—"

"You think he needs time away from his mama," Frankie interrupted, sharp. "I know. I get it. But, Christ on a stick, it's not like I *hover.*" She spun from the windows and set her glass on granite, nearly cracking the stem. "Where is he?"

Gwen tried not to grit her teeth. "Watching TV."

"Fine. We're going home." As easy as that, she dismissed Gwen, marched down the hall.

Sensing disaster, Gwen hurried after. "Francis, maybe give the kid a break. He's done nothing more dangerous than looking into his roots. Maybe don't go rushing in with your temper blazing."

Frankie wheeled at the end of the hall. She scoffed. "And you'd know all about roots, wouldn't you, Gwen?"

The bitter words were as tangible, as painful, as thrown stones. Gwen opened her mouth but couldn't force a retort past the obstruction in her throat. Frankie stood in silence, chest heaving. Her eyes were hard and bright. Her lower lip trembled. She took one long, shuddering gulp of air before exhaling. "You need to stay out of it. Stay out of it, Gwen. You can't understand." Then she marched off to find her son, leaving Gwen alone in the hall with only the dregs of her wine for comfort.

❦

Frankie suspected she was being colossal fool. And still, she couldn't help herself.

"I don't understand," she repeated for the third time. "Why now?"

Chris sat hunched at the kitchen table, chin propped on his fists. He stared down at the scarred wooden surface. "I told you: because I'm almost twelve."

"Is it because you're missing a guy in your life to do—I don't know —guy things with?"

"No."

"Because you know Jack loves you. And I know the two of you have a great time when you hang out together."

"Mom." Chris groaned. "I told you, I just wanted to see if maybe he'd come to debate finals."

"But the finals aren't until after Christmas." Frankie felt as though the top of her head might pop off at any moment. She didn't want to be hurt, or angry. But her heart had taken one too many sucker punches in the last month, and she felt bruised all over.

Give the kid a break, Gwen had said. And Frankie knew Gwen was right. But Gwen would also be gone the day after tomorrow. And once again it would be Frankie left behind to pick up the pieces of her heart, her family, her life.

"I wanted to give him a lot of time to make plans."

"But you don't even know for sure if you'll make the finals." It was probably the exact wrong thing to say. She was supposed to be her child's best cheerleader.

Get a grip, Frankie. This isn't about you.

"We will." For the first time, Chris looked up from the table. "We'll make the team finals, and we'll win. Because I'm team captain, and I'm good. And I want him to be there."

"I'll be there. And afterward, we'll do something special. We could drive into Richmond, have dinner, and see a movie."

"I want him to be there, too," Chris said stubbornly. "I wrote him an email and told him exactly when it would be and exactly how to get here. And I gave him our phone number, just in case. So if he calls, Mom"—he faltered—"you won't hang up on him?"

Tears pricked the back of Frankie's eyelids. She willed them away. "No, sweetheart, of course not. But, you know, your father is a very busy man—"

"So's Gwen, but she made time for me. Dad will, too. I know he will. It'll be great."

Frankie nodded and reached over to ruffle her son's hair. For once he didn't squirm, so she hugged him hard. "I hope so, bud. I really do."

And if he didn't, she decided, she would kill the man with her bare hands.

THE HOUSE WAS BIG AND DARK AND SPOOKY. NO LIGHTS ON IN ANY of the windows—not even a porch light or a lamp over the two-car garage. The rain had stopped, but the wind still screeched through the trees like an angry ghost. Overhead, disintegrating storm clouds rushed across a silver moon. Chris stood at the end of the long drive and tried to gather his courage.

For an instant, he saw the house as it had been when Edward was still alive: sagging around the edges, paint cracked and peeling, torn curtains in the windows, and mildew on the plaster walls. A great setting for a restless spirit, or two or three. Chris shuddered.

Pulling his coat tight against the wind, he glanced over his shoulder at Creek Lane and thought about turning back. But it was too far to walk, and he didn't really think he would be able to catch another lift this far off the main road. Besides, he reminded himself, it wasn't really all that late—just after nine. Gwen was probably at the back of the house, watching news on that monster TV. Maybe she'd turned off all the lights in the front of the house to conserve energy. Chris had heard through Roddy that people from the West Coast were all about going green.

Lifting his chin, Chris walked slowly up the rest of the drive, squinting against the wind. The butterflies in his stomach lessened a little as soon as he got close enough to see the new coat of paint his mom had put on the front door. The fresh paint reminded him that the house was practically brand new all over again, inside and out, and hardly haunted looking at all.

Anymore.

Besides, he didn't *really* believe in ghosts. His mom had spent hours in old houses—hours after dark, even—and she'd never seen one spirit. And just last Halloween, he'd walked through Bruton Parish cemetery in Colonial Williamsburg. Right at midnight he'd hunched down behind the ancient church, just waiting to see an old Civil War soldier come popping up from behind one of the moss-covered tombstones. But nothing had happened.

If he didn't have to be afraid of a Civil War-era graveyard, he certainly wouldn't let Edward's house frighten him away—even if it was really dark and empty looking. It didn't occur to Chris until he'd climbed the front steps that maybe Gwen had gone out. The Spyder wasn't in the drive, but maybe she'd just moved it into the garage and out of the rain.

Praying as hard as he could—because, please, God, he didn't want to walk all the way back home on a windy, creepy night like this one—Chris lifted his fist and pounded on the door.

His knock seemed to echo away into the distance. Chris leaned hard against the door, but he couldn't hear anything through the thick wood. He pounded again, and then, in desperation, pressed the door-bell over and over with his thumb. On about the seventh try, a light came on in the front hall. Chris puffed out a sigh of relief, burying his trembling fists in the pockets of his coat.

The door swung open with a creak that would have done any haunted house proud, but Chris was no longer afraid because beyond the square of light, he could see the floors his mom had redone, and he could smell lemon and beeswax and fresh paint. All scents that reminded him of his mother, and of home and safety.

"Christopher." That long, slow drawl made Chris want to smile. Southern as grits and sweet potato pie. He guessed that moving away to a place where people were weird about conservation and whales and the ozone layer couldn't really make a person less southern. "Where's your ma?"

Gwen shifted slightly in the doorway, peering over Chris's shoulder as if hoping to see Frankie on the driveway.

"She's not here." He did his best to sound casual.

Gwen didn't look like she'd been watching TV. In fact, she looked like she'd been sleeping. Her hair, usually so sleek and smooth, stuck up in clumps, and her feet were bare. She wore dark jeans and a rumpled T-shirt. Chris thought Gwen looked like she'd rolled out of bed and pulled clothes on at the sound of the doorbell. Except she had a beer bottle in her hand and—Chris looked more carefully—a gold pen stuck behind one ear. So maybe she hadn't been sleeping after all— just working. Suddenly, Chris felt just a little bit guilty.

"I didn't mean to bother you," he muttered, although that wasn't what he'd had in mind to say at all. "I know it's kinda late."

"Come in out of the wind." Gwen waited until Chris stepped into the hall, then shut the door firmly. "You drive yourself here, kid?"

"No." Chris tried to look as innocent as possible. "Took an Uber."

It was only a little white lie, really. His mom would kill him if she knew he'd hitched. Besides, it was the first time he'd dared, and he wasn't sure he'd ever have the guts to try it again.

Gwen's eyes narrowed. "Frankie know you're out?"

"No." He said it carefully. "She was asleep at the kitchen table. I didn't want to wake her." He didn't want to remember how he'd sat in the hall and listened to his mom cry herself to sleep, so he screwed up his guts and looked Gwen straight in the eye. "I snuck out. I wanted to talk to you."

Gwen's faintly puzzled expression didn't change at all. She stood so still and silent for so long that Chris had to resist an urge to wiggle. Then she grimaced and pointed the mouth of her beer bottle at the room off the hall.

"I've got a fire going in the parlor. Sit down and get warm. I'll join you in a minute."

"Where are you going?" Chris asked, although he could guess.

"To call your mom and let her know you're not dead on a back road somewhere."

Now he did wiggle. "She'll just come right over and pick me up." She would be all-fired mad, and she would probably cry again when she thought he wouldn't notice. The thought of her tears made Chris's stomach hurt. He bit his lip and reminded himself that he was almost twelve, and twelve-year-olds didn't get all sniffly at the drop of a hat.

"Then you'll have to talk fast," Gwen replied. "Go and sit down."

Chris trailed across the pine boards he'd helped his mom sand and into the parlor. The room was mostly empty except for a card table and two plastic chairs. Chris thought the furniture looked like it had been picked up at a garage sale. His mom had furnished most of the big rooms. Maybe Gwen needed help decorating the smaller rooms, too, if the parlor was any example. Papers covered the table in sloppy piles. A smooth little laptop hummed next to something that looked like a poster-size spreadsheet.

Chris picked the nearest of the plastic chairs and dragged it across the room to the hearth. He sat down, extending his feet to the fire, and closed his eyes. He sat as still as possible and waited for the sound of Gwen's return, but he'd forgotten his host was barefoot, and he didn't hear a noise until Gwen slipped into the room.

"I woke your mom up." She collapsed into the other plastic chair, thumping her beer bottle onto the table. "She didn't even know you'd gone. She was ready to rush over, but I told her to wait until she was clearheaded enough to drive safe. So you'd better tell me what this is about before she shows up and tans your hide."

Chris groaned. "She's really mad. Spitting mad, ever since this afternoon, ever since I told her I emailed my dad."

"You run over here to avoid a whuppin'?"

"She doesn't whup me." Chris said, shocked at the idea.

"She might after this stunt. You've made her feel pretty rotten, keeping this thing with your daddy a secret."

"She won't. She's not like that." Chris tightened his hands in his lap.

"And I thought maybe you could help me. I thought maybe you could explain to her so she'd understand."

"Me?" Gwen widened those really green eyes that Chris had first thought were colored contacts. "Why me?"

"Because you were dirt-poor once, too," Chris blurted, figuring maybe shortest was sweetest. "So you understand what it's like to be afraid."

Gwen's eyebrows almost disappeared into her hair. "You're not dirt-poor, kid. You've got a nice warm house and good clothes and food on your table every night, and a mom who's willing to pay for soccer lessons."

Chris's tongue felt stuck to the roof of his mouth. He stared at his fists so he wouldn't have to see the strange expression on Gwen's face as he rushed on. "But it wasn't always that way. When I was little, we were hungry all the time, and Mom had to to get our clothes at the mission." He picked at a hangnail. "She came from dirt-poor, and I know she hated it. She says we've been really lucky, but I guess she's afraid, too."

"Of?"

"Of, like, going back to the way it was," Chris explained as best he could. "She worries about it all the time. She wants me to go to a good college. That's all she thinks about. She's always scrimping and saving to put money into my college account—sometimes she goes without things like new work boots, even when they're worn down to nothing, or a new toaster oven that doesn't catch fire." It hurt to admit. "Sometimes she skips lunch to save money. And she's scared about what will happen if Chesapeake Reno doesn't work out." There was a crescent of dirt beneath one of his fingernails. Chris meticulously scraped it away. "Sometimes at night I'll get up to use the bathroom, and she'll be sitting at the kitchen, going over work bills. Sometimes she stays up all night long, worrying." Chris paused to see if Gwen was listening. She was, elbows propped on her knees, forehead wrinkled. Chris wished he could work out what she was thinking. "She thinks I don't know but I do."

"What's this got to do with your dad?"

This was the hardest part. Harder, even, than walking up the drive to a dark and spooky house. "My dad's rich," Chris explained. "He's really rich. Almost as rich as you, I bet."

"He told you that?"

"No." Chris felt the flush of embarrassment rise along his cheeks. "No, I don't think he remembers I exist. But he's a banker, in Richmond. And when I got his address off the internet, I showed it to some kids at school, and they said it's a real posh neighborhood. So he must be rich." When Chris looked up to check his audience a second time, Gwen didn't say anything. She just stared without moving. "Anyway. I thought maybe if I wrote him, maybe we could be friends or something. And maybe he'd think I was smart and good at school. He'd see how great I am on the debate team, and I could show him some soccer moves and my report cards. And maybe he'd like me enough to help out a little with college, since he's rich and all and I'm his son."

Still, Gwen didn't say a word. And Chris was too afraid to look up again. "I wouldn't ask him for much. And I'd have to do it secretly, because Mom never takes handouts." He tried to talk quickly, before all the fluttering in his stomach made him throw up. "Not for a car or anything like that. Just enough so maybe Mom won't worry so much. After all, he's got a responsibility to his kid . . . doesn't he? Child support, Roddy says." The last words were said with as much bluster as he could manage. Queasy with fear and embarrassment, he peeked up under his eyelashes and saw that Gwen was standing up.

"I thought maybe you could explain to Mom without hurting her feelings," Chris finished more quietly. "Because you grew up together, and she likes you, and she listens to whatever you say. You might make her understand without hurting her feelings about being poor," he said, repeating the most important point.

"That the only reason you wrote your daddy? For money?"

Chris had thought up a reply to that one while he'd stood out in the wind, hitching. Because he knew that if Gwen hadn't asked it, eventually his mom would. But he'd already told a fib once tonight—about taking a cab—and he just wasn't up to another.

"No," he said, hardly louder than the wind outside. "Mostly it was because of the money. But I wanted to see if I could make him like me.

Not all of the kids at school have dads, but those that do, they seem pretty nice. I guess a guy doesn't need a father to grow up right, but sometimes it helps."

"Sometimes," Gwen said, still staring at the flames. "But sometimes, kid, it's just not meant to be." That wasn't the answer Chris wanted to hear, but he was afraid, deep down, that it might be the truth, at least in his case. Not meant to be. And twelve-year-olds didn't cry over "not meant to be."

Still, he had to glare into the fire himself to keep his eyes and nose from running.

Chapter Fourteen

CHRIS'S MOM blew into the house with a bang and a clatter. Her footsteps were angry in the front hall. Chris squirmed in his chair and glanced over at Gwen, who stood still and straight in the middle of the room, one hand stalled halfway through smoothing her hair, eyes fixed on the door. Chris noticed the way the corners of her mouth twitched like she wanted to laugh. Or spit out an especially nasty cuss word.

Then Chris's mom stormed into the parlor, and he saw Gwen's face change, just for an instant. Her mouth stopped twitching and curved instead, and those weird green eyes went sharp as lasers. Chris thought she looked a little like a lady pirate or maybe a comic book superhero, bright and fierce and ready for battle.

But Frankie ignored Gwen completely. She swooped across the room, and the expression on her face made Chris clench his teeth tight. She was going to ground him *forever*.

"Christopher Allen Porter." She sounded gruff. From crying, Chris thought guiltily, or maybe shouting. Maybe she'd shouted her way all along the James, practicing her scold. "What are you trying to do, give me a heart attack?" She crouched in front of him, and he saw that beneath her client clothes, she'd exchanged high heels for yellow rain boots. The ache behind his breastbone threatened to turn into a hysterical giggle. Chris swallowed it down and shook his head. "Because if that's your goal, you've come mighty close. I can't take one more shock like this, young man; I just can't." Now her voice trembled.

Chris glanced quickly at her face, trying to determine whether the quiver was anger or tears. On the whole, he thought he preferred anger. "I left a note right on the kitchen table." He planned to keep quiet until she'd blown herself out, but he didn't want to look like a jerk in front of Gwen.

Frankie snorted. "'Be back in an hour,' it said. Not a word as to where you'd gone. And on a night like this!" The fire flared, and Chris saw the smear of dried tearstains across her cheeks. His stomach began to hurt again.

"I'm sorry." He balled up his fingers until they hurt, hoping he wouldn't puke in Gwen's parlor.

"You will be." She stood up. "We're going home."

This was when Gwen was supposed to break in, settle things down, start to explain what Chris didn't know exactly how to say himself. But Gwen remained silent, a shadow in the background.

"Wait!" Chris protested. If he could just figure out how to make her understand . . .

"'Wait' nothing," his mom snapped. She moved her hand to the small of his back, steering him to the door. "It's late and there're a few things to settle before either of us gets any sleep."

"Mom!" Chris set his heels against the wood floor. He tried to catch Gwen's eye. "Just wait a minute." He couldn't believe Gwen would fail him—not after he'd just spilled his guts. Maybe he'd made a mistake in thinking she was his friend.

"Francis." They were two steps into the hall before Gwen finally spoke. Chris felt his mom stiffen. She hesitated but didn't look around when Gwen followed them out of the room. "You're too worked up to go yet. The kid's practically in tears, and you're too mad to see any sense. And the wind's blowing so hard it's likely to tear my roof apart, let alone your ma's old car."

Frankie let go of Chris so quickly he stumbled. "Your roof's in no danger. It's forty-year shingle. And I walked every inch of it myself to make sure it was tight."

Gwen nodded. "Because you're a careful woman, when you're thinking straight."

Frankie huffed loudly. Chris almost closed his eyes in relief because that sound meant she was listening, even if she didn't like what she was hearing. Gwen must have understood, too, because she gestured back at the parlor. "Let the boy sit back down. Give him a chance to consider what he's done and whether or not he'll ever see his friends again. Meanwhile, come and help me start some tea. I've a hankering."

She stared to protest, but Gwen's hand drifted to her shoulder, barely squeezing. "You're still seeing crimson," Gwen murmured, quiet-like so Chris could barely hear. "Once you're calm you can go straight home. When I'm sure you can find the road past the blood in your eye, Francis."

Frankie huffed again. She gave Chris a freezing look. "Don't you move from that chair. We are not nearly finished."

For the first time in a whole day, Chris felt the muscles in his neck unclench. He nodded, relieved. Because Gwen was stepping up after all.

"I'll stay," Chris promised. And he kept his promise for almost all of five minutes. Then the butterflies returned to his stomach and sent him tiptoeing out of the room and down the hall.

⁔

"HE'S A GOOD KID." GWEN POURED HOT WATER OVER TEA BAGS. "Just a little mixed up."

"You know what he's thinking, do you?" Frankie took her mug with a snort. The steam wreathed her chin. "Because I haven't got a clue." Chris, hovering in the shadows just outside the kitchen, held his breath. His mom looked angry enough to boil the water in Gwen's kettle. "I just can't quite figure out how you've suddenly become an expert in my son and what he needs."

Chris winced. She looked mad enough to give Gwen a tongue-lashing. He wondered if Gwen would snap back and send her away. But she just leaned against the counter.

"I'm hardly an expert," she drawled. "He talks to me, I listen."

"Of course. He talks to you, which makes zero sense, as you've only been in town hardly over a month. He makes you his confidant, and he won't to talk to me, his mother. He talks to Jackson about sports. He talks to you about his feelings. He asks *me* what's for dinner." Frankie abandoned her tea. "Fine. What is it this time? Drugs? Booze? You can tell me. I can take it."

Chris's mouth dropped open. Did she really think he was doing drugs? He almost ran into the room to reassure her, but Gwen spoke first: "It's not drugs or booze. I told you, Francis. He's a good kid. He just wants to know his daddy." Chris waited for Gwen to explain about the money, but she didn't. Instead, she walked across the room until she stood next to Chris's mom, not quite touching. "I almost think you'd prefer drugs or booze."

"No." She sniffled. "Of course not. Though an ex-football hero, investment banker daddy with a tall, gorgeous wife is almost as bad."

"Only almost?" To Chris's surprise and relief, his mom laughed through her tears. Not a big laugh but still a real laugh.

"Listen." Gwen tapped her fingers on the kitchen counter. Her nails were painted a fresh green that reminded Chris of limes. "I'm having a party."

"Of course," his mom said in that stiff voice she usually used with clients she didn't like much. "To celebrate my failings as a mother?"

"Self-pity doesn't suit you, Francis." Gwen left her for the fridge, digging out milk. "A Christmas party. Usually I take my shareholders to Hawaii." She poured a dollop of milk into her tea. "This year we have a reservation at the Mauna Kea."

"Hawaii?" Frankie blew into her mug. "That's some party, Gwen."

"I've changed my mind."

"I imagine your checkbook will thank you." Chris's mom could make her tongue as sharp as a bee sting when she was pissed.

"I'm having it here instead."

Frankie didn't move, even when Gwen added a splash of milk to her own cup. Then she shrugged. "Okay. Williamsburg is lovely in the winter, especially if we get snow. Not exactly a tropical paradise, but CW does it up right with bonfires and holly wreaths and seasonal costumes." Frankie paused. "The hotels are probably all booked up by now."

"Not a problem, because I mean to have it here, in this house—which will need to be fully furnished—I'll want caterers and waitstaff, valet cars back and forth between here and Richmond, flagstones laid on the back lawn—a patio. Heaters, I think, and a tent for seating. We should have rooms set up to sleep ten, twelve if possible. Not everyone will want to stay in Richmond for the week."

Frankie choked on her tea. Once she could speak again, she demanded, "A whole week?"

"My shareholders expect big, Frankie, especially during Christmas; and it's my job to make them happy."

"I mean, I get that. But . . ." She trailed off, shaking her head.

"I need your help," Gwen said. "Don't make that face, Francis. You know this is exactly in your skill set."

Frankie tilted her chin. She stared at Gwen without speaking for so long that Chris thought she was trying to think of a polite way to refuse. But then she balanced the cup between her hands on her knee and nodded. "Sure, I guess. We can do the flagstone patio. It'll cost you to get it done, especially as the ground freezes, but we can do it if I juggle a few jobs around. And I'm willing to finish furnishing the house, but"—she held up a finger—"it'll cost you a pretty penny. Christmas is only two months away. You're practically asking for a miracle.

"As for the rest . . ." She shook her head. "I don't do caterers or transportation. I'm a builder. I don't do froufrou stuff."

"My assistant will handle the . . . froufrou stuff. I'd like you to concentrate on the house. Would you consider handling the seasonal decorations?"

"It's called Chesapeake Renovations. We're not party planners. Jesus. Jack wouldn't know a bayberry garland from a snake, and I've already got three jobs in the wings."

Gwen shifted slightly, glancing in Chris's direction. His heart stopped. He was sure he'd been seen, but Gwen only walked around the counter and dumped her mug into the sink. "How much work do you get done in the winter, really?" She turned on the tap. "I'll pay time and a half, so long as Pierce doesn't wrap my banister with adders."

Chris took a deep, very quiet breath. Time and a half was a good thing. His mom usually danced in the shower after a day of time and a half.

"Double time," she haggled. "I hate the Christmas rush. It complicates absolutely everything."

"Better start now, then."

"Double time," Frankie repeated coolly. "I'm not your fairy godmother. I can't work miracles without cash flow."

"I'll want multiple trees, decorated, eighteenth-century style." Gwen raised a finger. "No silly themes. I hate themes."

"I'll want twenty-five percent in hand before you fly back west," returned Frankie.

"I can do that. If you get me the bid by tomorrow."

"Done." Chris's mom slid off the stool and set her coffee cup in the sink. Then she just stood there next to Gwen, her back to the room, which was dumb because Chris was pretty sure she couldn't see anything in the dark past the kitchen window. He couldn't even see their reflections in the glass, as they stood shoulder to shoulder. The lights were too low.

But he was glad she wasn't crying anymore. Probably she was already thinking about work. And even though Gwen hadn't exactly said anything to get him out of the doghouse, it looked like she'd managed to scrub some of the mad off. Chris could tell that deep down, his mom was pleased, so maybe Gwen had handled things her own way, given Chris and his dad a little more time to make things right. Because Chris just knew that, somehow, they would.

They had to.

PIERCE LIVED ON SEVERAL ACRES OF LAND JUST OUTSIDE
Williamsburg proper. Gwen's car slipped on the muddy road before
clattering over a cow grate. Three big dogs greeted her arrival with
loud enthusiasm, herding the Spyder farther along until the road dead-
ended in a clearing occupied by a late-model Airstream and Pierce's
dingy truck.

Gwen braved the dogs—who were reassuringly well behaved for
their size—and rapped on the trailer door. When there was no
response, she knocked a second time. The trailer was silent, the door
securely locked. The dogs—Labs—sat politely in a row alongside the
truck and watched, tongues lolling. One brown, one yellow, one black.
Gwen suspected they might be laughing.

"Where's your master?"

One of the dogs barked sharply and bounded from the clearing. Its
companions followed, tails wagging. Somewhat less eager, Gwen
slogged through the high grass in their wake. Behind the Airstream a
trail had been mown into the grass. The dogs ran three abreast. In the
near distance Gwen heard the chop of an ax against wood. She could
smell wet sap and crushed grass and the faint sweetly acrid perfume of
a cigar.

The second hollow was smaller, clearing just begun. Felled pines lay
where they had dropped, waiting to be trimmed and split. Oak already
quartered, had been stacked in a neat pile. Pierce glanced up at the
dogs' arrival, then buried his ax in a pine log. He took the cigar from
his mouth and eyed Gwen warily.

"You're gonna ruin your shoes."

Gwen was pretty sure both her Gucci sneakers and Tom Ford jeans
were already ruined, but she was willing to make the sacrifice. "Nice bit
of land."

He stuck the cigar back in his mouth and spoke between his teeth.
"It suits my purpose."

"Which is?"

"Keeping unwelcome visitors out of my hair." He sucked in, then
exhaled a cloud of smoke. "Makes me wonder how you managed to
find my place."

"Why, Jack. I thought we were friends." When he only grunted, she added, "I asked Chris. He told me all about pizza nights in the trailer. And the woodshop he's going to help you build once you finish clearing the pasture."

"Damn. What'd you do, bribe him with dessert to get him to talk?"

Gwen hid a smile. "Something like that." Truth was, Chris had been eager to talk about Jack and his house in the woods. It was obvious he worshipped the man.

Jack whistled at the dogs and started back down the trail. "What do you want? I'm out of fancy beer, but I might be able to dig up a stale Coors."

"Kind, but no thank you." Gwen managed to keep her dignity as she sidestepped a large mud puddle and hopped a fallen log. "I have a proposition."

"You're not my type."

"Very funny." One of the dogs slobbered against Gwen's leg. She set a hand on the massive head. The dog wiggled with joy. "What I meant to say was: How would you like to be a star?"

Pierce stopped in front of his trailer, turned, and dragged again on his cigar, frowning. "What the hell are you talking about?"

"I've got a talent. But I can't do it all on my own. It's a two-way street." She braced herself. She'd known this would be hard. It had been a long time since she'd asked a virtual stranger for anything. "I need your help."

His eyebrows went up. Watching Gwen all the while, he fished a key from under the trailer's top step and used it to unlock the door. "Wow. Did that hurt as much as it seemed?"

"Like chewing nails," Gwen admitted. "But necessary. Will you at least listen?"

"This about Frankie? Of course it is. Nothing else would send you all the way out here." Pierce propped the door open with a chunk of what looked suspiciously like Carrara marble. Ducking his head, he disappeared inside the trailer. The dogs followed. Gwen stood in the grass and waited. She was wondering if she was expected to follow when Pierce ducked back out again, a bottle of tequila dangling from his fingers, the quenched stub of his cigar tucked behind one ear.

He looked less like a choirboy and more like a fallen angel.

"Fact is, I know all about your talent." He set two mismatched shot glasses on a stump that was obviously being used as a makeshift table. "I have one, too." He poured out the tequila. "And after our little party the other night, I decided to use it." He handed Gwen a full shot glass. "I've seen your birth certificate, your bank accounts, your books. I know what brand of toothpaste you brush with in the morning and your favorite tampon brand. I know you've got a scar behind your left knee and that you're allergic to penicillin. I also know exactly what you did on the streets before some Seattle tech king noticed you had a brain worth educating." Pierce lifted his own shot glass in a toast and drank. "Cheers."

Gwen said nothing. Pierce refilled his glass. "You didn't finish high school, and you didn't go to college; but you did get your GED, then an MBA. Impressive. You spent some time off the radar the year you turned twenty-one, but as far as I can tell, you didn't get into any real trouble."

"Not for want of trying," Gwen murmured. She couldn't decide whether she was pissed or impressed.

Pierce tossed back his second shot and smiled, teeth bared in an even white grin. "You had your wrist broken in a bar fight the day you turned twenty-three. After that, seems you settled down, mostly, and developed a talent for taking small less-than-profitable businesses and turning them into thriving branded entities."

"I like making money. Turns out I'm good at knowing what people want."

"And now you want to help Frankie out. You think you can take Chesapeake Reno and, do what? Turn it into some sort of national brand?"

"If Jo and Chip can do it, so can I," Gwen said easily. "It just takes finding the right spin. And it's not for Frankie, really. It's the kid."

"Chris." Pierce squinted. "Chris is doing fine. Chris and Frankie are doing fine, both of them. They don't need your help. Sure as hell don't need you sneaking around, playing Good Samaritan behind their backs."

Gwen let that pass. She said, "I know what it's like to worry about the future. I'd prefer they didn't have to." *And the kid should go to college.* "Happens I can see a way to make that worry disappear."

"Yeah? Happens I can see Frankie never talking to either of us again, we do this. I'm just not that stupid. You should know she doesn't take handouts." Pierce shook his head, poured another shot. "Drink up. That's my good thinking tequila, and I don't share it with just anyone."

Standing, Gwen downed the shot, grimaced, and set the empty glass back on the stump with a thud. Pierce drank a third shot, still smiling. "Another?"

"God no. I drove." *Thinking tequila.* "What are we thinking about?"

Pierce rolled his neck from side to side and then crossed his arms. "You've got a very expensive house on the left coast. The majority of your clients are located in Seattle, Scottsdale, and New York. Frankie's not going to pick up her kid and move him—not now."

"She wouldn't have to. I do plenty of work long distance. Besides, I intend to be out here as often as possible. Locations will be very important when it comes to branding, after all."

Pierce plucked the cigar butt from behind his ear, rolled it thought-fully between two fingers. "That so?" He met her eye. His were gray, like the sky before a thunderstorm. "Yeah, I watch *Fixer Upper.* So, what, we're Magnolia with an eastern twist?"

"More Christina and Tarek, I think. Emphasis on renovation; we'll avoid baking."

"And you want me to convince Frankie."

"No. That's my job." Gwen smiled. It was like stalking a vole on little cat feet. So long as she didn't pounce prematurely, she'd have her prize in the end. "Come Christmas, I need you to put on a tux and charm the fuck out of my investors. Because your woodworking magic is a big part of the punch—you've got unusual skills, and I like that. So will my clients. I could make you rich off cabinetry alone. But I've got bigger things in mind."

"You want me to put on a penguin suit and show off my wood."

"Aren't you a card. There will be plenty of details to discuss, of course. But for now, I just need to know you're agreeable."

"For Chris's sake. Not because you get a nice cut when—if—we go big."

She supposed she'd earned that. He had, after all, somehow seen into her bank accounts. Which meant she needed to make some angry phone calls as soon as she got home.

"For Chris's sake," she said. "But also because you and Frankie are a rare commodity, and rare commodities are my specialty. So. Despite all appearances, I suspect you're a man with both sense and ambition." She held out a hand. "How about we deal?"

Chapter Fifteen

SEATTLE WAS EXACTLY as Gwen had left it: gray and wet, and smelling of fish and flowers and gasoline and leather. And money—always money. She could almost inhale the perfume of new wealth as she navigated the rain-drenched streets. It was in the brilliant glass palaces being built into green hillsides, in the jazzy electric cars skipping from lane to lane on the freeway, in the low-lying strip malls catering to health nuts and astrophiles, and in the boxy corporate factories sprouting up between pine trees.

Money was Gwen's game. She had a knack for taking small businesses and turning them into multimillion-dollar brands, and it had served her well. She was accustomed to the small measure of fame success had brought, used to the articles with her name in bold. She'd even become used to the numbers in her bank account.

But she never forgot the girl who had grown up in Edward's basement, and she never let herself assume that the bank accounts would continue to grow on their own. She still worked as if her future depended on it—as if every penny was her first, every multimillion-dollar deal signed her last. She was good at what she did. She enjoyed turning a profit—for herself but mostly for others. It made her feel powerful, and it made her feel needed.

She was looking forward to time spent back in the office—or so she told herself. And her head agreed, preferring logic to frustration any day of the week, but her heart registered continued, painful protest. She felt like she'd left a solid half of it on the other side of the country.

She buttoned the collar of her coat against the rain as she dashed from the car to her condo, pausing only to greet the doorman. Mirror, chrome, and shiny black granite—the building was the height of Seattle architectural style, at least for this year. She wondered what Frankie would think of the stark surroundings and decided they would have to take time to find out. Maybe in the spring, when the Sounders' season started up again, she could convince them to fly out to catch a game.

Someone had affixed a wreath of fall flowers to the penthouse door —probably Gwen's housekeeper. The man seemed determined to fill her home with blossoms and potpourri. The wreath was crooked, but it was also pretty, and it smelled of nutmeg. Gwen straightened the orange and yellow leaves as best she could and decided she would leave it up for as long as the flowers lasted. Frankie would approve of the color.

She unlocked the door and shoved it open with her foot. The foyer was black-and-white marble, completely bare of decoration. Gwen had never before noticed quite how cold it seemed. She stood for a moment, feeling oddly lost, then tossed her keys and her coat onto the single black lacquered bench that served as both a seat and mail depository.

She shucked off her heels and went in search of dinner. The very expensive and incredibly beautiful bromeliad she'd picked up in March at a local farmers market drooped in its pot on the kitchen counter, near death. The orchid she'd nursed for the last five years looked like it had already succumbed. And the shelves of her industrial fridge were bare.

"Hell." Gwen scrubbed a hand through her damp hair. Her house-keeper had a mind like a steel trap when it came to clean toilets and spotless windows, but when it came to some basic needs, he could be severely lacking. Gwen turned in a baffled circle. The huge state-of-the-art room she'd been so proud of now seemed cold and sterile. Full of echoes, empty as the front foyer, gleaming and free of dust but about as welcoming as a tomb. Every utensil she owned had a place behind closed doors. Only the two suffering plants and a single blue glass vase adorned the counters.

She'd forgotten there were no windows. Somehow, she'd come to expect sunlight in her kitchen.

Restless, Gwen cranked open the kitchen tap and let water rush into the sink just to hear the sound of it. Frankie had smiled when she said goodbye, adorable in grease-stained dungarees and workman's boots. She'd kissed Gwen on her cheek in front of her son, then turned away, focused on the plans she had drawn up for the new flagstone patio.

Kissed Gwen on the cheek as if they hadn't fucked like rabbits on a wild late-summer night. The tips of her fingers remembered every inch of Frankie's body, every angle and swell.

Get it together, Gwen. You knew this wasn't going to be easy.

Scowling, she set the bromeliad gingerly into the filled sink. Once she was sure the pot wouldn't tip over in two inches of water, she reached for the sleek black concierge phone that hung on the wall alongside the fridge. Dinner, first. Takeout—Chinese, and lots of it. Then work. Which was just fine because she didn't think sleep would come anytime soon.

VOICE MAIL SPOOLED FROM GWEN'S PHONE AS SHE STOOD IN HER office and watched the sun rise above Lake Washington. Here, the windows were floor to ceiling. Black vertical blinds parted around her body as she set her palm against the cool glass.

She'd been missed but not catastrophically. Gwen had laid well-oiled tracks, and Pinnacle chugged along as it should without her. She was both pleased and—for the sake of her ego—a little disappointed.

"Gwen?"

"Speak of the devil." She turned from the window to greet her assistant.

"Should my ears be burning?" Thin and wiry, Mike Windsor tended to overcompensate for lack of bulk with color. He wore a bright-yellow tie and a wide grin. He carried a paper shopping bag over one arm.

"I was just thinking you did a wonderful job keeping things on track while I was away."

"Thank you." Windsor's smiled died. "Can't say our shareholders were happy to have you out of state."

Gwen's heels clicked on marble as she crossed to the desk and picked up a file. "They'll have to get used to it." She weighed the file in her hands, then passed it over. "Notarize these, will you? And then get back to me. I'll have a memo out before breakfast. And I'll need you to draw up a list of caterers in the Williamsburg-Richmond area." It galled a little that she was already looking forward to December with an intensity approaching desperation.

Mike nodded. "Maui's a hard one to give up. But a white Christmas might be a nice change." He set the shopping bag on her desk without comment. She'd asked him to make a run to her safety deposit box, described what she wanted in careful detail, and it was to his credit he didn't ask any questions.

"Good. Spin it like that." She sat down. "Snow, evergreens, blah-blah, hot toddies in front of a crackling fire . . . et cetera, et cetera. Oh, and fireworks on the Palace Green. They'll love it."

"Not a problem. I'll have everyone singing 'White Christmas' in no time at all." He tossed Gwen a jaunty salute. "It really is good to have you back."

He left the office, shutting the door behind him. Gwen regarded the shopping bag with indecision, then gathered her courage and peeked inside. The small neatly wrapped gift box was exactly how she remembered it, the daisy-print paper faded with time, the yellow ribbon wilted from more than a decade in storage. She positioned it carefully on her desk, turned it this way and that with one finger, thinking.

"Good to be back," she said to the empty room, determined to make it true. She set the box aside and got to work.

&

For the first time in as long as Frankie could remember, it snowed on Halloween. Snow fell in sheets, covering the skeletal woods in clean drifts. Gray clouds in the darkening sky made the evening dour.

Spooky, Frankie thought in appreciation. A truly ghostly night—perfect for the holiday.

Although, as she stood in the driveway and lifted her face to the blizzard, the air felt decidedly more like January than October. Still, the turning seasons always brought her joy, and she whooped a little out loud as she whirled in a circle. Chris would have a snow day or two. And maybe she would actually splurge on a fresh farm-raised turkey for Thanksgiving this year instead of settling for a processed breast. She would find the time and energy to whip up mashed potatoes and sweet yams and pecan pie.

As far as she was concerned, nothing beat a snowy winter. Never mind the fact that her clients would not be pleased by weather delays. Frankie wasn't worried. She always found her way around any bump in the process.

The more snow the better, she decided as she hurried to the house. Snow to shovel, snow to play in, snowmen and hot cider in the kitchen of her snug little home. Not that Ma's old house was exactly weather-proof—but that was another project she would tackle later, when the inevitable slow season set in. She and Chris would blow insulation into the attic, fix the cracks in the storm windows. She would nag Jack until he agreed to find her a refurbished oil tank, one that didn't leak. Maybe they could finally be able to get rid of the old electric heaters.

She hummed as she climbed the porch steps. They already needed shoveling. Two huge pumpkins, carved into a grotesque vampire and a friendly mummy, watched her from either side of the front door. Smiling, she dug around in her tote for a matchbook and, crouching, carefully lit the candles in each pumpkin. Flames danced up behind their gaping eyes and toothy mouths, turning the gourds into ghouls. The flicker sent yellow light across the porch and turned innocent corners into spooky hollows. Pleased, Frankie dropped her tote on the porch and sat down next to the basket of candy she'd put out earlier in anticipation, content for the moment to watch the falling snow.

She had the ghostly night all to herself. Chris was out at a school mixer, masquerading as Zorro with an old rubber prop sword Frankie had found in a secondhand shop. The sword wasn't exactly period, but Chris loved it. Her child had been happier lately. She wasn't sure whether the mood change was due to the roll of the seasons, the hours he spent boating on the creek, or the new video game console Jack had bought for the Airstream.

Chris still jumped when the phone rang, and Frankie knew he was hoping for his daddy at the end of the line. But if Richard had read Chris's email, he hadn't bothered to respond, hadn't bothered to pick up the phone.

The same could not be said of Gwen. Frankie cupped her chin in her hands and watched the flickering candlelight on the stoop. Gwen's weekly calls had become anticipated events: Sunday night, six o'clock sharp, as reliable as the Chesapeake tide. She always asked for Chris first. Frankie didn't know what they talked about; she'd been determined not to eavesdrop. She only knew the calls made her son smile, and she was grateful for that.

And every time the telephone rang on Sunday night, Frankie's heart galloped in a frantic rhythm. Even from the West Coast, Gwen turned her life edgewise.

They chatted about easy things: work, the weather, the house, and the party. Small talk. And it *was* easy—sometimes they spoke for hours about nothing, got to know each other all over again, as grown women. Gwen was taking a cooking class—something called Asian Fusion. She made Frankie laugh with dry descriptions of her less-than-talented classmates. Sometimes she read to Frankie passages from the book she kept by her nightstand. Lately it was *From a Land Where Other People Live*. She'd never thought Gwen would develop a taste for poetry, but she read it out loud beautifully, with emotion she rarely showed otherwise.

Just the sound of her voice was a gift to take with her into a long workweek.

Or it should have been. But Frankie always hung up the phone with a pit in her stomach. She missed Gwen more than she had expected.

She'd known it would be bad, of course, but she assumed it would get better as time passed. It hadn't.

She missed Gwen as she'd never missed Chris's father. She missed her with an intensity that made her knees shake at the oddest moments. That made her eyes well up for no reason, just as they had when Frankie had been sixteen and Gwen had been the first to break her fragile heart.

Well. Frankie's heart wasn't fragile anymore. She'd gone into the thing headfirst, eyes wide open. The sex had been good. Great sex. Incredibly great sex, but still—just sex. And if it had only been the sex, maybe it wouldn't be so hard to hang up the phone every Sunday night.

It wasn't just the sex. It was all the rest of Gwen, too. Her stubborn streak, her quick smile, her sharp wit. The way she tried to overcompensate with fancy clothes and a silly little car. That she still preferred beer over champagne, and pie over anything else, and four-inch heels no matter the weather.

Gwen had taught herself to cook because it was practical. She'd taught herself to build a boat, for Chris's sake. She got all croaky when she read good poetry. And when Gwen looked at Frankie, Frankie felt *seen*.

"Well, Jesus." Frankie reached for a handful of Halloween candy. She'd loved Gwen once, with a girl's quick, deep passion. Frankie knew she loved her still. And she suspected that she'd never stopped loving Gwen in between.

BY THE END OF NOVEMBER, SNOW COVERED WILLIAMSBURG IN A thick blanket. Unused to harsh weather, the town ground to a halt for days each time new snow fell. Plows had to be shipped over from Richmond and salt brought in from farther north. The College of William and Mary closed for Thanksgiving break. By that time the local high schools had already used most of their allotted snow days.

Chris loved the unusual weather and spent every free moment out in the cold, building ice forts or racing around on borrowed cross-country skis with a group of boys from the debate team. He spent one weekend learning how to ice-skate at the local mall and decided he desperately wanted to join Williamsburg's junior hockey league. His eagerness had Frankie setting aside spare change toward the purchase of hockey blades for Christmas.

Frankie's client list grew in spite of the cold weather. She had a professor who wanted the kitchen in his old cottage restored to its former glory and a senator who wanted his sprawling home on the James completely refitted with period light fixtures. She had one woman who wanted her garden walk redesigned and another who couldn't decide whether she wanted tile or hardwood in her basement. She'd become more attached to her phone than ever; texts and emails pinged from early morning until late in the night.

She had the phone with her one dreary afternoon as she chopped wood beneath a light dusting of snow. She was expecting a call from a contractor, but when it rang, the sound shrill in a landscape muffled by snow, she almost dropped her ax.

"Porter!" she barked, pressing the phone against her cheek as she stripped the gloves from her fingers.

"Ms. Porter?" The voice was bland, dry, and very familiar. "Mike Windsor. I trust you have a moment?"

"Mr. Windsor. What a pleasant surprise." Frankie made a face at the chopping block as she balanced the phone between shoulder and jaw, tucking fingers under her armpits to keep them warm. "I didn't expect to hear from you until the weekend."

"Yes, well." Gwen's assistant cleared his throat. "Something's come up."

Something always did, Frankie thought as she watched her breath turn to mist in the cold air. She'd had her share of paranoid clients, but Mike Windsor took the cake and then ran with it. She wasn't sure what the trouble was. In the beginning she'd assumed the man just didn't trust her to do the job. He phoned her almost daily, no matter the hour, checking on this and that and the other thing. He didn't like the amount she billed for furniture. Her food budget was definitely too high. His transportation budget, on the other hand, was too low. And did she really think they needed boot warmers in the front hall?

Frankie had tried to be understanding. The man was detail orientated and obviously good at his job. But the calls kept coming, even after she'd proved—to herself, at least—that she didn't need a nanny. Maybe he just didn't like her, although he always kept the calls professional and upbeat. And as much as Frankie hated to admit it, she'd begun to look forward to his check-ins because Mike's nitpicking only meant that nothing had changed and, come Christmas, Gwen would be home, if only for a little while.

"Ms. Porter?"

"Yeah. Yes, I'm here." Frankie blinked and focused. "I'm here. What can I do for you today, Mike?"

"Gwen asked me to phone. She's away on business for the next few days, but she asked me to relay a few lighting specifications."

"'Lighting specifications'?" Unlikely. Frankie thought it probable Gwen had never paid attention to "lighting specifications" in her life.

"Yes. Christmas lights, for the eaves of the house. Gwen saw the ones she wants in a catalog. I've sent you the link. Please take a look when you have a minute."

"Okay." Frankie frowned down at a piece of split wood. Last Saturday it had been tree skirts, holly bushes, and dining room furniture. Someone—probably Windsor—was definitely feeling the Christmas spirit. "What kind are they?"

Mike hesitated just long enough to have Frankie bracing herself. "LED-rainbow icicles. I believe she described them as 'gay and fabulous.'"

Frankie winced. While "gay and fabulous" was usually a plus, she'd promised Gwen Williamsburg traditional, and that was definitely not rainbow LEDs. "Um. Remind her we need Twelfth Night candles in each window. Candles plus outside lights on the eaves might be a little too much."

"I'll tell her." As usual, Mike sounded awfully chipper. "Oh, and I'm supposed to remind you that Gwen is out of the country for the next week and that she'll phone or text you after the first of December, once she's home. Meanwhile, I will of course continue to be at your disposal."

Frankie frowned. Still balancing the phone, she worked her stiffening fingers. "I remember. Gwen's either remarkably brave or remarkably stupid. Party's on the eighth. She waits too long, there'll be no time to fix any screwups."

"I assure you Gwen has no doubts as to your ability and skill. And as I said, I will continue to be—"

"At my disposal," Frankie said, rolling her eyes at the snowy woods. "I get it. You can tell her I've cleared up the mess with the Hampton caterers."

"I'm sure she'll be pleased to hear it. Have a good evening, Ms. Porter."

"Gee, thanks!" Frankie tried for Mike's unnatural level of cheer, but the line was already dead against her ear. Shaking her head, she went back to chopping wood.

Chapter Sixteen

FRANKIE CALLED GWEN ON THANKSGIVING, late in the evening after she and Chris and Jack had polished off half a turkey, one quarter of a Virginia ham, and half a pumpkin pie. The cider she and Chris had imbibed all through dinner fizzed cheerfully in her belly. The boys' boisterous laughter in the kitchen made her tiny house feel like a home. The holiday had been almost magical; she didn't want to roll into bed without telling Gwen all about it.

But the call went straight to voice mail, which she hadn't expected. Gwen was usually very prompt about answering Frankie's infrequent calls and returning her texts. Frankie knew Gwen was trying to make a point: three thousand miles would not change her commitment to their friendship.

Frankie wrinkled her nose as the greeting played over the phone. Gwen's voice was clipped, professional, most of the South smoothed away. It was almost like listening to a stranger. Unaccountably nervous, Frankie disconnected.

Adrenaline made her mouth dry and her palms sweaty. It felt distressingly like she was back in high school and trying to work up the courage to ask handsome Johnny Parker to the junior prom. Johnny hadn't answered the phone, either. Frankie had given up after only the one try.

"No." Frankie knocked her knuckles against her temple, willing the strange anxiety away. "No. You are not seventeen years old, and Gwen is not Johnny Parker, and it's generally acceptable to phone friends on Thanksgiving."

Chris stuck his head into the room, eyebrows raised. Frankie waved him back into the kitchen, mouthing: "One second." Then she dialed again, mentally prepared to leave a brief, cheerful, perfectly *friendly* holiday message.

It didn't help that her pulse was pounding in her ears, and the fizzy cider was threatening to erupt in a nervous burp. She was regretting her greedy share of pumpkin pie when Gwen picked up.

"Francis." Her slow, sweet drawl, so different from Professional Gwen on the voice mail, magically made everything easy again. *Bad sign, Frankie. Very bad sign.*

She didn't care. "Happy Turkey Day, Gwen. I was just about to leave a message. In case you were busy."

"I am. Very. With a serving of crème brûlée and a glass of twenty-year scotch. Happy Thanksgiving to you. How was the traditional Virginia ham?"

"Not as good as crème brûlée, I'll bet. You're not at home." Frankie had forgotten, in the festivities, that Gwen was working through the holiday. "You're meant to be out of touch until the first. Slipped my mind; sorry."

"Four Seasons Scottsdale," Gwen purred, smug. "And don't apologize. I was actually going to ring you and Chris after I finished dessert. Lovely crisp weather in Scottsdale. How about your neck of the woods? Plenty of the white stuff, I hope."

Frankie grinned into the phone. "Snow up to our ears. Like something on a postcard."

"Wonderful. Couldn't be better." Gwen paused. Frankie imagined her taking a bite of pastry or a slow sip of scotch. "A white Christmas fits the bill nicely. And what do you think of my icicle lights?"

"They're too much." Frankie leaned against the wall, slid down until she was sitting on the floor, closed her eyes. It was easier to conjure Gwen's face against the backs of her eyelids. "But I suppose your assistant already told you that? He's worse than a hen with one egg."

"I pay him to be a hen. I'd hoped to change your mind about the lights. Admit it: they're fabulous." Another pause, the clink of silverware against porcelain, a hum of pleasure that made Frankie's toes curl even though she knew damn well Gwen was doing it on purpose. To remind Frankie of what she was missing.

And damn if it wasn't working.

She cleared her throat. "The Twelfth Night candles are enough. You don't want to overdo it. Trust me."

"Oh, I do. Let's scandalize the neighbors just a tiny bit. How about on the gazebo? Put my pretty rainbow lights on the gazebo." It sounded suspiciously close to a plea. "We both know that Creek Lane needs more gay in Christmas."

Frankie smothered a lough. She opened her eyes and rolled them at the cracked plaster ceiling. "On your head be it. I thought you wanted a traditional Christmas. Rainbow LED icicle lights on a gazebo are not really traditional, Gwen."

"I did. I do. I know. But I've seen them, and now I want them. Don't make me go over your head."

"To whom? I'm the boss," Frankie reminded Gwen. But it pleased her that Gwen was taking an interest, so she relented: "If you're so in love with the lights, we might find a way to use them. Not on the house. The gazebo probably works."

"Thank you."

"You're welcome."

Gwen hummed but didn't speak. They sat for a moment in silent companionship. Frankie imagined Gwen finishing her dessert, sipping her drink, waving the waiter over for a refill. She was probably dressed in the latest Arizona chic, a jewel on display in the hotel's meticulously decorated dining room. Frankie had never been to a Four Seasons.

"Francis?"

"Yes? I'm still here." She probably should have passed the phone to Chris by now, but she was reluctant to let go.

"I miss you." Simple. Warm. Wistful.

Bittersweet. "I miss you, too. And Chris. He can't stop talking about your visit. Party's only days away, Gwen." She felt jitters rising, firmly squashed them down.

"Listen. I'm landing in Richmond, nine o'clock the night of the first. Pick me up?"

"I'm not your Uber, Gwen. I have half a million things still to do to get everything ready."

"Please." Again, it was dangerously close to a plea, and much too close to unspoken honesty.

"You never ask me for anything. And now twice in one phone call. Are you feeling all right?" She meant it as a tease, to make the both of them laugh, to keep the call light. Honesty, spoken, was for later, face-to-face and not across three thousand miles.

"What can I say?" Gwen hesitated. "I really love those lights."

"Idiot," Frankie told her fondly. "Fine. Richmond, nine o'clock. I'll try."

THE LAST MEETING WITH THE FLORIST MIKE HAD FOUND IN Newport News took less time than Frankie had budgeted, so she took the free hour and drove out to the creek. The winding road up to the house had been cleared of snow, sanded, and plowed. It was still slicker than she liked. She drove carefully, keeping her eye on the road and her foot on the sluggish brake pedal. When she turned onto Gwen's drive, traction was better but not by much. She made a mental note to put a call into a clearing service and schedule ice removal for the duration of the party. She didn't need intoxicated drivers playing bumper cars in the drive, ruining the aesthetic she'd worked so hard to create.

And it *was* picture perfect. Frankie threw the Mercedes into park and took a long moment to appreciate her work. She wasn't usually self-congratulatory, but she knew that this time, she had outdone herself.

Fresh white snow covered the front lawn, the flowerbeds, and much of the roof. The temporary miniature evergreens she'd planted on either side of the drive looked as if they had sprung naturally from the earth and not hidden planters. A single candle glowed in every window. Icicles hung from the eaves in glistening spirals, reflecting the afternoon light.

"She wanted icicle lights," Frankie grumbled as she stepped into the cold. Snow crunched beneath the soles of her boots. "We've got the real thing."

She climbed the front steps, one hand on the cold iron rail. She would have to remember to ask the service to de-ice the stairs. It wouldn't do at all if a guest slipped on slick brick and took a tumble.

Through the sidelights around the front door, she could see the vague red shadows of the poinsettias she'd set in the entryway. Tomorrow they would be joined by swathes of evergreen and mistletoe. The florist had promised delivery at 8:00 a.m. sharp.

Frankie paused on the top step, turned to look back over the yard. She felt as though she were standing smack in the middle of a Norman Rockwell painting. The snow across the lawn looked so very fresh. She had to ignore a gleeful urge to run back and forth across the white expanse and leave a trail of zigzagging footprints.

No. Everything had to stay pristine and lovely, at least until Gwen arrived. Frankie knew she would be happy with the results. More than happy.

"She'll be knocked right out of her fancy heels."

Frankie discovered she had the edge of a thumbnail in her mouth and yanked her hand away. She'd been chewing her nails voraciously lately. It was a habit she scolded her son over, and she needed to stop. It was Gwen's fault, driving her to distraction all the way from Seattle.

No, it was her own fault. For hoping that if she got this party just right—just perfect—maybe Gwen would stay. And that was bananas, unhealthy thinking, and she didn't need a therapist she couldn't afford to tell her so.

As she frowned at her ragged thumbnail, a flash of red shot in a streak across the edge of her vision. Frankie lifted her head, then held her breath. A cardinal, scarlet and royal, danced on the air just above the snow. The bird swooped over the lawn several times before settling on a bare branch just across the drive.

A cardinal—a final bright spot of beauty in the paradise Frankie had built on Edward Cook's ugly legacy. She wished she dared reach for her phone and snap a picture, but she was afraid to move. The bird stayed on his branch for another five minutes, waiting as the sunlight warmed and the icicles began to drip. Frankie stood just as still, worries forgotten in the beauty of red feathers, until a cloud passed over the sun, and the cardinal stretched his wings and dove from his perch, away into the afternoon.

Chapter Seventeen

GWEN WAS PREPARED for light and color and an abundance of festive details. She'd had, in the back of her mind, pictures from magazines and images of Christmas at the White House or the grand holiday celebration at Monticello. Two beautiful old houses done up elegantly for the winter.

She had supposed Frankie would treat Edward's mansion with the same elegance. But the truth of the matter knocked those preconceived images, along with every sensible thought, straight from Gwen's skull. Elegance abounded, yes—all the festive details she could hope for. And the furnishings Frankie had chosen were certainly tasteful and period enough to grace the pages of any magazine. Gwen saw Jack's handiwork in some of them.

But Frankie had added something more. Something Gwen definitely hadn't seen on those elementary school White House tours.

Frankie had added a . . . feeling. An impression. A *feeling* Gwen couldn't quite pin down. Homey, maybe. A sense of welcome and belonging. The promise that, no matter how lovely the overstuffed chairs, no matter how stylish the pewter knickknacks or how extensive the greenery, a person would always find a warm nook to relax in, a comfy chaise to share with a book. And there would always be something comforting simmering in the kitchen.

The house had room enough for any number of visitors, but Frankie had taken something cold and made it cozy, made it ready. Ready for family, clients, children. A cat, Gwen thought foolishly as she touched the polished banister. She wasn't entirely sure, but she thought a cozy house needed a cozy cat.

God help them both, Frankie had turned the place into a home. Full of furniture and easy clutter, the rooms were unrecognizable. Already Gwen longed to take a nap on the parlor sofa in front of the crackling fire, sit down to supper at the new dining room table, explore the wine cabinet and sideboard. She was dying to know if those were real presents under the tree in the dining room, under the tree in the master bedroom, under the little fir in the corner of the kitchen. And then there was the library. Frankie had stocked the library with real books.

It wasn't the sort of house one rented out between summers. It was the sort of house one lived in, loved in. And Gwen saw Frankie in every room of the house; in every piece and detail; in every painting, fabric, and rug. She thought she'd prepared herself. She was wrong.

"So." Frankie stood with her back to the fireplace, warming her hands. Gwen didn't miss the slight furrow between her brows. "You're awfully quiet. What do you think?'

Gwen left the banister and walked into the front parlor. She touched the tapestried wings of an armchair. For once the right words escaped her, refused to come easily to her tongue. Shaking her head, she abandoned the chair and stood alongside the twelve-foot Douglas fir that stood twinkling in the center of the room. Fingering a bundle of needles, she inhaled. The entire house smelled of the Christmases she'd never had.

"You don't like it." Frankie sounded very calm. "All right, then. We've still got time. Not much but some. What do you want changed?"

Gwen shook her head again. And then, glancing down between her Louboutins at the velvet tree skirt, she said the first thing that popped into her head: "Are the presents real?"

"I—What?"

"Are the presents real? The gifts beneath this tree? And the ones upstairs? The tree in the kitchen?" She was as eager as a child to know.

Frankie blinked. Nervous, Gwen realized.

"The ones under this tree are party favors. One for each guest, as per your instructions, through that hen you call an assistant. The ones under the kitchen tree are prizes for the games you wanted planned, again through your assistant, who is not only a hen but also a tightwad—"

"I pay him to be a tightwad," Gwen interrupted pleasantly, trying to hide her amusement.

"Fine, whatever." Frankie made a sound of indignation. "You saw the basement, the pool table, and the roulette and darts."

"It's all wonderful." She broke a needle from the tree and rubbed it between her fingers. "I suppose I'll have to sleep upstairs, in a real bed.

"I guess so. Is that a problem?" Frankie's blinking grew owlish.

"No. I think, at last, I've outgrown the basement." She smiled wryly at the needle in her hand.

"The fridge is stocked, of course, with enough snacks to keep you happy. The caterers will start carting in the nonperishables tomorrow. The rest will be ready by Tuesday."

"Wonderful," Gwen repeated. "What about the presents under the tree in my bedroom?"

Frankie's eyes widened, a look that said she'd been caught, but her expression remained professional. "From Chris and me. Just little things."

A pulse of warmth behind her ribs made Gwen smile. "Kind of you."

"Chris's idea."

"Of course. They're beautifully wrapped, all of them. Service?"

"No." She wet her lips. "Turns out I'm handy with a bow."

"They're lovely." Casually, Gwen crossed the new blue-and-green Oriental rug, stretching her fingers to the fire.

"Thank you."

"And the strands of pearls and the little stars in the trees."

Frankie's cheeks were pink, whether from the heat of the flames or the press of Gwen's body. Experimenting, Gwen edged closer.

"I'm glad." Frankie was staring hard at something past Gwen's left shoulder. Gwen resisted the urge to look around, see if the Ghost of Christmas Past had made a sudden appearance.

"Francis." Gwen squeezed Frankie's elbow until, finally, she gazed up at Gwen's face, lips parted in a silent question. "I love it," Gwen said. "Every bit of it. It's perfect. More perfect than I could have imagined."

"Perfect," Frankie echoed, and the corners of her mouth curled slowly upward. "I wanted it to be perfect."

"You succeeded. I'm struck almost speechless." And because Gwen wasn't one to let opportunities pass her by, she dared to steal Frankie's hand and tuck it against her forearm. "You're also very quiet. Ever since you chased me into the car at the airport, I've heard hardly a word. Everything okay?"

"I was worried." Her breath tickled Gwen's collarbone. Gwen's fingers tightened involuntarily. "I don't usually get worried. This time I was. I wanted you to like it."

"And I do. I knew you'd make something wonderful, but I had no idea . . ." Gwen trailed off, gratefully inhaling the perfume that was simply Frankie. "Francis. Stay awhile?"

"I need to be going." Was that regret Gwen heard? "I promised Chris I'd help him with his homework." She leaned briefly into Gwen's embrace before stepping back with a sigh. "He's got a huge history exam tomorrow."

Gwen grimaced in sympathy. She'd flunked her fair share of history exams as a kid and couldn't imagine revisiting that torture as an adult. "I'd hoped maybe he'd be at the airport."

Frankie reached for the floppy canvas bag Gwen had begun to associate with her work. "Jack's keeping an eye on him until I get back."

"Pierce." Jealousy reared its ugly head. She'd almost forgotten how it felt. *You need to get over it, Gwen.*

"Oh, don't make that face. You'll worship the man once you see what he's done to your back lawn. The flagstone patio is gorgeous."

"We'll see." Dismissing Pierce—for the moment—Gwen recaptured Frankie's hand. "Come upstairs before you run off. I've something I want to show you." Frankie's eyes narrowed. Gwen laughed. "Christmas presents," she clarified. "For you and for Chris. Things are about to get very busy around here, and I don't want to run out of time. Come up, just for a minute."

Frankie didn't resist when Gwen led her up the curving stairway. Each item in the master bedroom bore eloquent witness to Frankie's aesthetic: A polished mahogany desk stood against one wall, perpendicular to the windows. Behind the desk a carved chair crouched on slender legs. A simple cherry bench sat at the foot of the bed, supporting a stack of neatly folded faded quilts. Ivory candles sprouted on a wardrobe, and an evergreen bough tied with green ribbons hung on the four-poster.

Gwen had abandoned her luggage on the floor by the bed. She tugged Frankie across the room, then released her hand long enough to sort through the cases. It took several tries to find what she wanted. Without ceremony she handed Frankie the large flat box.

Frankie blinked at the box in her hands, then shook it lightly. Curiosity wrinkled her brow. "What is it?"

"Open it," Gwen suggested.

Frankie shot her a skeptical look but unfastened the thin cardboard flaps. The box fell open. Frankie's gasp was loud in the room.

Her hands trembled as she unfurled green silk, her mouth curled softly when she held the dress up against the light of the window.

"Just a little something I found in a vintage shop in Scottsdale." Gwen watched Frankie's face with rapt attention. She saw disbelief and yearning and love at first sight, and she was pleased.

"It's not the traditional Christmas gown, but I knew you could carry it off."

"Christmas gown?" She held the silk against her chest, cheeks pink. Gwen was absurdly happy. "This goes with it." She plucked a linen envelope from the box and put it in Frankie's hand. Frankie set the gown gently onto the bed and broke the seal.

"Party invitation," Gwen explained when she remained quiet. "I'd hoped—will you come as my guest?"

She stared down at the invitation as if she expected it to bite. "I don't think—"

"You and Pierce," Gwen added gruffly. "He's got his own invitation. It's a sound business decision. You've done the work; now put your face forward. Show off your skills a little."

Frankie gnawed at her lower lip. "Jack in his Carhartts and Wolverine boots?"

"I'm not buying Pierce a gown," Gwen said, deadpan.

"Fair enough." At last Frankie looked up. Her eyes were bright. "A sound business decision. You're right; it would be."

"And this is for the kid," Gwen continued in a rush because she wasn't 100 percent sure she'd gotten it right, and she really wanted to get the kid's gift right. "A Sounders jersey. But not until Christmas. He has to wait."

"Grinch." Frankie set the second box next to her gown. "He'll be over the moon. No invitation?"

"A party like this is no place for a kid. Trust me." Gwen couldn't resist. She reached out, brushed the damp from Frankie's cheek with the tips of her fingers. She hastened on: "Don't cry. You never cry, remember?"

"Not even over a skinned knee." Frankie turned her cheek against the palm of Gwen's hand. "We've missed each other; I'll give you that. And distances do funny things. But nothing's really changed, has it?"

Gwen thought of the sheaf of papers in her carryon and was surprised by a sudden curl of fear. *"She won't like it,"* Jack had advised several times. *"Trust me; she won't thank you for interfering."*

"It's Christmas." Gwen pressed a kiss against the crown of Frankie's head. "What do you say we just enjoy the holiday and not worry about anything else?"

"You're right." Frankie squared her shoulders, stepped away, retrieved her packages from the bed. "I'm stopping by Hampton Delicious tomorrow to taste test the canapés, then running by the bakery to pick up the order of gingerbread men. You're welcome to come to make sure everything is how you'd like it."

Gwen thrust her hands in the pockets of her floral Gucci duster. Her fingers found the small box tucked away in the left, touched it as if for luck. In the last few weeks, it had become her touchstone, her talisman. "Mike's flying in early. We've a bit of business we need to complete before the guests arrive. He'll be settled in by dinner. I'd like to see Chris, spend some time with you." Only a lifetime of stubborn pride kept her from begging. "Come to dinner?"

To Gwen's relief, Frankie nodded. "Sure. He's eager to see you. We'll come for a little while. School night."

She would take what she could get. "Of course. An early dinner, then. How is he?"

"Better. Busy. Richard hasn't bothered to pick up the phone, but I suppose he's told you."

"Boy's better without him." A rough declaration but as far as Gwen was concerned, the honest-to-God truth. "Better than fine, with you as his ma."

"I hope you're right." But her quick smile eased the knot of nerves in Gwen's chest. "See you tomorrow. I'll bring dessert. Think a welcome-home cherry pie fits the bill just fine."

THE MAN WHO OPENED THE DOOR TO CHRIS'S ENTHUSIASTIC KNOCK wore a bright-green bow tie, matching suspenders, and a wide smile displaying astonishingly even teeth. He was not at all what Frankie had imagined.

"Mike Windsor," he offered, pumping first Frankie's hand and then Chris's. "Delighted to finally meet you. Come on in." He took her coat and Chris's windbreaker, then hung the garments neatly in the nearby coat closet. "Gwen's waiting for you down in the game room."

"Game room? Cool." Chris dashed away down the hall.

"Ah, to be young and full of energy," Mike said. Then he turned his full attention on Frankie, executed a courtly and—to Frankie's mind—completely unnecessary little bow as he took the cherry pie from her hand. "My compliments on your achievement, Ms. Porter. Chesapeake Renovations exceeded all expectations."

She wondered if he expected her to say something polite like, *I couldn't have done it without your help*, but since that wasn't true, she said,

"Thank you." To her surprise he seemed satisfied with that and simply waved her ahead down the hall with another of his funny bows.

She caught up with Chris in the kitchen, where he was bent over, inspecting the presents beneath the small Christmas tree. "The house turned out awesome, Mom. It looks really great."

"It does, doesn't it?" She matched his pleased grin.

"Does Gwen like it?"

"Gwen loves it." The sweet southern drawl preceded its owner up the basement stairs. Gwen stuck her head into the kitchen and winked at Chris. "Gwen likes it very much."

Her son didn't exactly fly into Gwen's arms, but he did accept her quick hug without complaint.

"Come downstairs." Gwen put her arm around Chris's shoulders. "We've got billiards and Italian—spaghetti with extra meatballs. You play snooker, kid?"

"No. Some of the kids at school wanted a table for the gym, but it cost too much."

"You'll love this table. It's a doozy." With a glance over her shoulder at Frankie, Gwen ushered Chris into the basement. "Come and eat, and then I'll teach you a few moves."

Frankie followed more slowly, enjoying the moment. Lights blazed in the game room. A fire jumped behind a glass screen. She'd installed shaded fixtures over the billiard table, and the wash of light made the space glow. The table itself was a work of art: all green felt and wood so dark it was almost black. Luxe but not overdone. Frankie had known, when she had first seen the table in a showroom, that it would fit Gwen's taste to a T.

"Wow!" Chris stood in front of the table, enthralled. "It's really nice. How'd you ever get it down here?"

"Trade secret." Frankie laughed when her son made a face and, because her stomach had started growling at the mention of spaghetti, went to investigate dinner.

Italian takeout overloaded two round tables. Frankie knew the inlaid tops could be flipped over to reveal roulette wheels. She took a paper plate, chose a hot calzone, and carried her dinner to the soft leather couch dominating one side of the room. She sank into the cushions, kicked off her boots, and took a healthy bite of dinner. The cheese was almost—but not quite—hot enough to burn her tongue. Heavenly. She closed her eyes in bliss.

"Good, isn't it?" Gwen held out another plate overflowing with pasta. "Try the meatballs. Hole-in-the-wall place down on Richmond. Yelp recommendation. I haven't tasted better in a long time."

Too hungry to be bashful, Frankie accepted the second plate, tucking in. "I think I forgot lunch."

"Eat up, Francis."

She did while Gwen showed Chris how to arrange the balls on the table and how to hold the cue. The click of billiards and Chris's whoop of laughter when he made a shot might have been the best Christmas present Gwen could have given her—better even than a vintage silk gown.

"There's soda and beer behind the bar, if you're thirsty." Gwen told Frankie when they paused to take a break and load up a plate for Chris.

"I'm good," Frankie said, thinking if she added anything more to her stomach, she would burst. "I can't remember the last time I ate so much in one sitting."

"I've discovered I like feeding you." Gwen brushed the top of Frankie's head with her mouth. The shock of her touch felt dangerously like lust. Gwen turned away quickly, leaving Frankie dazed and blinking.

Eventually, Frankie stacked her plates on the floor and stretched out on the couch. She watched the clash of egos, listened to the crack of balls and the friendly insults. She counted as Chris downed four servings of pasta. He had the proverbial hollow leg. Growing boys, she thought, were a mass of conflicting miracles: nerves like drawn wire and stomachs of steel. She snorted when the burping contest began. Gwen could belch as well if not better than most of the boys they'd grown up with—a contradiction in cashmere, a lewd twinkle in her eye. Sometime after Chris took decisive victory, Frankie fell asleep. The darkness was safe and warm and smelled of the creek, of home.

"Francis."

Frankie burrowed more deeply, away from the sound of her name.

She had been having such lovely dreams. Dreams of sunshine and flight and—

"Frankie." There were fingers in her hair, stroking, teasing. Lips on the hollow of her neck, nuzzling. Frankie's flesh tightened in reaction. Still half-asleep, she stirred and sighed and pressed closer. "Francis. Open your eyes."

She might have, but she didn't want the dream to end. Murmuring, Frankie turned her head, found Gwen's mouth. Gwen inhaled sharply. Her hands stilled and then began to move again, caressing lower, stoking fire under the collar of Frankie's shirt. Frankie gasped and twisted, searching, yearning—wanting more.

The draft of Gwen's sudden retreat startled Frankie fully awake. Flushed, short of breath, she sat upright and found herself buried in a nest of blankets and haloed in firelight. The overhead lamps were off, the billiard table silent. Only the dim glow on the hearth brightened the room. Gwen stood against the billiards table, a blacker patch of life in the dark room. Frankie could just make out the gleam of her eyes.

"Where's Chris?" She brought a hand to her throat. Had Gwen kissed her?

"Upstairs. Putting away the last of dinner."

Frankie tasted only tomato sauce on her lips, not the earthy tang of desire she remembered so clearly. But Gwen's fingers had worked magic, and her nerve endings were still tingling. "What time is it?"

"Getting late." Gwen shifted in the shadows. "I hated to wake you, but—"

"Homework," Frankie said, then groaned. Mortified, she fumbled around until she found her boots. "You should have woken me earlier."

"Chris was having fun."

"I'm glad." Frankie stood up on legs that wobbled, caught her balance. "Ugh. No, don't worry. I'm a mom. We go from sleep to wide awake in thirty seconds."

"You're exhausted." Gwen didn't move, but Frankie felt her gaze track her as she groped for her tote bag and adjusted the strap across her shoulder.

"The cold will wake me right up. I just needed a little nap. The party—"

"Only six days away; I know. Are you ready?"

"Of course." Frankie lifted her chin because she was ready, more than ready, to show off what she'd accomplished, make a name for herself and her business. "I'm going to blow their minds."

"Don't I know it." Gwen's teeth flashed in the firelight.

Frankie barely resisted kissing the grin from her face. Her body was warm with arousal. She wanted more. She *wanted* to kiss Gwen until she couldn't tell where one ended and the other began. *Two halves of the same coin.*

But Gwen was already turning away and climbing the stairs, her bare feet ghost silent on the new carpet.

Chapter Eighteen

IN HER DOUBLE-WIDE, Frankie tried on the gown in front of Ma's ancient mirror. The silk was too thin for winter, but the cut was genius, and the fabric slid over her body like a second skin. It was a far cry from her usual uniform of work shirts and denim, but silk didn't make the woman in the mirror any less capable. In fact, she seemed to glow with confidence, ready for anything.

Fingering the high mandarin collar, she turned slowly in front of the glass. Delicate gold beads glittered along the hem and bodice. She thought maybe she would splurge a little on a wrap for warmth. She knew she had a pair of neutral shoes in the closet that just might work with the bold color.

Gwen was right—the dress suited Frankie. It didn't camouflage her athletic build or overpower her small stature. It wasn't flashy, but it wasn't boring, either. It was . . . elegant. Frankie knew elegance when she saw it. It was part of her job to recognize sophistication. She'd just never thought the word applied to her.

Was this how Gwen saw her? Elegant, confident, *sophisticated?*

It made Frankie feel bold to think so, and she practiced another spin in front of the mirror.

She'd heard Gwen whistling in the kitchen earlier that morning.

Whistling Christmas carols and once or twice breaking into muted song. And she'd had to wipe her eyes again, foolishly, right there in front of the florist who had come to drop off the last of the flower arrangements, because Gwen sounded carefree. And Gwen had never been carefree. Wryly humorous—often. On a good day, playful. But carefree? No.

Frankie remembered Gwen laughing loud and often, usually at herself. Yet she'd never before seen real joy on Gwen's face until she followed the singing into the kitchen and discovered Gwen serenading a row of sugar-dusted gingerbread men. She'd clammed up at once, turned sheepish. But then Gwen had fed Frankie a gingerbread cookie with such tenderness that Frankie had almost broken.

I'll always make my way back to you.

Frankie had seen the declaration written openly on Gwen's face and had had to turn her own away.

"Mom!" The bedroom door flew open. Her son stuck his head into the room. His jaw dropped. "Wow."

Frankie's tremulous smile spread to a grin. She pirouetted one more time. "You like?"

"Wow!" he said again. "You look great! Where'd you get a fancy dress like that? You look like a movie star."

Frankie wrinkled her nose at her reflection. "It was a Christmas present from Gwen. She brought something for you. It's under the tree, but you can't open it till Christmas Eve."

"Mom!"

"Not my fault Gwen's a grinch. She made me promise."

Chris slipped into the room and stood at her side. She studied their reflections and realized that he'd grown again. Soon enough her son would top her by several inches.

"Are you going to stay out all night?" he asked.

"Probably. The party runs through breakfast." She put a hand on his shoulder. "I'll stop by in between things, if I can, just to check in, okay?"

"Mom." He made a face. "I'm twelve. I can stay one night by myself. Just text."

"We'll see." She thumped his shoulder lightly. Whatever crisis Chris had suffered over his delinquent father seemed to have passed. "Gaming all night is fine but no guests. No pizza delivery. You don't open the doors to anyone. Jack and I both have keys. And if your microwave mac and cheese catches fire, you run out the door to Mrs. Witherspoon's house and *then* call 911."

"Mom! I know! I'm not a baby." He tossed his head in disgust.

Frankie poked him in the ribs. "Day after tomorrow we'll go see the Illumination fireworks. Okay?" He nodded. "It'll be fun." She hugged him about his hips, drew him close, and leaned her head against his curls, memorizing the pretty picture they made in the mirror. "Now, the question of the hour: What should I do with my hair?"

"Jeez!" He groaned.

Frankie kissed him on the nose before he could scoot away. "There'll be school Monday. You should do some homework tonight before the video game marathon."

"There won't be school. It'll snow again." He said it with certainty. "Anyway, I was going to call Roddy and see if I could get a ride to the rink."

"Homework first," she told him. And then put on her "Mom" face when he opened his mouth in a silent plea. "Give me an hour; then we'll see if we can get the Mercedes to start, and *I'll* drive you to the rink. Roddy can meet you there."

He ducked his head. "We need a new car."

"When we win the lottery." She smoothed the gown about her waist. "When we win the lottery, we'll get a new car. I'll even let you pick."

"A Spyder like Gwen's," he said. And then, quick as a flash, changed his mind. "Or maybe a convertible. Or one of those new Audi SUVs."

"Keep hoping, boyo." But he was already darting away. She stood alone with her twin in the mirror. "A movie star." She snorted a little at her son's imagination and then stripped down, quickly and efficiently, and hung the gown in her closet. Until tomorrow.

"And tomorrow," she promised herself, "I'll enjoy every splendid minute."

GWEN COULDN'T HAVE WISHED FOR BETTER WEATHER. THE STORM dumped enough snow to make the woods a winter wonderland. Luckily the Weather Channel promised the worst of it would pass just in time for her guests' arrival. Her clients would have the white Christmas Mike had promised them and would hopefully forget to miss island paradise. Assuming the Richmond airport remained up and operational, things were falling nicely into place.

As she waited in the library for Mike's daily briefing, Gwen browsed through the books Frankie had chosen for her shelves. The room smelled of leather and lemon oil. Oriental rugs, deeper in color than the ones downstairs, were arranged in a haphazard manner on the floor beneath a divan and matching armchairs. Again, Frankie had hit every right note, managed to please every sense.

Gwen slid a volume from a high shelf and read the title. *Of Mice and Men*. She remembered struggling with the book in school, but in the end, she'd loved it. Did Frankie remember?

When she heard Mike's footsteps on the carpet outside the office, she slid the book back in its place. Mike knocked once before marching into the library with a general's precision. The man wore a subdued gray shirt and black trousers. His patent-leather loafers were bright red, shiny as Rudolf's nose. Gwen used fashion as armor; Mike used it to make a statement.

"So?" Gwen said when her assistant didn't speak at once. "What's the update?"

Mike dropped into one of the armchairs, spreading papers across his lap like a fan. "Airport's open. Richmond says they can handle the weather. I don't anticipate any problems in that direction."

"Good. And the drivers? You've got all the schedules?"

"Down to the minute. I called this morning to double-check with the limo company. I also rented a tasteful sedan for yourself, should you need it." Mike crossed and uncrossed his legs, red loafers shining. Were they Jimmy Choos? If so, Gwen was paying the man too much. "As for today's little matter"—he lowered his voice as if worried the walls had ears—"it took more convincing than we expected."

"But it's done?"

"Signed, sealed, and now delivered." He held out a plain manila folder. "You've broken the news, I imagine? Will we be celebrating tonight?"

Gwen inspected her manicure: Christmas-Berry Red. Bold and festive all at once. "Not yet," she murmured.

Mike paused halfway out of his chair. "I beg your pardon?"

"I said I haven't spoken to her yet. I haven't had the opportunity." Because she had made one.

"Jesus, Gwen. Get it done and smoothed over before the guests arrive. We don't need a blowup in front of the money, and there's no guarantee Pierce will keep it quiet."

Gwen winced. "Frankie will see the good sense in the transaction. There's precedent, after all."

"Sure, she will. But just in case she blows your ass to kingdom come . . ." Mike shook his head. "I, for one, would prefer it didn't happen in front of the Pinnacle Group. "

GWEN GAVE FRANKIE THE SMALLEST OF THE GUEST ROOMS, A SNUG triangular space under a peaked roof that had windows facing the front of the house. It was comfortable and warm, and it was distant enough from the center of the house to afford her some privacy. She thought Frankie would probably need it.

FOR THE NEXT SEVEN DAYS THEIR EVERY MINUTE WAS SCHEDULED, doled out to clients and guests and the duties of a host. Gwen knew from experience how draining it could be to throw a good client party. She had every confidence Frankie could handle the emotional stress and the physical work and come out the other end smiling. But Gwen couldn't help feeling protective. The party had been her idea—a whim —and if even the smallest thing went wrong, Chesapeake Renovations would take as much flack as Pinnacle. And unlike Pinnacle, Frankie's barely blossoming company was in no position to withstand bad press. Especially as Gwen hoped to pitch it to HGTV come the new year.

Well, they would just make sure everything went smoothly, wouldn't they? Because more than anything, Gwen wanted good things for Frankie. And Christ, she hoped those good things included herself, because she couldn't imagine life without the woman she loved. Had always loved. *Would* always love.

Now Gwen just had to convince Frankie that she was in for the long haul, in for the *forevers*. And, more importantly, she had to do it without pissing Frankie off.

§⋆

FRANKIE SNATCHED A HALF HOUR SHE DIDN'T HAVE TO SWATHE Chesapeake Renovations in ribbons and greenery. She hung lights in the front window and a wreath from the door. She was balanced on a ladder—zip ties between her teeth and florist wire in her hands—when she heard Jack calling her name from the floor below.

He took the stairs up two at a time, as he always did, and then helpfully plucked the ties from her mouth. "Looks nice. Too bad we won't have time to open up until after the holiday."

Frankie twisted the wire, securing boughs to the balcony railing. "It'll make a good impression, and that's the point, isn't it? To make a good impression?"

"The guy at the tux shop would agree." He squatted to help secure the branches. Frankie laughed.

"Good man. Did you remember a cummerbund?"

"And shoes. They pinch."

"Not more than mine, I assure you."

The last decorations in place, Frankie dusted her hands on her trousers, tilted her head in thanks. "I'm sure you'll look very handsome. The ladies will fall at your size-twelve feet."

"Huh." He looked down his nose at her.

"What?"

"You seem good. Better than you have for weeks."

She ducked so he wouldn't see her face, gathering up her spool of wire. "The Cook job's all but finished, and we actually pulled it off. Even the annoying bits like food and linens and flagstone patios in subzero temps."

"That all?"

"What else?"

He took the spool from her hand. "I'm thinking the lady herself. You wilt all autumn like a neglected fern, and then as soon as Gwen jets back into town, you unfurl."

"Unfurl?" She snorted in amusement. "Nice metaphor, partner. But no one's been unfurling around here."

"Simile."

"What?"

"Simile," he repeated, and then of all things, he shuffled his size-twelve feet. "Listen, Frankie. You know you're the best part of my life, right? You and Chris both. That's not ever going to change."

"Okay." Of course she knew, or she never would have made Jack Chris's godfather.

"Partnering with you these last few years has taught me a lot. Christ, it's been everything, honestly. I was in a pretty bleak place when we met. You gave me a reason to keep busy, helped me realize I still had it in me to make beautiful things."

"Okay," Frankie said again, more slowly. She peered up into his face. "Where's this coming from? You okay? Because this is sounding suspiciously like a goodbye and, Jack, you know I've got a thing about people running out on me."

"No, not a goodbye." He squeezed her shoulders in gentle reassurance. "Just a reminder. We do good things together. I'm feeling grateful, is all. Must be the season. Christmas spirit and all that. You know how I get."

Frankie didn't, but maybe that was because she hadn't really taken the time to notice before. And *that* was a realization she didn't like.

"I've been taking you for granted." Hadn't Gwen implied as much? Handyman, partner, babysitter, best friend. Jack was all those things because Frankie expected him to be.

"Maybe." He smiled. "But until you hear me complaining, it's all good. You know I can't do without pizza nights."

She nodded, gave him a tight hug. "You know we'd never have gotten this far without you, right?"

"Now you're getting maudlin." He shifted, embarrassed. "Thank Jesus you decided to forego the kissing ball this year."

Frankie snorted into his ribs. "Only because last year all our best clients were lining up to peck your cheek. I don't think you got a lick of work done. Merry Christmas, Jack."

He brought his big hand down on her head, patted gently. "Merry Christmas, Frankie."

Chapter Nineteen

GWEN'S GUESTS arrived in trickles, then in droves. Frankie took shelter in the kitchen with the herd of caterers. She would be much too busy to make a social appearance until dinner, but she couldn't help a healthy curiosity. For the next several days, the entire house would echo with the comings and goings of people who were if not Gwen's friends, then certainly her compatriots. Frankie couldn't help wondering what the faces who matched the voices looked like and whether or not they would be properly charmed by the house.

One of the caterers, a stocky college boy with golden curls and freckles, stumbled against the kitchen counter, barely holding on to a tray of hors d'oeuvres. Frankie caught the tray as it wobbled, saving stuffed mushrooms from a premature demise.

The boy's face fell. "Oh shit. Sorry."

"No harm done. I don't think anyone noticed." Frankie gave him a sympathetic smile. "First time?"

"Yeah." Anxiously, he rubbed his chin. "It's actually my girlfriend's. The job, I mean. But she's sick, and I promised to fill in for her, and I've never even folded a napkin before." His forehead was damp with sweat. "I'm kinda nervous."

"Me too. Nerves do terrible things to my stomach." To fill the queasy hollow in her gut, she stole a warm mushroom from the tray and popped it into her mouth. "Lord, that's amazing." Ignoring the chef's distant grumbles, she closed her eyes and enjoyed the brief taste of heaven. "If all the food is as good as this, dinner might just be worth the trouble."

"Didn't you arrange our menu?"

Frankie's eyes popped open. The awkward caterer had vanished along with the tray of hors d'oeuvres. In his place stood Gwen at her smuggest, wearing an innocent grin and a tuxedo so expertly tailored it looked like she'd been born in it.

"Your tight-ass assistant and I went over the menu with a fine-tooth comb," Frankie replied, licking mushroom from her thumb. "But the food's only as good as the chef and his kitchen. So far, I'm not worried. I built the kitchen, and I've met the chef." She gave the man in question another wary stare. "He's as temperamental as they come."

"I'm told that's a good sign." Gwen bent close and lowered her voice to a whisper. "What's he doing now? Looks dangerous."

"Something to do with the pecan pies."

"Pecan pie." Gwen's face lit up.

Frankie licked her thumb again to keep back a laugh. "What's a holiday party without pie? What are you doing back here? Shouldn't you be tending your—our—guests?"

"We've had a lull. Mike's showing our latest couple to their room now."

The green heat of approval in Gwen's stare made Frankie's insides flutter. "Really." She caught herself nibbling her thumbnail. "So you've got a couple of free minutes."

"One or two." Gwen drifted across the gleaming tile. "Problem?"

"No problem." A tiny pulse beat hard in Gwen's throat. Frankie couldn't seem to look away from the flutter. "Just a question about the last of the sleigh bells."

"You're my guest, now, Francis. As of this morning, your contract's up. Leave the bells alone."

"I need to put them somewhere," Frankie protested. "They're bothering me."

"Fine. Put the damn bells wherever you like," Gwen murmured. She lifted a hand, trailed her thumb along Frankie's jaw and up, brushing her lower lip. Frankie trembled, losing her train of thought. *Jesus.* She wanted Gwen to take her right there in the kitchen, among the hors d'oeuvres and centerpieces; in front of clients, caterer, and temperamental chef. Beneath her T-shirt, her nipples pebbled in anticipation.

They stared at each other, sleigh bells forgotten. The caterers, the temperamental chief, the guests in the other room—everything else receded. Only Gwen mattered, so close Frankie knew they were sharing the same breath. And then at last she could taste her, as Gwen covered her mouth with her own, crushing, delving deep, questioning.

In answer Frankie leaned into the onslaught, opened her mouth wider as an invitation. Gwen's groan vibrated through her body.

The kiss quickly became molten. Gwen pulled until Frankie overbalanced, then caught her up against her chest. Her thumb found one of Frankie's nipples through cotton and stroked. Frankie gasped, hips stuttering against Gwen's thigh. She wanted—needed—more. She reached up behind Gwen's neck, dragged her head lower, arched in encouragement.

Gwen dragged her mouth away. "Frankie." She gasped. "Wait."

Frankie had waited long enough. To hell with being afraid. Hadn't they spent the last few months relearning each other over the phone, hours upon hours spent in conversation? This was the woman she loved. This was the woman she wanted, in her bed and in her life.

She pressed the palm of one hand against Gwen's sharp cheek. "Let's go upstairs. I want to try out that bed. Surely you can take a few minutes."

"Francis." Gwen swallowed. "Listen, I want that more than anything. But first there's something we need to discuss." She laughed weakly when Frankie made a noise in irritation, and then suddenly she stiffened.

Heart sinking, Frankie's turned to follow Gwen's stare.

"You're needed," Mike said apologetically from his place in the doorway. If he felt any embarrassment at catching the two of them sucking tongue, he didn't show it.

Gwen swore under her breath, separated from Frankie. "What is it?"

"Mr. and Mrs. Lawrence Duncan are in the foyer. Apparently, they forgot to book a hotel room in Richmond, and of course all the rooms in CW are already reserved."

"Of course," Gwen replied blandly. She turned her green stare Frankie's way. "Finish up whatever you're doing, Francis, and then come find me. It's time for you to relax and enjoy yourself, don't you think?"

Frankie could only nod. Dazed, she watched as Gwen followed Mike out of the kitchen. She brought a shaking hand to her forehead, wondering if the heat she felt in her face showed.

"Amore," said the chef from behind her. When Frankie blinked at him stupidly, he added, "Love. Best to go with it, but not in my kitchen." He waved a solid-looking spoon in her direction. "Now get out."

Frankie fled.

<hr>

THE AFTERNOON RACED BY. SHE MEANT TO DO AS GWEN SUGGESTED and find time to relax, but there was always something more to do, and time slipped away. She spun from room to room so she could keep one eye on the caterers and another on the workmen hanging the last string of rainbow icicle lights around the gazebo. She ran through the few unoccupied rooms with a rag and a can of furniture polish and then discovered that the Christmas trees needed more water. She rechecked the twine anchoring swathes of greenery to the banister, then scraped a fresh batch of snow from the porch. One of the heaters under the patio tent needed an adjustment. She found Jack and set him to the task with only a little twitch of awkwardness. Then she went back to attend the caterers.

Somewhere in between doing this and checking that and pretending that her nerves weren't jangling, Frankie developed a monster headache. When the pain became impossible to ignore any longer, she paused between watering baskets of amaryllis and reknotting the bow on the kissing ball hung in the upstairs hall, and decided she needed to sit. Halfway down the hall to her room, she passed a young woman wearing an understated velvet jumpsuit and whimsical, dangling earrings that were—Frankie took a second peek to make sure —definitely large pretzels.

"Oh, hello!" The woman said in a stage whisper. "So sorry to bother you, but can you point me toward the Toile Room? I think I'm lost."

Luckily there was only one bedroom in the house done all over in toile, an overly floral Schumacher reproduction that Frankie secretly adored.

"No, you're fine," she told the woman. "Just keep going; last door on your left."

The woman nodded, paused, gave Frankie a longer look. "I hope you don't mind," she ventured, still in a whisper, "but I know that look well. My dad gets migraines all the time. Do you have something? Sit down." She gestured at a nearby settee. "I always carry something." She indicated the roomy purse slung over her shoulder. "What with three children and the in-laws and, well, you know . . ." She trialed off, digging in her purse.

Frankie dropped gratefully onto the settee. Really, her room was only a few more steps down the hall, but she couldn't recall if she'd packed any aspirin. And bright stars were beginning to burst like fireworks on the edge of her vision.

"Ah-ha." The woman proudly displayed a pill bottle and a travel-size water. "Here we go. I think sumatriptan always works best; Dad always says so. Here you go." She handed Frankie the water and two pills, watched until Frankie swallowed the medicine down. "I'm Liz, by the way. You know, the Pretzel Queen."

Frankie didn't know, but she nodded anyway. "I like your earrings. Thank you so much. I'm Frankie."

"Frankie!" Liz clapped her hands together in theatrical excitement before sinking onto the settee at Frankie's side. "Imagine that. I've been looking for you literally everywhere. Wanted to see what new trick Gwen has up her sleeve. I'm her first, you know, and I'm always *so* excited about the next hookup."

"I bet," Frankie said weakly, trying to work out whether she'd seen Liz on Gwen's arm in any of those annoying paparazzi pictures. Come to think of it, the woman's pixie-like face did look vaguely familiar.

Had Gwen really invited an ex to their party? "You two know each other quite well, then?"

"For about six years, yes. Ever since Gwen tasted my first Soft Knot, right off my cart in the Bronx, and said the world couldn't do without. The secret's in the yeast, you know. It's my grandmother's starter." She patted Frankie's knee with a familiarity that should have made her bristle, but the pills were starting to make a dent in her headache, and the woman seemed genuinely happy to see her. "I've met Jack already," she continued. "I was expecting another Chip Gaines, but your partner is really very stoic, isn't he? No matter. I'm sure Gwen will polish him right up."

"Chip . . . Gaines?" Unobtrusively, Frankie pinched the inside of her wrist. Had she somehow fallen asleep sitting up? Was she having a stroke? What was this odd woman talking about? "Chip Gaines, the lifestyle-television star?"

"Why, more than just a television star. They're a *brand*, darling. Just like Soft Knots. Just like you'll be once Gwen's finished with you." She leaned in. "Now, you, dear—*you* I can see. Not quite as tall as Jo but just as pretty, and from what I've seen just today, loads of talent. Can you bake?"

"I . . . not really," Frankie confessed, completely befuddled. "I mean, I can do a pie in a pinch. But mostly we stick to peanut butter on toast."

"Oh dear. Well." Liz patted Frankie once more before rising. "Don't you worry. Gwen will put us in touch, and I'll share a few of my best baking secrets. No, don't get up. You just sit here until that migraine eases. You've got the entire Grand Canyon on your forehead. And I'm off to call the kids before bedtime; they get so sad if I miss. Lovely to meet you, J—I mean, Frankie."

Frankie watched the strange woman until she disappeared into the Toile Room. Then, when she was sure her head wouldn't fall off her neck, she rose and slowly made her way down the remainder of the hall to her room. It was time to call her own child, make sure he wasn't up to any mischief. Grateful for the closed curtains and dim light, she sat on the bed and dialed Chris. It connected immediately to Chris's voice mail. Frankie hung up without leaving a message, tossed the phone onto the bed. He was probably asleep in front of the television. Or in the shower, pretending to shave the bit of peach fuzz he'd recently become so proud of. She wouldn't let herself worry.

Don't hover, Francis. Give the kid some space.

Frankie stood and wandered over to the windows, twitched back a corner of the drapes. The sun was going down over the gazebo; the icicle lights were already beginning to sparkle. The modern LED rainbows, so at odds with the rest of the traditional decorations, made Frankie smile.

"'More gay in Christmas.'"

She wondered if Chip and Jo would approve.

"WOODEN PEGS, YOU SAY?" IGNORING THE RUSH OF BUSY CATERERS, the woman crouched smack in the middle of the kitchen and studied the cabinets. She'd introduced herself as Rachel Duncan when she stormed the kitchen, shaking the startled chef's hand and demanding to see "the Pierce cabinets." Frankie's lips quirked. Rachel was short and dark and definitely tenacious. Her long velvet gown bunched as she shifted from a squat to her hands and knees. Rachel didn't seem to notice.

The chef sulked over his range, shooting glares their way. The caterers ignored the woman with professional aplomb.

"Yes. It's called mortise and tenon," Frankie explained. "Jack happens to be the local expert. He puts each one together by hand." Frankie hunkered down by the woman's side. A diamond the size of a gumdrop gleamed on Rachel's hand as she tapped her fingernails on the wood. "He's in demand up and down the coast."

"Amazing. How long does it take?"

"Quite a while," Frankie admitted. "But he does all the work himself, from top to bottom—the molding and stain. And he hand-smiths all the hardware."

Beyond the kitchen, Gwen's party was in full swing. Someone had tuned in to and turned up *It's A Wonderful Life*, and Jimmy Stewart's lovable laughter seemed to rattle the walls. Dinner—all three courses—

had been met with highly favorable reviews. After-dinner drinks were now being guzzled at an astounding rate, and the caterers were trying their very best to distribute dessert. Frankie silently wished them luck. She had never seen so many people in one place in her entire life, never imagined so much energy could be contained in one spot.

Gwen's friends and clientele made up a large and diverse group with an eclectic mix of young and old, hemp and satin, diamonds and leather; they mingled together in a soup of holiday cheer. Frankie had seen one man in jeans and a floor-length leather duster. Another proudly displayed a spiraling tattoo along the curve of his jaw. A pair of identical twins in matching black dresses danced together in the foyer while a cluster of men in Armani business suits discussed knitting beneath the parlor Christmas tree.

Relaxed and happy. As far as Frankie could tell, Gwen's party was a huge success.

She knew she should be celebrating. But she felt nothing at all.

"They're gorgeous," Rachel said, regaining Frankie's attention. The woman managed to keep her dignity as she crawled about on hands and knees. "I'll have something similar, I think."

"For your kitchen? We can do that."

"For my *kitchens*." Rachel climbed carefully back to her feet. "I'm having an old home split into condos in Tucson. Four kitchens."

"Jack will be delighted, I'm sure." *Over the moon!* "Let me just see if I can find him." She poked her head into the hall, scanning the crowd. She'd seen him from a distance off and on all day but never managed to be in the same room, which must have taken some maneuvering on his part. "There he is." She steered Rachel from the room. "Let me just introduce you."

Gwen took a welcome break from mingling sometime after the Patek Philippe on her wrist registered 2:00 a.m. Weaving her way between crowds of well-wishers, she made it to the basement without spilling the beer she'd lifted from a caterer's tray. Collapsing onto the currently unoccupied sofa, she exhaled gratefully and kicked off her heels. She was used to long nights, but this one seemed in no hurry to wind down.

She recognized several of the people grouped around the billiard table as enthusiasts and wasn't surprised when the betting became quietly serious. Behind the table a game of roulette spun on to a chorus of shouting and giggling and general ruckus. Past the roulette, a blackjack dealer waited for interested players. Blackjack wasn't Gwen's game. Roulette could wait. What she wanted most was bed—bed and a moment alone with her thoughts.

But in Gwen's world, profit often depended as much on the sales-person as the product. She'd worked hard to polish her people skills. To smooth out her backwoods accent, dress like money she eventually began to earn, drive the right cars. She'd made herself over, clawed her way off the streets, become corporate Seattle's rising star. She'd made her reputation and guarded it like a cat with one kitten.

So, because she knew it was expected, she finished her beer, slipped her heels back on, and inserted herself into a game of billiards. The table was sweet, the stakes to her taste, and her companions free with both money and booze. Time rolled on. Gwen caught her second wind. Her opponents were decent players, and the caterers kept the drinks coming. She made sure to win only occasionally, and winning wasn't as easy as she'd assumed. She enjoyed the challenge, the small talk, and a casual flirtation she struck up across the table with a pretty brunette in a sequined gown: lawyer, San Diego area, specialized in environmental issues. Gwen started having fun. When she finally glanced at her watch, it was after four.

She deftly lost what little money she had on hand and excused herself. Scrounging up a bottle of mineral water from behind the bar, she loosened the collar of her tux. The room had filled up since last she'd noticed, grown stuffy. The blackjack table ran smoothly. She couldn't see the roulette wheel past a cluster of boisterous onlookers. She felt a burst of pride. It looked like the party was already a legend in the making.

Suddenly, fiercely, Gwen wanted to see Frankie. She sucked down a last gulp of water, thumped the plastic bottle back onto the bar, and shrugged her way through the crowd, searching.

She found her on the new patio, perched with a cup of tea on a folding chair in the warmth of a glowing heater, protected from a light fall of snow by the sturdy awning overhead, deep in conversation with a dapper mustached octogenarian in a plaid Christmas suit. Two younger men smoked thin cigars a few feet away. The octogenarian was Frederick Burgan. Frankie had helped him make quite a lot of money off what, at the time, had seemed a revolutionary idea: DVD vending machines in airports and train stations. The two younger men were new investors, and they were obviously out on the porch so they could surreptitiously ogle Frankie.

Grace appreciated their good taste, if not their lack of good manners.

After the warmth and noise of the house, the patio seemed muted. Gwen turned one of the white rental chairs backward and sat, content to wait. Frankie glanced her way but said nothing. Gwen realized with a pang that her silk gown afforded little protection against the winter. But Frankie didn't seem bothered. Her cheeks were flushed, her voice animated, and as Gwen watched she laughed at something her companion said. Frederick Burgan had a quick mind and a generous spirit.

As Gwen listened, he questioned Frankie closely about the work done in the master bathroom, about Chesapeake's future projects. Frankie answered in low tones. Gwen lost herself in the moment, content for once simply to exist. She admired the gleam of the early morning on undisturbed snow. In the distance she could hear the bubble of the creek, made sluggish by winter.

Frankie laughed, and Gwen caught the exchange of business cards. Good. By the end of the week she would be known coast to coast. Things were going exactly as Gwen had hoped—better, even.

When Frederick left the patio, Gwen chased the entourage of cigar-smoking young men away with a single look. The kitchen slider hissed shut behind them. Silence wrapped them like a blanket.

Gwen took in a breath of crisp air and tilted her chin at the card in Frankie's hand. "How many of those have you given out?"

"Business cards?" Frankie shrugged, tucked her feet up beneath her thighs. "Twenty or thirty. Not as many as Jack. Everyone loves Jack. He's like spilled soda pop to sugar bees: constantly surrounded."

The consternation on Frankie's face was puzzling. "That's a good thing, isn't it?"

"Sure." She sniffed, made a wry face. "You smell of alcohol, even from here. Are you drunk?"

Gwen's hackles rose, just a little. She wasn't Edward. She was allowed to indulge occasionally. "No. Buzzed, maybe. It's been a long night."

Frankie retorted, faux prim and proper, "A lady doesn't get tipsy when she's trying to impress." She shook her head. "Or so Ma always said."

"We're neither of us our parents," Gwen said firmly. "Look around; look at us both. We're doing just fine, Francis. More than fine."

"Seems that way." Frankie's expression turned guarded. "You want to tell me why people I don't know keep pulling me aside to say they're pleased to see I have both marketable talent *and* a face for television?"

"Ah," Gwen drawled carefully. "Well, the television bit isn't necessarily essential."

"Essential for what, exactly?"

Taking a moment, Gwen adjusted the cuffs of her sleeves, then peeked up through her eyelashes. Frankie's scowl was not encouraging. "I did say I thought it would be a good idea for you and Jack to show yourselves this week, show off the house and the work you've done. That there'd be opportunity to impress."

"Uh-huh. A woman wearing gigantic pretzel earrings said something about a lifestyle brand. Said she couldn't wait to see how I polished up after 'you were finished with me.'" Frankie's eyes blazed warning.

"The Pretzel Queen!" Gwen said with false cheer. "Yes, she's very enthusiastic about new projects. Overly enthusiastic, really."

"Is that what I am to you? A project? Just another money-making scheme? What the hell, Gwen. Chesapeake Renovations is *mine*, and we're doing just fine. Keep your 'Midas touch' to yourself, thank you very much."

Shit.

"It's not like that." Gwen watched Frankie warily. She didn't think she would start throwing things in front of an audience, but the Porter temper ran deep. She'd really hoped to do this in private.

"Oh, stop it," Frankie snapped. "I can see what you're thinking. I'm not a child, Gwen. As much as I'd like to make a scene, I think I'll just walk away." She rose. "Mostly because I think you prefer it when I yell; and anyway, I can't stand to look at you right now."

"Francis—" Gwen jumped to her feet, but the slider hissed open before she could speak again. A wave of noise broke from the kitchen, and a redwood in a penguin suit stepped onto the patio.

"Frankie!" Pierce held out Frankie's old phone. "It's Mrs. Wither-spoon." Brow creased, he added, "She says was getting her first cup of coffee and happened to glance out the window and see Chris leaving the house on a dirt bike with Roddy Green."

"LET ME COME WITH YOU," GWEN DEMANDED FOR THE THIRD TIME.

"No." She shook her head when Pierce grabbed his coat from the front closet. "I'm his mother. You'll both stay."

"It's almost dawn. No one will care if I disappear for an hour or two or however long it takes." Gwen reached for her own coat.

Frankie shot her a look of disbelief. "Of course they will. Stay here. I'll be back as soon as I can. He can't have gone far. I talked to him just before dinner." She stomped into the boots she'd hidden in the closet. "I thought we were over these stupid stunts."

Pierce closed her hand around a set of keys. "Take my truck," he suggested. "Even in this weather, it's a fair bit safer than the wreck you drive."

She nodded blankly and stepped into the morning. Sunrise was still slow to come, but already the day seemed several degrees warmer, soft as spring. The ice on the drive had melted to slush.

"Be careful," Gwen called, but Frankie didn't respond. Gwen drove her nails into her palms to keep from running after. Anxiety prickled her skin. She made herself inhale and exhale before turning back to the house.

There was no reason to panic. The kid was just acting out. Wanting attention. Wasn't that why teenagers made bad choices? Frankie would find him. Probably ground him for a year, but that was Chris's problem, not Gwen's.

No reason to panic. Then why did she feel like her lungs were full of water?

&.

GWEN DIDN'T HEAR FROM FRANKIE AGAIN UNTIL JUST AFTER DAWN. The house was mostly silent, the majority of her guests gone to bed. Only the faint mumble of Frank Sinatra from the game room hinted at one or two stragglers. Gwen sat alone in the master bedroom, backbone propped against one carved bedpost, phone balanced on one knee, eyes glued to the screen.

A few of her guests, she knew, would rise with the sun. And then the networking would begin all over again. It was a cycle she was familiar with—a cycle she loved. The busy light and sound, the dance of etiquette, contracts signed, deals closed, terms broken and mended. She had several nice deals on the table even over the Christmas holiday. If all went as planned, they would close before the end of the week.

But she couldn't concentrate on work, not with Chris missing. Her mind kept spinning out worst-case scenarios. Had the kid even thought to wear a helmet? Motorcycle deaths made up roughly 20 percent of traffic accidents. Gwen knew because she'd googled it.

Was this what it was like to be a parent? How the hell did Frankie do it? Gwen had sat in on multimillion-dollar buyouts that were less anxiety inducing than this.

She supposed she should try to get some sleep. Or order up breakfast. Instead, she blindly willed the phone to ring. When it finally did, she answered with her heart in her throat.

"Kid okay?"

"He's not here, Gwen. He's not anywhere in the house or on the property." She sounded choked and out of breath. Gwen popped off the bed, unable to sit still.

"What does the neighbor say?"

"Only that they took off together early in the morning. On Roddy's Yamaha." Frankie paused. "I found a letter on his bed, under his pillow. From Richard's secretary." Her voice turned to steel. "The bastard had his secretary write because he doesn't have the time to deal with us himself. Too busy, can't spare the effort right now to come for a visit."

Gwen paced in a circle around the room, silently cursing Tilletson. Obviously, the man was too stupid to recognize the gift he'd been given. Too stupid, as far as Gwen was concerned, to walk the earth. "What a bastard. No wonder Chris did a runner. He just needs some time to cool off, Frankie." She hoped she sounded more convincing than she felt.

She sighed. "You're right. I know you're right. It's just . . . I'm going to call a few numbers. See if he's bunked at a friend's house, if anyone's seen them. Damn Roddy. I'm half-afraid to leave the house in case Chris comes home."

"Then don't. I'll drive the back roads, see what I can see. I want to," she interrupted when Frankie protested. "Please. Let me help."

Frankie relented. "Thank you. If you find him, don't scare him to death. That's my job. Just bring him home to me." She disconnected before Gwen could make any promises.

The kid couldn't have gone far, Gwen told herself. Chris was angry, not stupid. Gwen remembered what it felt like to be full of rage and betrayal. The boy would run until the pain eased, and then he'd hole up somewhere safe.

Gwen started stripping off her tux, dug in her closet for clothes more suitable for search and rescue. Halfway dressed, she paused, frowning. Jeans in hand, she wandered back to the window, where the sun was coming up over the woods.

"Somewhere safe," she murmured, narrowing her eyes at the gray spread of trees sheltering the creek.

Chapter Twenty

CHRIS HATED the smell of stale cigarettes. Especially stale, damp cigarettes. Like moldy leather or campfire ashes, it made him want to sneeze and cough at the same time. And after several hours spent cramped in a small space with Roddy, the stink was stuck in his clothes. Chris made a face, flapping the hem of the flannel shirt he wore beneath his jacket, trying to air the fabric out.

There was no way he was going to get that smell past his mom. He wished Roddy had brought his e-cig, but they'd both thought it would be cooler to go old school. It wasn't. The stale smoke made his eyes hurt. Or maybe it was just the sleepless few hours spent out in the cold that made the backs of his eyeballs feel sore and itchy. He couldn't sleep.

Unlike Chris, Roddy was out like a light and snoring. Sometime after his third cigarette and fourth beer, he'd fallen asleep on his back under their borrowed tarp. And he snored like a chainsaw—so loud Chris was afraid someone would hear.

Chris rolled onto his back. He couldn't get comfortable. The wooden floor bruised his ribs, and his legs had gone stiff. And he was pretty sure the sun would be all the way up soon. If he didn't wake Roddy, eventually someone would notice they'd gone missing. They'd promised each other they wouldn't leave their post until sunrise, just in case something extra cool happened.

Chris was pretty sure something extra cool wouldn't happen in the next thirty minutes.

Most of Gwen's guests had disappeared into the house, and the party, which had still been rocking when he and Roddy had snuck into the gazebo before dawn, had finally quieted down. But he didn't want to break their pact, so he let Roddy snore and occupied himself with thoughts of breakfast. He would make oatmeal and French toast because he was good at that. And hot chocolate, as close to boiling as he could get it because he was freezing. Even the canvas tarp he'd filched from his mom's car hadn't helped much.

Smoking old cigarettes had, for a while. After his second, though, he'd begun to feel sick and decided he never wanted to smoke another. He hadn't felt a buzz or anything—just a pain in his gut that he figured might be more guilt than tar. He hadn't even tried the beer. Old Edward's addiction was still too clear in his mind for that.

A nailhead dug into Chris's elbow through his coat. He shifted a little to the right, bending his knees to avoid clipping Roddy in the balls. Overhead, gray had finally spread to pink. And he couldn't hear even a whisper from the house.

It had been his idea to spy on the party, make a peepshow of Gwen's clients. He'd hoped some of the gods of the computer industry would put in an appearance, because he figured Seattle was full of them. He and Roddy had spent the first third of their adventure pressed against the side of the house, up to their knees in snowdrifts, peering into the glitz and glamour through the parlor window. Only it hadn't been all that glamorous. Chris had seen a few faces he thought he recognized from his computer magazines, and Roddy had sworn he'd seen Dave Matthews, but they hadn't been able to hear anything exciting over the blare of the Christmas music.

They'd talked of getting into the house and stealing some of the awesome-looking food, but even Roddy couldn't figure out how to do that without getting noticed. Because Chris's mom was everywhere, and Gwen was everywhere else, and where they weren't, Jack was. So they'd retreated along the edge of the yard and bundled up on the floor of the gazebo to listen to muted laughter and music and watch the cool rainbow lights.

And smoke cigarettes. His mom would kill him if she found out. He hadn't cared much the night before. He'd been too filled with piss and venom after reading his dad's letter. He'd been really angry, ready to kick a hole in the wall or do some damage with his fists. And once he'd stopped swearing and punching his pillow, he'd wanted to cry.

He'd gone looking for distraction instead, and Roddy always provided distraction. It hadn't taken any effort at all to get his friend to agree to an adventure. And it had been totally awesome to race that old dirt bike on the back roads and through the woods, wind howling in their ears. Another reason for his mom to kill him. She hated motorcycles—said they were death on two wheels.

Roddy mumbled in his sleep. Chris's feet were numb. The wind was coming back, rattling the trees, but it was an easier breeze, warmer than the bitter cold of night. It was time to go home. If they waited much longer, his mom or Jack would get there first; and when they noticed the house was empty, the shit would hit the fan.

He sat up, intending to kick his friend awake, then squeaked in terror when a hand reached around the white latticework and grabbed his jacket.

"Come on out." Gwen leaned into the gazebo. The hazy beam of her phone flashlight lanced through the early morning, illuminating Roddy's sleeping face. "Both of you."

Chris thought he would die from the shock of it. He still couldn't quite catch his breath, and when Gwen traced the flashlight over empty beer cans and a small pyramid of cigarette butts, his heart jumped into his throat.

"We'll clean it up," he said quickly. He scraped as much of the mess as possible onto the tarp. "All of it."

Gwen's face was a shadow behind the light. She sounded grim. "I don't doubt it. How long have you been in here?"

"A little while." No way was he going to admit to playing Peeping Tom through the parlor window. "Not the whole time. We went down to the creek some, to test the *Wolverine* out."

"I thought she was the *Tilletson*."

"I changed her name," Chris muttered, struggling to regain some of his composure. "I can do that, can't I? I mean, we haven't painted it on her yet or anything."

"You can call her whatever you want. But you sure as shit shouldn't be out by yourselves on the creek in winter, especially in the middle of the night." She played the flashlight around the gazebo. "You unplug the lights?"

"Yeah." The LEDs had begun to give him a headache soon after Roddy started snoring. "They're not broken or anything—just unplugged." Chris nudged Roddy again, harder. "Hey, wake up, will you?"

Roddy mumbled and rolled onto his stomach.

"Your buddy's playing possum," Gwen said. She reached down and grabbed Roddy by the collar of his windbreaker. Roddy let out a shriek and sat upright, fists clenched, scattering beer cans with his Doc Martens.

"It's okay," Chris assured him quickly before his friend could freak. "It's just Gwen."

Gwen's shadow stretched over Roddy's knees. She wore a dark knitted hat over her hair and a long black trench coat over jeans and a sweater. All done up like Neo from *The Matrix* or something. "Funny, you don't look sixteen."

"He's twelve," Chris said when Roddy didn't answer. "But his dad lets him dirt bike on the back roads." Truth was, Roddy's had no idea, but if he did, Chris knew he wouldn't give a shit.

"I suppose it's a better solution than hitching," Gwen said, resigned. "Where did you park the bike?"

"Up Creek Lane." Chris wished Roddy would stand up and behave instead of blinking like a dumb owl. "Right off the asphalt, where nobody would hit it. We wore helmets and everything. And Roddy's a good driver."

"Is that so? He's not driving back this morning." Gwen hoisted Roddy upright. She was stronger than she looked because Roddy definitely wasn't putting his legs into it. "Your friend's drunker than a skunk. No, leave it," she added when Chris began to gather up the tarps. "You can clean up later this afternoon."

Chris winced when an empty beer can rolled out from between the canvas folds. "I can walk him home," he said, hopeful. "It's not that far."

"I don't think so," Gwen said in a tone that could have frozen hell. Grunting, she lifted Roddy into her arms. "Come on. Time to face the music."

They had to stop once to let Roddy puke into a boxwood tree and then once again when he tried to kick Gwen in the stomach. By the time they reached the house, Chris was miserable and embarrassed. The last thing he wanted was for Gwen to think him a no-good boozer, and a sneak to boot. Even worse, Jack was waiting for them on the back patio. He didn't say a word, but the look on his face made Chris hunch his shoulders.

They crossed the porch in a group. The house was sleeping; most of the lights were dimmed. Two men were passed out in front of the parlor television, and the oldest woman Chris had ever seen was dozing in a needlepoint chair pulled up against the banister. He remembered the chair, remembered how happy his mom had been when she'd found it at an estate sale. He hoped the old lady didn't drool on the needlepoint.

"Upstairs," Gwen told him. He started upstairs, trying not to drag his feet. Gwen followed after, still lugging Roddy. Following behind, Jack was already on the phone to Chris's mother. Chris tried not to listen to what was being said, because he figured it probably wasn't anything good.

Chris focused on Roddy's dangling feet so he wouldn't have to think about the trouble he was in. The Doc Martens his friend wore were scuffed and worn about the soles. Chris knew the boots were a gift from Roddy's granddad, but Roddy liked to tell everyone he'd stolen them from Macy's. Roddy wasn't quite as rough and tough as he wanted everyone to think. But Chris, being a good friend, kept his secret.

The long hallway came to an end. Gwen stopped.

"In here," she said. Jack reached past Chris and turned the knob. Chris fumbled until he found the light switch. The room was small, with one bed and a rocking chair. A fire burned low in the grate, and his mom's work clothes were hanging in the open closet.

Gwen dumped Roddy onto the bed and left the room without a word.

Jack said, "There's a bathroom down the hall, if he needs it. Better not let him sick up on your mother's rugs."

Chris winced. "Where are you going?"

"To sit and wait," Jack replied coolly. "You'd better do the same. I imagine you'll spend the rest of the year explaining this one away."

Chris peeked at Jack's face and wished he hadn't. Even so, he was his mother's son and had her pride. "I had some things I needed to take care of," he explained, chin high.

Jack bent over until he could look Chris in the face. "I suppose you did," he said. "And I'm not saying I don't understand. But you could have chosen a better time to piss into the wind."

Chris stared at the floor. "Do you think Gwen's very mad?"

"Gwen?" Jack snorted. "Can't say. But I'll tell you, Christopher, I wouldn't want to be in your shoes tonight. Or tomorrow, for that matter."

∮♠

FRANKIE SAT IN THE DELICATE ROCKING CHAIR, MORNING LIGHT streaming through the window at her back, and watched the two boys sleep.

Roddy Green slept in the fetal position, arms wrapped around his knees. He snored like a chainsaw. Chris was sprawled on his stomach in a straight line, hands above his head. She could still see the tracks of dried tears on his cheeks.

He'd been defiant and then apologetic. He'd tried excuses and explanations and promises. And then, when she'd refused to soften, he resorted to crocodile tears. But what had started out as carefully crafted drama had quickly turned to real heartache. He'd crawled into her lap and wept against her shoulder, the first real tears she'd seen him shed in a long time. Angry as she was, Frankie had been glad to see the dam burst. Her son had sobbed out all the loneliness and frustration and fear of a boy abandoned by his daddy, and then he wiped his nose and cussed until he was red in the face. And she'd let him, just this once, because she thought maybe the occasion called for a bit of healthy Porter anger.

"He's a no-good son of a bitch," Chris had muttered, staring hard at the dying embers in the fireplace grate. "He wouldn't even give me a chance."

She'd stroked the damp hair from his brow. "His loss, kiddo. I'm sorry."

"He didn't even write the stupid letter himself." Chris's mouth set in a stubborn line as he brushed the lingering tears from his lashes. "It was his secretary—his *fucking* secretary!"

The emphasis made Frankie want to laugh and cry at the same time. "I think you've used up your dirty word allowance for the year, champ."

To her relief he'd smiled slightly before he rested his head back down against her shoulder. "I'm sorry I ran off," he muttered a few minutes later. "I didn't think you'd find out. Can't believe Mrs. Witherspoon was spying."

"Moms always find out." She hoped he would believe that white lie for a few more years.

"Yeah." He'd heaved a sigh that sounded suspiciously like relief. "Jack's pretty mad. Think I've earned a whupping?"

"Maybe." Frankie bit her lip to keep the amusement back. They both knew Jack couldn't hurt a fly.

"You wouldn't let him, would you?"

"After this stunt? I just might."

"He wouldn't really." His smile had died. "Not sure about Roddy's dad, though. Maybe we don't have to tell him?"

"No," she'd agreed soberly, remembering the lengths she'd gone to in order to protect Gwen from Edward's fists. Her anger at Roddy softened a notch. "No, we don't have to say anything. This time."

Now, as Roddy grunted in his sleep, Frankie decided she would have to take him aside at some point in the future and ask some gentle questions. If the boy was truly living in an abusive household, she didn't intend to look the other way. Gwen hadn't had any real options, but times had changed and thank God for that.

Chris stirred and almost rolled off the shared mattress. Frankie waited until he settled back to sleep and then climbed to her feet, stretching her cramped muscles. She hadn't had time to change out of her party clothes, and now she felt awkward in the flimsy green silk—the glamour of the night fading with the sunrise. She chose practical cords and a soft flannel the color of Christmas instead.

The house was quiet when Frankie slipped from the bedroom and into the hall. Some of the guests would be waking soon. Glancing out a window, she was relieved to see the caterers' van parked in the drive below. If all went as planned, breakfast would be steaming on the sideboard before the first of Gwen's clients stirred. She hesitated for a moment at the top of the stairs when she heard the murmur of voices from below. She didn't want to interrupt any important business. But then she recognized Jack's growl and Gwen's lighter sarcasm.

Tiptoeing as she descended so as to not wake any light sleepers, Frankie felt a moment of pride at a job well done. The floorboards didn't betray her with a single squeak. Two silent caterers were cleaning up evidence of the night's frivolity. Two more were busy laying out fresh linens in preparation for breakfast. A young man dusted down the kitchen countertops, and another swept up the snowfall of cocktail napkins littering the floor. Frankie lifted a hand to the caterers in thanks, then followed the echo of voices down the front hall to the parlor.

The door was shut, but they either weren't trying or had forgotten how to be quiet; she could hear the argument from beyond clear as day.

"I work at my own whim, and I'm not interested in living by a schedule," Jackson said in the gravelly voice Frankie knew meant trouble. "You can't rush art."

"I'm not asking you to schedule your life any more than you already have. From the looks of things, your usual clientele is more than willing to wait on your work. But things have changed. Some clients—Rachel Duncan, for instance—*just might* be willing to pay a premium to move to the top of the waiting list." That was Gwen, sounding clipped and irritable.

"Because they know they're waiting on a one-of-a-kind piece. Look, even I know there's a difference between a lifestyle brand and a *franchise*."

Frankie set her hand on the door and pushed. Neither of the two looked up when she stuck her head around the door—probably because they were too busy staring each other down under the Christmas tree.

"Not a franchise. Just a slight uptick in production. People need to know you're out there. Stickley didn't become a household name because the man hid behind his pride."

Jack turned on his heel, took three long strides across the parlor floor, and then returned to the Christmas tree, only to scowl at the decorations. "Stickley's an unusual case. And no one was threatening to put his artistic process on television."

"Media has changed just a little bit in the last century," Gwen retorted. "The trick is to walk the line, and that is my particular specialty. I'll make sure your rarefied skills are a coveted commodity."

Jack opened his mouth, but Frankie beat him to it: "Damn right, he's coveted. By me. And I'll thank you to stop trying to dip your fingers into every one of my pies, Gwen."

Jack's mouth twitched. Gwen turned from the tree, both brows raised.

Frankie rushed on, "Listen, whatever it is you're up to, we're not doing it: The television thing. The brand thing. Chesapeake is our thing—mine and Jack's. And you can't have him. So just let him be." She hugged herself around the middle. Chris's little adventure had been enough to distract her from Gwen's interference. Now the ache of betrayal came rushing back.

Gwen's brows rose impossibly higher, almost disappearing under her neat fringe. "'Let him be'? You're jumping to conclusions again, Francis. Pierce is already on board, one way or another."

Frankie might have called her a liar if not for the expression on Jack's face: embarrassed, guilty, and maybe a little smug. And that smugness felt like another betrayal, as painful as a slap.

"I got a lot of interest in my cabinets, that's all," Jack told her quietly. "Quite a lot. And I got to thinking maybe I could stop some of the handyman shtick and concentrate on woodworking. You know, become a real craftsman. Gwen's got some excellent ideas. She knows how to get small businesses noticed." He stopped when he saw Frankie's expression.

Worse than a slap. They'd gone behind her back and were planning a future without her input. Her first love and her best friend, leaving her behind with no say in the matter. Again.

"We were supposed to be partners," she blurted at Jack. "Build the business together, you and I. I trusted you to have my back. We're doing just fine without as we are. And you"—she wheeled on Gwen, fists balled at her side—"you and I, we're done. Just stay out of my way from now on, you hear?

"I'm finished with the both of you."

Chapter Twenty-One

FRANKIE MARCHED PAST BAFFLED CATERERS, out the kitchen door, and down the porch steps to the creek. The sky was clear and bright, the air warming. Melting snow seeped through her thin shoes. In some places a few solitary drifts lingered, higher than her ankles, clean and white until she marked them with her footprints. She passed the gazebo, where tiny icicle lights twinkled again. Just ahead she could see the edge of the woods. The trees grew up bare and skeletal, black against the cloudless horizon.

Another time she might have been impressed and deliciously frightened by the spooky picture they presented. But for the moment she only wanted to hide, to escape. To scream and shout and punch something. And maybe, to shed a few tears undisturbed.

She slid to a halt beyond the edge of the woods. Just down the slope, the creek gurgled sluggishly. Ice melted on the branches above her head and fell like rain onto the ground below. Beneath the trees the ground was free of snow. Muck and leaves and mud swirled in patterns around pale trunks, sculpted by wind and rain. Sunlight trickled through branches, sparkling on the damp leaves.

The woods were beautiful and except for the patter of dripping ice and the bubble of the creek, very quiet. Safe. Frankie walked farther under their canopy. Her sneakers were unsuitable for tromping over winter ground. She slid twice, cursing. Her heart throbbed in an angry beat.

The boathouse loomed up at the bottom of the slope. In the wash of the morning, the creek appeared molten as it wound past dormant ferns and exposed gray logs. A second shadow crouched just to the left of the boathouse. It took Frankie's eyes a moment to adjust before she realized it was Gwen's skiff, wedged between two trees, propped up in a V-shaped cradle made of two-by-fours and cinder blocks. Someone had covered the little boat with a blue canvas tarp.

Frankie touched the canvas. The fabric was rough and smelled of teak oil. Tears leaked from the corners of her eyes. She brushed them away with an irritated grimace. From up the slope, she heard the murmur of distant voices and the bang of a door—more voices and laughter and then a muddled version of "Jingle Bells." The morning seemed to be steaming along just fine without her. The distant door banged again, and the off-key singing seemed suddenly louder, moving close.

Fingers trembling, Frankie shucked off her shoes, abandoning them to the mud. She knew from long experience the boathouse was easier to climb in bare feet.

The bricks were cold and slick, but Frankie found the old cracks without trouble. She scaled the building easily. The hem of her shirt caught on the corner of a splintered shingle and almost tore. She jerked it free.

Up on the roof a smattering of snow had collected and then melted into gray slush. The soles of Frankie's feet stung as she crossed the shingles. Up so high—almost above the trees—the air seemed much colder, and she shivered. If she turned and looked back up the slope, she would see the lights of the house, warm and welcoming, and Gwen's rainbow lights on the gazebo.

Her nose was running. Snuffling, Frankie rubbed it with her forearm. She snuffled again and then walked until she stood on the lip of the roof that hung over the creek. The waters, always deep near the boathouse, were high with rain and melting snow. The waves lapped along the face of the bricks and swallowed several inches of the bank.

Leaves swirled on the current, black against the water. Despite the slush she sat down on the edge, legs dangling over thin air, and watched the water as it swirled below her feet.

She reached for the Porter temper, wanting the comfort of rage, but she couldn't find the spark. Instead, she felt numb, cold as the creek below.

Jack came after her first, stood in the mud on the edge of the water and rocked back on his heels as if to see her better. Frankie felt a burst of childish satisfaction. He wouldn't dare risk his bulk up on the old roof. Too dangerous by far, and Jack was always cautious. It was one of the reasons they worked so well together.

Had worked so well together.

She kept her eyes pinned on the water below.

"You should know," he began after several long, cold minutes, and she knew him well enough to hear how carefully he picked his words, "that when Gwen came to me with her plans for Chesapeake Reno, it was about Chris, not her wallet." He kicked lightly at the side of the boathouse. "Well, about you, too, I guess. But I don't think she would have considered interfering except for Chris. We knew you'd be pissed. We should have said something sooner, but . . ." He trailed off into silence.

"If you knew I'd be pissed, you shouldn't have gone whispering behind my back," Frankie told him coldly. "Gwen. Well, Gwen's Gwen, and she thinks she's all that, and maybe she can't help interfering. But I trusted you, Jack. If you're unhappy working for me, you should have said something."

"Jesus, I'm not unhappy, Frankie. Didn't I say so? You and Chris and Chesapeake are the best thing that ever happened to me. I'm just saying Gwen's not wrong when she says we're a rare commodity and"— he prodded the bricks again with his boot—"maybe I think the opportunity's a good one, for all of us. And, hell, maybe I also wouldn't mind being a real artist and not just a handyman."

"And you think Gwen can do that?" Frankie retorted. "Make you an artist?"

"No, Frankie. I already am an artist. I'm just ready for the rest of the world to realize it. And unlike some people, I'm not averse to accepting a leg up."

She didn't think the ice in her veins could run any colder. "A hand-out, you mean."

His sigh was loud enough to carry over the breeze. "I'm sorry for you, Frankie, if you're going to let old wounds get in the way of a good thing. Especially if you can't look past your pride and see this is Gwen's way of giving back." He turned his back on Frankie and retreated up the creek bank, disappearing in the direction of the house.

Gwen came soon after, making more noise than a moose in the underbrush, cursing loudly at the mud and tree roots. The commotion was probably meant to give Frankie warning, because they both had learned as children how to walk silently under the trees when they wanted to go unnoticed, which was most of the time.

"Fuck, it's a witch's tit out here," Gwen said when she reached the boathouse. "Jesus. I just finished lecturing your son on the very same thing. At least he had the good sense to wear a coat." Gwen wore a shiny silver puffer coat over jeans and a turtleneck sweater, carried her long black trench coat over one arm.

"I told you," Frankie said between teeth that had started chattering at least fifteen minutes earlier. "We're done."

"Of course it's the boathouse. It's always *up* when you're trying to escape, isn't it, Francis?" She kicked off one black rubber rain boot, then the second. "You ever stop to wonder about that? Because I know I have." She peeled off her socks.

"What are you doing?"

"You are my future," Gwen said grimly. She slung the trench coat over her shoulder and began to climb. "My heart and my home. You always have been, and you always will be. I need you to know that. Fuck!" she added with feeling when mortar crumbled under her fingers.

"Gwen!" On her knees on the shingles, Frankie peered over the edge. Gwen stared back up at her, eyes wide and frightened, mouth a flat line. Terrified.

"You're okay," Frankie told Gwen firmly, because even though Gwen was really the last person she wanted to see, she couldn't let her oldest friend suffer. "It's really not that high. Not even fifteen feet. The bricks will hold; I promise. That's right." She smiled her most reassuring smile when Gwen began to inch upward again. Despite what she'd said, a fall from fifteen feet was nothing to laugh at. Something she'd never worried about when scaling the bricks, but now that Gwen was making the climb, fear trickled through her veins, chasing away numbness and turning her mouth dry.

"You're fine. Doing great." She promised when Gwen stopped again. "Almost there." And too far to make it easily down again. How the hell were they going to get Gwen down? Once she was safely on the shingles, there was no way Frankie was going to let her go over the edge again. "Stupid, stupid," but she said it fondly. "You know you can't do heights."

"Opposite sides of the same coin." Gwen panted. Her jaw worked, and then she seemed to find a burst of strength, because she was up and over the edge of the roof in a frantic heave, scrambling on the shingles, shaking like a leaf.

They sat for a moment without speaking while Gwen, still shaking, calmed her breathing—high up above the creek, caught between the earth and the tops of the trees.

"Squirrel's eye view," Gwen said at last. "Can't say it's my thing."

"Then why?" There was the anger she'd excepted, rising in a flush up her throat, warming her cheeks, making her shiver.

Gwen edged closer, wrapped the trench coat she was carrying around Frankie with trembling hands. The leather was surprisingly heavy—a warm, comforting weight that smelled faintly of citrus and cinnamon.

"Pierce said you were out here without a coat. So I brought you one. Because, like I said, cold as a witch's tit. Also," she added before Frankie could reply, "I needed to tell you and know that you were listening. What I said. Even if you really are done with me." She glanced up at the skeletal branches above their heads, then over at Frankie. Then she released a long sigh, and the tension went out of her body. Her shoulders relaxed, the shaking stopped, and she met Frankie's glare with a small nod.

"You kept me alive when we were kids. Maybe you think you know that, but you have no idea. What it was like to grow up in that house. Always afraid. Always ashamed. Waiting for the next angry word, the next blow. Cowering in the basement like some sort of frightened animal, living in the dark. The only time I saw a glimmer of hope was in your smile, Francis. I lived for your smile." She dipped her head, examined her hands. "Definitely not healthy, that reliance, but, hell. I'm still here, so who am I to judge? Plenty of times I thought I wouldn't make it, but then there you were, tiny but mighty." Her smile was wistful. "Ready to take on the next bully, the next god-awful baking project. Whatever the challenge, you never backed down. So neither did I."

When Frankie still didn't answer—because the boulder-size lump in her throat made it all but impossible to speak—Gwen nodded as if to herself before continuing, "And, yeah, I ran out on you. And I wish I'd done it differently. Because I realize now how much it hurt you, and I see it wasn't fair." She scrubbed a hand over her face and through her hair, mussing her raven-wing strands. "And, hell, I don't regret running, because that also probably saved my life. But you should know I always meant to come back." She gestured at the trench around Frankie's shoulders. "There, in the left lower pocket, if you wouldn't mind? Just a little present."

"More presents aren't going to make me less pissed off, Gwen." And because she wasn't a complete jerk, she added in a low voice, "I understand now why you ran. And I guess it took a lot of strength. I don't blame you, haven't for months. And even though you're an interfering clothes snob with an ego the size of a sports car, I'm glad you're alive." With more heat, she added, "But I don't need a fairy godmother in my life, Gwen, granting wishes I haven't made. I just need someone I can depend on. I was actually starting to think you were that." *You're an idiot, Porter*.

"I am that. I can be that. Look in the pocket, Francis. Please."

It was the "please," so rare out of Gwen's mouth, that did it every time. So she dipped her fingers in the left side pocket, drew out the small box wrapped in faded daisy-print paper and tied with a pretty yellow ribbon, and felt her heart stop.

"I kept it. One of the few things I took with me when I ran. I told myself I just needed time to heal up, that I'd be back in a few weeks, then a few months, then . . . Well, truth is, maybe I just couldn't come back while the old bastard was still alive. I'm not as strong as you think."

"All this time." Frankie turned the box over and over, unable to look away. "My birthday present."

"Go ahead." Gwen snorted, breath fogging in the cold, then bumped Frankie's shoulder with her own. "Might as well open it." She sobered. "Whatever happens next, I want you to have them."

The ribbon came away easily between Frankie's fingers. The wrapping paper was more difficult. The old Scotch tape was surprisingly stubborn. Frankie used a thumbnail to split the seal, then carefully unfolded the paper to reveal a worn velvet-covered box.

"Don't get too excited; they're not Mikimoto or anything like," Gwen hedged as Frankie gaped at the little jewelry box. "But they're real. One of the few things my mother left behind. I hid them away the day of her funeral before Edward could get it in his head to pawn them. Thought I'd wear them one day; then I decided I wanted you to have them instead. You'll see why. I still want you to have them." She bumped Frankie's shoulder once more. "Come on, don't be shy. Open it."

Breath held, Frankie opened the box.

Pearl studs, gleaming on black velvet like two moons in a starless sky. Speechless, Frankie brushed one with the tip of her finger. Pearls, she knew, were not as smooth to the touch as one might think. Their surface was gritty, layered, naturally produced. Exquisite.

Gwen said roughly, "To go with your ma's strand. They could almost be a matching set."

"But Gwen!" Frankie wiped tears from her lashes with the sleeve of Gwen's coat. "They were *your* mother's. They're yours . . ."

"To give to the girl I loved. The woman I love. My heart and my home, my always. If you can forgive me for being an interfering couture aficionado who is planning to turn her ego-size sports car in for a nice reliable truck at the soonest opportunity."

You're such a goddammed softie, Porter. It didn't matter. Frankie did what felt right and threw herself into Gwen's arms. "I love you, too, you idiot."

&

"They look good on you," Gwen proclaimed a minute or an hour later as they sat huddled together at the top of the world, the trench and the puffer coat wrapped around both of them for warmth. Her fingers had been light as butterflies affixing the pearls to Frankie's lobes. "And you'll think of me every time you look in the mirror."

"There's your ego talking."

"You love me in spite of my ego." Gwen looked supremely pleased with herself. "Which means eventually you'll forgive my sticking my fingers in your business. You're right about the fairy godmother thing. The Midas touch. It's just what I do. Helping people. Because it makes me happy." She bent forward, brushed a kiss across the tip of Frankie's cold nose. "And it's the only way I know. We can fight as much as you like over Chesapeake's future—"

"I'm not going on television."

"How about YouTube?" When Frankie sputtered, the corners of Gwen's mouth curled upward. "Negotiable, I see. We'll work on it. You and Chris are one thing, and I'll step off if you decide that's what you want; but Pierce is another. The man's an artist, Francis, and he's eager to make something of it. Don't rain on his parade."

"It feels like—"

"He's doing a runner, I know. And God help us when Chris goes off to college. But you have to understand Jack's not going anywhere. And neither am I. In fact, having a nice little project here in Williamsburg is just the excuse I need to start shifting Pinnacle's headquarters east."

Frankie sat up so abruptly she just missed crunching Gwen's chin with the top of her head "Really?"

"And for true. These last few months were hard. I don't want to be away from you and Chris, Frankie. I want to be more of what you need . . . *dependable*. I can do that. Mike's due for a promotion anyway. It will take some time, and I'll still have to do my fair share of traveling, but the truth is, I can work from anywhere." Gwen huddled under the coats, turning plaintive. "Except up in the bloody sky. Honestly, this is my idea of hell. Can we please get down now?"

"I suppose everyone's looking for you by now," Frankie said. She hated for the moment to end, this small slice of time alone with the woman she loved. *The woman who loved her*. But if Chris wasn't already awake, he would be soon. "But, Gwen, are you really okay to climb down?"

"Of course not," Gwen answered, brows raised in wry disbelief. She dug into her puffer, pulled out her phone. "Which is why I'm calling Mike for help. Stop laughing. Goddammit, Francis, *stop laughing*."

Chapter Twenty-Two

SNOW STARTED FALLING late in the day and continued until long after dark. In Gwen's house the lights still burned, her guests settled in for a quiet evening. Tomorrow there would be walking trips through Colonial Williamsburg, a bus tour to historic Jamestown, or cross-country skiing at one of the local resorts. For the moment Gwen's guests were more than content to rest their lingering hangovers in the parlor or over a quiet hand of poker in the game room. Bing Crosby played on in the kitchen, a backdrop to muted conversation; the caterers were busy laying out a light supper of cold cuts and soup; and the Seattle Mariners' latest young superstar stood in front of Frankie's fancy stove, pinching spices into what was surely an Alfredo sauce made from scratch.

"I'll admit the party's worth the price of the tux," Pierce said from behind Gwen. "You've got an interesting assortment of friends."

"I do." Gwen showed him her teeth. Pierce wore a snow-covered parka and cap. "You've been out?"

"Home, checking on the dogs. Roads are rough but not impassable. Decided to come back and see if Chris is interested in an overnight in the Airstream."

"Frankie's napping." Gwen couldn't quite help the surge of possessive joy. She'd been wakened by the dip in the light or a distant sound and had spent uncounted minutes watching Frankie sleep. She'd thought about waking her up, tumbling her again in the warm sheets until they were both limp and breathless with want, but Frankie was smiling in her dreams, and Gwen hated to disturb her.

"Chris is in the library," Gwen told Pierce. "Writing a formal apology to his ma and to Roddy Green's dad."

"She's forgiven you, then."

"For the moment. I expect we'll be butting heads for the rest of our lives, but she loves me for me, and that's all that really matters."

Pierce couldn't quite hide the wry turn of his mouth. "I'll take Chris home and wish you luck in the fray. Say a kind word or two on my behalf."

"You're her family, Pierce, and you always will be. Frankie knows that."

"Yeah, well. And don't you forget it," Pierce replied. "Because I'm beginning to like you well enough, Cook; but you hurt either of them, and I'll bury so deep in my woods even the dogs won't find your bones."

CHRIS LOVED CHRISTMASTIME IN WILLIAMSBURG. HE LOVED THAT the Historical Foundation decorated the houses along the Royal Mile exactly as the colonists would have, with real wreaths on every door, fresh garlands hanging from peaked roofs, and decorations made of apples and oranges and pineapples beneath every dormer. On the Royal Mile even the air tasted of cinnamon and apples. The tourists were all smiling. The interpreters wore sprigs of greenery on the front of their historical costumes or sold ginger cakes from baskets.

Chris especially loved the Grand Illumination. He knew he would never outgrow the torches burning on every street corner or the guards parading in ceremonial gear in front of the Governor's Palace. Fife and drum bands marched up and down the Palace Green. Muskets went off, cracking in the dark, to welcome the Yule. This year the snow made everything especially pretty. The night was cold as hell, but Chris didn't mind. He was warm enough in the heat of the torches as he stood on the edge of the crowd and waited for the fireworks. He would have liked to have edged through Gwen's guests to get a place up front, closer to the show. But he was already on Double-Secret Probation, and he didn't want any of his Christmas gifts returned on account of another misstep. Besides, he wanted to be sure Santa wouldn't put an orange in his stocking instead of the Nerf gun he was hoping for.

Chris glanced out of the corner of his eye at his mom. She stood just ten feet away in her overalls and work boots and her favorite fisherman's sweater. He could tell she was happy. Her eyes sparkled, and she laughed at something one of the interpreters said.

Most of Gwen's guests were too dressed up for the Illumination, the ladies in long coats and diamonds and the men in ties. They looked sort of silly and out of place. He wondered if they noticed the stares they were getting.

"Cold?" He started guiltily when Gwen ghosted up behind him. How did she move so quietly in heels a mile high?

"No."

"Bored?" Gwen stared straight ahead over the crowd at the unlit tree. Her mouth looked like she wanted to laugh.

"Maybe." Not even a little bit, but it wouldn't do to admit he was enjoying the festivities, just in case Gwen thought Christmas was for little kids.

"My favorite part was always the fireworks," Gwen said. "I never could afford a ticket, so I'd sneak up Francis Street there, to just behind the old Magazine. Used to be a stump in the ground. I'd sit over there in the dark, and nobody ever noticed. I always thought I had the best seat in the house because they used to light the rockets almost at my feet."

"Really?" Chris bounced on his toes. "I love the rockets! What do they light 'em with? A really big match? Or one of those gas-torch things?"

A shout of laughter interrupted Gwen's reply. One of the party guests, a man Gwen had introduced earlier as Dr. Gates, was talking to Chris's mom while Jack stood nearby, listening in with a smile. Chris knew his mom and Jack had been working through *business issues* the last few days, and sometimes those business issues made Frankie swear and call Jack a *stubborn jackass under her breath*, but Chris wasn't worried. He knew they'd work it out because they were family and his mom always said family was the most important thing.

Jack said something and Dr. Gates laughed again, loudly, waggling his fingers in the air. He was ancient and covered with wrinkles, and if you got too close he smelled of tobacco and laughed a little too loud, but he seemed to have an okay sense of humor; and Gwen had said he was a doctor of engineering and not medicine, which made him interesting.

Chris shifted and glanced sideways at Gwen, but Gwen was busy watching Chris's mom and smiling a real smile, the kind Chris had only seen on her face once or twice before, when they'd been working together on the skiff. Gwen's smile seemed to grow even wider when the doctor gave a great big belly laugh and chucked Chris's mom under her chin like she was a little kid. Gwen's eyes, dark green like the needles on a Christmas tree, grew all soft and warm. Then she slipped her arm around Chris's shoulders so casually it almost seemed like an accident. But it wasn't.

Chris's stomach flopped. A silly, gooey feeling spread from his toes to his cheeks. He thought maybe he should feel embarrassed, but instead he felt warm and safe, and for some stupid reason, he almost started crying again. Good tears, not bad.

Gwen gave his shoulders a quick squeeze. "How about after the show, I'll walk you over and we'll take a closer look? Bet the guys would love to tell you just how many times they came this close to losing a hand on a bad rocket."

"Cool." Chris wiped his nose on his sleeve, and instead of squirming out from underneath Gwen's arm, he leaned just a little bit against her side. "Maybe next summer we can launch a few out over the creek."

"If your mom says yes." Chris felt Gwen take a deep breath. "I'm thinking of moving back into the old house after the holidays. For good."

"For good? Really?" Chris couldn't believe it. Trade Seattle for Williamsburg?

Gwen nodded. "I've been a long time away, and I'm ready to come home."

The gooey feeling in Chris's stomach turned to excited butterflies. Still, he thought he should be honest. "Williamsburg isn't exactly Seattle, Gwen. We don't even have a real baseball team. And what about Pinnacle?"

"I'm thinking about expanding east."

"Okay."

Gwen looked up at the tree. "I wondered if maybe you and your mom would like to move in with me. If, you know, she thinks it's a good idea. There's plenty of room, and the house gets lonely." From behind the crowd Chris heard the piping of the fife and drum band, a sign that the ceremony was about to begin. For once he didn't rush to get a spot as close to the tree as possible.

"Mom would like that," he managed after a moment, hoping his voice wasn't as squeaky as it sounded in his own ears. "Between you and me, she thinks of that house as her second baby."

"We'll christen the skiff as soon as it warms up, paint her name on the bow," Gwen continued. She sounded strangely hoarse, but when Chris peeked up at her face, she seemed engrossed in the night sky. "Until then, there are plenty of things to do—skiing, hockey. Your mom said maybe you'd like a pair of blades. It's been a long time since I've skated. We could pick up a few pointers together."

"Cool." Chris wiped his nose again before Gwen noticed his snuffling.

"There's that room on the second floor at the end of the hall. I thought you might like it as your own. It's small but it's got a great view of the front lawn, and a fireplace. Plenty of room for your things."

Chris could see the room in his mind's eye. The view was pretty neat, and he'd never had a fireplace of his own. "Sure."

"So. Sound good to you?" Gwen asked as the breeze blew the merry sound of pipes over their heads.

"Yeah." Chris thrust his hands into the pockets of his jeans. "Sounds good to me."

Gwen's arm tightened until Chris thought his ribs might crack, like maybe she wasn't used to giving hugs and was overdoing it. For a moment Chris was afraid she might say something mushy or ruffle his hair the way his mom did when she couldn't think of the right words. But Gwen only smiled. Her smile was like a shared secret, wide and bright and full of mischief. And that smile was even better than her hug.

♨

FRANKIE THOUGHT THEY WERE BEAUTIFUL, HER LITTLE FAMILY. With their arms linked and their faces upturned, washed in the glow of the thousands of lights shining on the tree. Gwen had her arm around Chris's shoulder, and Chris didn't seem at all inclined to move away. As she squeezed her way toward them through the cluster of tourists and party guests, she realized with a tiny pang that her son had grown again. He was almost as tall as Gwen.

She managed to duck through the crowd and throw her own arm around Chris. "Pretty fancy, huh?"

He was pretending to be bored, but she could see the flush of excitement on his face. "I don't think there were so many lights last time."

"You were just knee-high last time." She looked over the top of his head at Gwen and winked. "Wait until the fireworks."

Gwen smiled a slow, lazy grin that made Frankie remember the afternoon hours they'd spent in her carved antique bed. She wrinkled her nose in return and then ruffled Chris's hair. "This year the fireworks are supposed to be extra loud. Better plug your ears."

"Mom!" Chris rolled his eyes. He squirmed away from her hand. Frankie laughed silently. Gwen's mouth twitched. And then the air boomed with cannon fire as rockets flowered overhead.

"Awesome!" Chris bounced in excitement. "I bet they use real gunpowder!"

Frankie could barely hear her son over the bang and pop of fireworks. Flashes of red and green, blue and yellow and white, tore through the sky in spirals and petals and comet-shaped blasts. But the best entertainment stood at her side. Chris's breath fogged out in puffs as he stared up at the sky. His hands were buried deep in the pockets of his jeans, and he swayed a little on his heels. Every time a rocket exploded, he quivered and held his breath until the pattern formed.

On her son's other side, Gwen stood motionless, attention on the heavens. Her hand on Chris's shoulder was light. Although Gwen didn't jump when the fireworks exploded, Frankie thought she saw her blink several times in wonder.

"I love you, Gwen Cook," Frankie whispered into the noise and light. She didn't suppose Gwen would hear, not over the boom of the show and the shrieks of the crowd. But she did. She looked away from the night, watching her with such tenderness that Frankie had to bite her lip to keep her heart from stuttering.

❧

MUCH LATER, WHEN THE HOUSE WAS STILL AND QUIET BENEATH A midnight snowstorm, Frankie pressed Gwen down on the old antique bed, atop the linen sheets and the cloud-soft duvet, with only the twinkling lights on the Christmas tree in the corner to see by.

"So many buttons," she complained, nuzzling into the crook of Gwen's neck as she worked at the front of her fancy silk pajamas. "Why did you even bother with PJs?" She herself was naked as a jaybird, could think of nothing else than feeling Gwen's bare skin against her own.

Gwen snorted, and then moaned when Frankie nibbled a line along her collarbone. "It's been a long day. I thought we were planning on sleep." She gasped, arched when Frankie finally found a nipple beneath all that silk, rolled it between her thumb and forefinger. "Francis."

"Mmm," Frankie agreed, smiling to herself. Gwen's nipple was a hard pebble against her hand. The crook of her neck smelled of the citrus and cinnamon, and faintly of winter on the creak. Of home. Reluctantly, she rocked back on her heels, putting distance between them.

Gwen's green eyes were half-lidded, dark with arousal. They sharpened when Frankie moved away. She sat up, unbuttoned silk sliding down her shoulders and onto the duvet. "What are you doing?"

"Taking my time," Frankie said, smile growing when Gwen huffed displeasure. "There's no rush, is there? Show me your hands."

"What? My hands?" She was actually pouting, dark hair ruffled, lips swollen from Frankie's earlier kisses, eyes gone narrow. Frankie half expected her to bristle and hiss. "What about my hands?"

"Well, I've heard all about them." Mock serious, Frankie held out her own hands, palms up. "More, honestly, in the last few days then I ever need to hear again. 'Midas touch', isn't it? What I want to know is, can you really turn everything you touch to gold?"

"Of course not." But Gwen set her left hand on Frankie's right, palm on palm. Gwen's hand trembled. "That's all hype. This isn't a fairytale."

"We'll see." Frankie linked Gwen's fingers with her own, brought them to her mouth, kissed her knuckles one at a time. "Magical hands? I think we should make sure. A sort of. . . experiment."

"Oh," said Gwen, blinking when Frankie sucked on her thumb, and then her index finger. She couldn't seem to look away from her fingers in Frankie's mouth. She rocked forward, silk-clad knees parting on linen sheets. Frankie felt a rush of heat between her own legs, groaned as she released Gwen's hand.

In answer Gwen pulled Frankie abruptly into her lap. Her breath came in pants, tickling Frankie's ear. "An experiment," she agreed. It was her turn to skim her teeth along Frankie's collarbone, as her hands cupped Frankie's naked breasts, pinching and kneading until Frankie gasped in pleasure. "God, Francis. You're amazing, you're perfect."

Gwen made Frankie breathless, wordless. Frankie's head fell back as Gwen dipped lower, past her belly button, down along the inside of her thigh, fingers sliding into wet and heat and *need*.

"How's that?" Gwen whispered, lips working against the shell of Frankie's ear, fingers working at her center. "My love, my other half, my heart. What do you feel?"

Frankie couldn't answer, could only make sounds of disjointed pleasure as her orgasm peaked with surprising speed, clenching hard and fast, quaking through her bones, leaving her quivering in Gwen's embrace. Flying high.

Gwen was quivering, too, but with quiet mirth. "Well, then," she said, in her smuggest southern tones. "I'm not so sure. Did that feel like magic to you? Because, now that I think about it, maybe it's not *all* hype—"

"Ego the size of an elephant," Frankie proclaimed gruffly, before shoving Gwen over into the duvet. Loose, languid, happy, she straddled her oldest friend and lover, showed Gwen her teeth. "Let's see what happens when we keep those hands over your head like *this* . . ." She pinned Gwen's wrists. "And I taste you like *this*." She licked around one of Gwen's nipples, then the other. "For safety's sake."

"Fuck." Gwen's hips bucked but she couldn't dislodge Frankie. "Yes. Did I already say. Jesus. That you're perfect."

"Several times," Frankie replied as she began to take Gwen apart in the glow of the Christmas tree. "Say it again."

About the Author

Sarah Remy/Alex Hall is a nonbinary, animal-loving, proud gamer geek. Their work can be found in a variety of cool places, including HarperVoyager, EDGE, NineStar Press, and SkullGate Media.

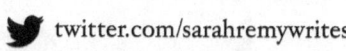 twitter.com/sarahremywrites

instagram.com/s_a_remy

Also By Alex Hall

Beastly Manor

Earnest Ink

As Sarah Remy

Stonehill Downs

The Bone Cave

Across the Long Sea

The Exiled King

ANTHOLOGIES

Fairly Twisted Tales for a Horribly Ever After

Achten Tan: Land of Dust and Bone

Remedy

Reed Androku hated early mornings with the passion of a person forced regularly and by necessity to rise before dawn.

The passion, Reed though glumly, standing at the kitchen counter in crisp boxers and a baggy SPBU sweatshirt, palms pressed flat against granite, waiting for the water in the ancient coffeemaker to boil, *of a thousand white-hot pre-dawn suns.*

The coffeemaker had come with the apartment and was far below Reed's standards— Reed's standards being simply 'no appliances older than fifteen years'—but the apartment was otherwise so completely fantastic, the opportunity so unbelievable, that Reed had supposed they could forgive Kate Griffin the bargain-basement Mr. Coffee until there was time to pop into New Haven and pickup something better than just serviceable.

Reed had supposed wrong. Because working for Kate Griffin was turning out to be an every-hour-of-every-day sort of job, which left Reed with barely any time to spend on their own small herd, and zero time to pop into the city for even the most basic of supplies. And the ancient Mr. Coffee, after eight solid weeks of hard use, was sounding what Reed supposed was the electronic equivalent of a death rattle.

At 6AM on a Monday morning. And not just any Monday on Tulip Farm, either.

"Come on come on come on," Reed begged the coffeemaker in the Russian of their childhood, the language of their father, the one they used to encourage a flagging horse. They tapped their fingers on the granite countertop. "One cup, that's all I ask. One cup. You can do it."

The coffeemaker gurgled, hissed, and in a final effort of good will dribble 10 oz of steaming black coffee into Reed's favorite mug, an old Rumph Pottery classic in the shape of a Pegasus.

"Thank you, God." Reed patted the Mr. Coffee in heartfelt gratitude. Lifting the mug to their nose, Reed inhaled coffee-scented steam, waiting for the liquid to cool enough to sip. Outside the kitchen window, Tulip Farm was still mostly dark, the pastures and outbuildings sleeping. Safety lights illuminated the gravel walkways between Barns A, B, and C, as well as the curtain of rain falling steadily from the sky.

Spring, Reed thought with a sigh, was taking its own sweet time in coming. Though most of the bulbs and annuals planted around the farm were beginning to send up brave shoots, and the old magnolia tree in front of Barn A had begun to unfurl red-green leaves, the sky hadn't cleared for two weeks at least, and the pastures were more bog than field.

Reed took a cautious sip of coffee, groaning out loud and curling bare toes in pleasure as the caffeine hit their system. Yes, that would do for now. And maybe later they could convince once of the grooms to drive the farm pickup truck into New Haven on an appliance run, maybe bring everyone back lunch from Café Atticus , Reed's treat.

Christ knew they'd all need a boost by mid-day, once Senior finished making the rounds. The man was a strict taskmaster on a normal day. Three weeks off the farm, three weeks away from the business, there was no doubt in Reed's mind that Senior would come blazing through barn check ready to take names and kick some ass.

Gabriel Senior was a perfectionist, and Tulip Farm flourished under his tutelage. Reed couldn't take issue with the way he put everything he had into the job. Senior's reliance on intimidation to keep his staff in line, on the other hand—

Well. Reed was just glad that Barn A was strictly Kate's province. Because Reed didn't tolerate bullies, and it was hard enough to keep their mouth shut when Senior started going at the rest of the staff within ear shot.

You need this job. Tulip Farm is a dream come true. Don't muck it up over one sour apple. His son's just out of hospital, for Christ's sake. The whole family is under a tremendous amount of stress.

Out the kitchen window, past the dark pastures and sleeping barns, lights burned in the first-floor windows of the main house: the MacAuley Griffin clan already up and about, like Reed, preparing for a Monday that wasn't an average Monday, a morning that promised to be bittersweet.

Because today Peter was coming home. Their golden boy, the ex-Olympic hopeful. Come home in the back of an ambulance because none of the farm vehicles were wheelchair accessible, and the van the family had rented for next few months hadn't yet arrived.

Reed sketched the sign of the cross in the air—another old habit taken from their Orthodox father. They swallowed down the last dregs of still-hot coffee, rinsed the mug in the kitchen sink, and padded into the bedroom in search of rain-proof clothes.

🖎

Dressed warmly in an anorak and Wellies over jeans and a soft thermal, Reed bypassed the freight elevator—excruciatingly slow even on a good day—and thumped down the four flights of stairs from Barn A's upper apartment to stable level. The perfume of farm life, always a muted presence upstairs, hit Reed like a solid wave. The earthy stink of horse manure, the sweeter smell of hay and bedding, leather and saddle soap, and the warm, wild musk of the animals themselves. Reed loved the smell of barn the way some people enjoyed the scent of Chanel daubed on a delicate wrist or behind one ear. It was seductive, sexy, full of promise.

"Morning, Boss!" John Dotty, Reed's assistant and groom in charge of morning feedings, was already tossing hay and checking water buckets. "Word from the main house is no turnout today. It's a pisser!"

Reed cracked a smile. "Isn't it just? Much more of this I'll have to break out my pool floaties."

Rain pelted the barn on all sides as if in agreement, rattling plank siding. The horses, snug in their stalls, nosed contentedly at the hay John tossed their way. Most nickered greeting when they heard Reed's voice. They appreciated John for the hay, but Reed was in charge of doling out morning grain, and that was the real treat. Down the aisle, Pritchard and Bob pawed their stall doors impatiently while Annie, taller at 17 hands than any other horse in Barn A, stuck her dark, wedge-shaped head over the stall divider and whinnied.

John, ignoring the ruckus, threw Reed a wink. "Don't worry. Just as soon as you think we're all going to drown for sure, the sun will come out and bake everything dry. Mid-summer you'll be praying for a piece of rain."

He'd know. John was a local who, like Reed, had grown up with horses and knew his way around a farm. Unlike Reed, he had dreams of a future in the big city and was working for Senior only until he'd saved enough money to pay his own way toward an accounting degree at the University of New Haven. A wiry kid in his early twenties, John wore Carhartt dungarees over vintage band T-shirts no matter the weather, and never missed a shift.

He'd accepted Reed from day one, never giving Reed's dye-tipped hair, thick eyeliner or preference for flowery scarves and bright nail polish a second glance, or pretending not to understand Reed's heavy accent. Small things, but rare enough that Reed would be forever grateful, and counted John a good friend though they'd worked together only a handful of weeks.

Now they moved through the barn in quiet companionship, John filling water buckets with a long hose while Reed pulled the feed cart down the aisle, measuring and dumping grain into individual buckets, adding supplements scooped from plastic containers and metal tins. Sport horses, even semi-retired sport horses, were athletes and like their human counterparts, needed a wide variety of nutritional support to keep their bodies operating at maximum efficiency. Reed dosed their small herd daily with organic supplements hand selected for each animal's individual need. And ever since Peter's Annie had been shuffled off to Barn A to recover from the accident, Reed had switched the mare off her old big box feed store regiment and onto organics.

"She's feisty this morning," John told Reed as they passed in front of the mare's stall, long hose and four-wheeled cart meeting but not tangling. "She's realized something's up. Horses are like that. Betcha she knows *he's* coming home today."

Reed studied the mare through the bars as she tucked eagerly into her grain, ears pinned, black tail swishing. 'Feisty' was not unusual for a horse who'd been confined to stall rest for the past month, but Annie was taking it harder than most. Though Reed had managed to keep her coat shiny and her weight on, still she was losing muscle without regular work, and her friendly nature had taken on a grumpy edge.

She was bored, Reed knew, and lonely despite the genial presence of the other six horses. She'd been born to work but she'd been put up on the shelf and forgotten while she healed.

"I emailed Senior last week." Reed grimaced. "About starting her back to work. No response yet."

John grunted unhappily. "Got other things on his mind, I guess. Could be he blames her some for the accident, which isn't fair. But Senior can be that way." Together, they watched Annie lip her grain bin and flick her tail. "Would be a waste not to bring her back, for her own sake. Mare like that needs something to do." He flicked a glance Reed's direction. "Seems to me that would be right up your alley, wouldn't it?"

"Hmm." Reed had been thinking the same thing. Lying awake at night, in fact, imagining how they'd start her again, with chiropractic manipulation before, slowly increasing exercise, massage and ice after. Suspensory injuries could be tricky, but luckily Annie's was only a bad pull and not a tear. With the proper care, she would recover. Which was why Reed had emailed Senior in the first place. Because it seemed criminal to let any horse, but especially a horse as talented as Annie, languish and fade.

"Seems to me," continued John, with the certainty of youth, "that maybe there was a reason Kate had that mare moved to this barn, your barn, your *rehab* barn. Doncha think?"

"Hmm," said Reed again, though they both knew John was right. Reed was learning it was just like Kate to dangle a challenge in front of a person's nose until they bit, and Annie was exactly the sort of case Reed liked to sink their teeth into.

Speaking of juicy treats; One by one along the barn aisle Reed's own special projects, having inhaled their grain, were peering through the stall bars, anticipating a morning tidbit. Fishing in the pocket of their anorak for the ever-present Ziploc of freshly sliced apple, Reed doled the wedges out one at a time, opening stall doors a crack to pat noses or stroke ears. They were all visibly pleased to see Reed. Pritchard, a bay gelding with ears like a mule's and a temper to match, tried—and failed—as usual to take off a few of Reed's fingers with his slice. Bob, a gentleman chestnut who had raced long enough to earn his previous owner a nice chunk of change and had the stress fractures to prove it, lipped his treat gingerly off Reed's palm. Angel kicked up bedding with her one hoof, more interested in ear scratches than apple. The big-boned black mare had spent more than a year alone and neglected in a backyard pasture before Reed had found her. She was a glutton for attention.

Ingrid and Charlie, the newest additions to Reed's little family, had both come off a farm near Saratoga, and shared the same sire. They looked enough alike they might have been a matched set, with red bay coats and wide, white blazes from forehead to nose. Ingrid had four white socks. Charlie had only three. Neither had seen the racetrack. Charlie panicked in tight spaces, which meant the large foaling stalls in Barn A suited him better than the usual 10 by 10. Ingrid simply didn't have speed in her—if given the choice, she'd rather walk than run. She'd make someone a lovely show pony or trail horse once Reed had taught her not to bolt every time she saw a whip.

"Good morning, beautiful." Reed stroked her face while she ignored the apple they proffered and instead nosed at their pockets. Laughing, Reed relented, allowing her one of the sugar cubes they kept on hand for the babies.

"You spoil her," John teased, rolling up the hose. "My dad always says treats breed bad habits."

"She deserves a little spoiling," said Reed fondly. "They all do."

Although they suspected John's dad might be the primary reason the kid wanted to ditch the country for the city, Reed knew better than to outwardly criticize what he'd learned of Mr. Dotty's approach to horse care. Sometimes it was better to teach by example.

Giving Ingrid one last pat, Reed secured her stall door and zipped the front of the anorak firmly all the way up to their chin. If the continuing pelt of rain against Barn A was any indication at all, the shallow roof covering the breezeway between building and the back wing where Reed's other charges lived would provide slim protection.

John said, "Good luck out there! See you at barn check."

"Even if I have to swim," Reed agreed. Taking a deep breath, they ducked through the heavy barn door and into the storm.

Rain and wind lashed Reed's shoulders as they ran across the breezeway, spattering their eyes and cheeks even under the hood. Water pooled on the gravel walkway. It splashed in angry gouts under Reed's wellies, ink black in the pre-dawn. The safety lights alongside the path flickered in and out as the wind gusts increased dramatically, and the clatter of rain against the breezeway roof sounded suspiciously like hail. Reed's breath hit the frigid air in puffs of smoke.

Chris Jesus. Reed shivered even beneath two warm layers. *Spring in Connecticut shouldn't be this cold. Goddamn climate change.*

The breezeway was only fifteen feet long, but it felt like twice that. Reed hit the door to the foaling barn at a run, punched the code into the security lock, and blew into the building on a blast of wet air. They groped for the light switch nearest the door before realizing—half a second late—that the overheads were already on.

That was wrong, because Barn A was Reed's responsibility. For the sake of precaution Reed was the only member on staff who knew the unlock code to the building. Even John didn't have unsupervised access. Tulip Farm made most of its money in sales and stud service. The eight babies under Reed's care were quite literally worth their weight in gold. It was no small thing that Kate Griffin trusted Reed—who up until two months ago had been a perfect stranger—with their wellbeing.

A person stood partway down the aisle, half-turned Reed's way as if in surprise. Reed reached automatically for the baling knife kept sheathed always on their belt. Bone-handled and a good five inches long, the knife was a necessary tool when it came to daily barn chores.

It was also, Reed had cause to know, a nice security bonus when in the hand of someone trained, as Reed was, in self-defense.

"Woah." The man in the aisle said, raising both hands in surrender as he turned the rest of the way toward Reed. "Hold up. There's no call for bladed weapons, Harry Potter, especially as I left mine at home."

"Wands." Reed relaxed a fraction but kept the knife in hand, a reassuring weight against their palm.

The man's brows went up. Now that Reed's eyes were adjusting to the change in light and they could see the intruder clearly, panic eased. If the very faint lilt of Ireland —a generation removed —wasn't a giveaway, his features were. He had Aine MacAuley's distinctive violet eyes and ink-black hair, worn long enough to brush the collar of the Burberry trench coat protecting his suit. Neither the coat nor the expensive-looking suit did anything to hide the sturdy, long-legged Griffin build beneath.

"Sorry?" he said. Reed noted the way he kept his hands loose at his sides, visible so as not to provoke, deceptively inoffensive. In Reed's experience a man who knew enough to sham harmlessness in the face of a knife blade generally also knew how to hold his own in a fight.

"Harry Potter," Reed explained while at the same time taking a quick glance around their surroundings, "used a wand, not a knife." As far as they could tell nothing had been disturbed. In fact, from the trail of wet leading from the door halfway along the aisle to where the fellow stood, pooling in drips and drops beneath the hem of that fancy coat, Reed guessed they'd entered the wing within minutes of each other.

"Whatever. Mind putting yours away?"

"Not quite yet." Reed showed his teeth in a dry smile. "I can see you're family, and because no horseman would be stupid enough to wear those city shoes out into the barn even if it wasn't raining buckets, that makes you the lawyer."

"MacAuley Griffin," he agreed, violet eyes flicking from Reed's face to the knife in Reed's hand and back again. "Mac, if you like. And you must be the Russian. Katie mentioned you. Androku, right?"

"Thing is," continued Reed, still smiling, "Kate *didn't* mention you were coming into town, or that I'd find you standing in my barn at 5AM on this pisspoor May morning."

"She doesn't know I'm here. Yet." Mac confessed, "I drove down last night because I wanted to be here to welcome my brother home. Only, I couldn't sleep a wink from the nerves. It's been a long time since I was on the farm. It makes me restless, coming back. So, I got up too early, as one does before a big day, which meant I'm here long before I'm needed." He shrugged. "I always used to come to Barn A, when I was a kid, when I was feeling low. To see the babies." His mouth turned up at the corners, a much more pleasant smile than the one Reed wore. "It just lowers my blood pressure, you know? The cute-ness overload."

Reed got that. But still, there was the matter of security.

"Kate changes the door code every month. If she doesn't know you're here, how'd you get in?"

"Sure she does. But what you might not realize, as you've only been on the farm for a short time—and I must say you're exceeding expecta-tions already, because you're still holding that knife and it looks to me like you're just a little too willing to cut me if necessary. Senior would be so pleased—is that my sister has been using the same door code every May for the last ten years. Also, in consistent rotation: June, July, August, September...Well, you get the picture."

Reed sheathed the knife. "I did know that," they said. "And if you do, too, then you're probably who you say you are, and I won't have to cut you." Pushing back their hood, scattering more water, Reed flashed a genuine grin. "Wasted opportunity."

The man in the fancy suit and expensive coat relaxed for real this time, subtle lines of tension easing from his shoulders and face. He shoved his hands into the pockets of his trench. "Sorry. For startling you. And the early hour, and the 'pisspoor' weather. It followed me all the way up from New York."

It was Reed's turn to shrug. For safety's sake they'd learned early on how to read people, and MacAuley Griffin didn't seem a bad sort. Sure, he dressed like a man with too much money and too little good sense, but he seemed genuinely pleased to make Reed's acquaintance, and although Reed hadn't missed the start of surprise Mac had tried and failed to hide when he'd glimpsed Reed's face beneath the hood, he'd passed quickly from bewilderment to comprehension and then blasé acceptance.

"Katie," Reed imagined the younger brother would say to his sister over the breakfast table, *"you mentioned the new barn manager was Russian, but forgot to mention he was so...progressive."*

And Kate, always conscientious, would reply, *"They, Mac. Reed's nonbinary and prefers they/them pronouns."* And everyone at the breakfast table would nod, probably baffled and maybe disapproving, but willing for the sake of farm PR to play the part of enthusiastic allies.

But possibly that was unfair, because Mac offered a hand and when Reed took it, he shook in what seemed like honest welcome.

"I'll stay out of your way. I know how it is. Civilians just get under feet during feed time."

Reed unlocked the grain room. "Thought you grew up on the farm?"

"I did," Mac agreed, head tilted as he watched Reed measure out grain. "Moved away after high school."

"Then you know how to feed," Reed guessed, and from the flicker of resignation on Mac's face, they'd guessed correctly. "So, make yourself useful." They indicated the feed trolley. "You've already made me late, and barn check's at six."

Mac whistled softly. "Old man's still a tyrant, I see." But he gripped the trolley handle, tugging it out of the grain closet, Burberry coat flapping damply around his ankles. Reed had to a completely unprofessional urge to laugh at the sight.

"Senior's dedicate to the farm," Reed replied, hoping he sounded less doubtful than he felt. "I'm told everything else comes second."

"Exactly." A muscle in Mac's jaw clenched. "And how well do you think that worked out for my baby brother?"

Look for REMEDY in early 2021
from Madison Place Press and Alex Hall.

www.ingramcontent.com/pod-product-compliance
Lightning Source LLC
Chambersburg PA
CBHW030141180626
46812CB00002B/790